THE BLOOD-DIMMED TIDE

ANTHONY QUINN

NO EXIT PRESS

First published in 2014 by No Exit Press,
an imprint of Oldcastle Books Ltd,
P.O.Box 394, Harpenden,
Herts, AL5 1XJ, UK

noexit.co.uk
@noexitpress
Editor: Martin Fletcher

ISBN
978-1-84344-465-7 (Print)
978-1-84344-466-4 (Epub)
978-1-84344-467-1 (Kindle)
978-1-84344-468-8 (Pdf)

2 4 6 8 10 9 7 5 3 1

Typeset by Avocet Typeset, Somerton, Somerset
in 11.5pt Ehrhardt with Copperplate and Captain Howdy display
Printed in Great Britain by Clays Ltd, St Ives plc

DEDICATION

For John Paul and Kerri-Louise Quinn –
Little brother, shining bright,
Now I look up to you

'The hills shall be torn down, and the sea shall have red waves, and blood shall be spilled, and every mountain valley and every moor shall be on high, before you shall perish, my little black rose'

Anonymous Gaelic Poet

CONTENTS

CONTENTS

UPON ATTENDING A SÉANCE

IF it is your wish to mingle with the denizens of the spirit world, you must begin by discarding any preconceived notions you might have about our ghostly companions. Firstly, it is incorrect to believe that they float in a state of radiant enchantment, or that they experience no suffering in their ethereal realms. Their world is riddled with just as many labyrinths of love and hate as ours, and is governed by the same unfulfilled longings and restless fears that afflict the world of the living.

More importantly than this, to make contact with a ghost you must be prepared to relinquish the very idea of your own existence. For most seekers, everything exists because they exist. They believe that whatever they see and whatever they hear must be real, and thus, conversely, that what they cannot see or hear must not be real.

Instead, you should adopt a view of the world based upon your non-existence. Then you might hear or see things as surprising as a field of rainbows bursting from a darkened sky.

In fact, with the correct training in the rituals of the occult, it is possible to guide your mind through the gates of forgetting that separate this realm from the next. Only then will you see that we are all wandering spirits, overcrowding a dark continent of emptiness, and that our fears and longings are so numerous they intermingle with those of the dead.

1

IRELAND, NOVEMBER 1917

ACE OF PENTACLES

A ROUGH hand grabbed the captain's shoulder and shook him from a sleep so disturbed it was worse than no sleep at all. The sentry shone a lamp in his eyes and urged him to get dressed at once. He jerked awake with a gasp and cursed, but right away sensed there was danger. The night terror he had tried to shake off had left his reflexes jagged and tense, but his mind felt sharp. Beyond the round flare of the lamp, he detected the sentry's presence, a pool of interrogating watchfulness in the dark.

He shielded his raw eyes. 'Damn it, man. I can't see a thing.'

The lamp swung away from his face, and its holder became a single reeling shadow moving about the room. He swung his legs out of the narrow bunk with a grunt. The sentry's stench of sweat and stale alcohol climbed up his nose and distracted him as he fumbled putting on the uniform. He cursed again. In his haste, he had poked his big toe right through a hole in one of the socks, tearing the darned patch he had sewn on the previous night. Breathing heavily, he fumbled in a drawer for a fresh pair.

'You haven't got time', warned the sentry.

'Of course I have time', he replied, but he hurried as quickly as he could.

When fully dressed, he searched out his revolver and thrust it under his shirt. The cold press of its muzzle against his flesh made his heart gulp. It had been months since he had experienced the chilling sensation that someone might soon try to kill him.

The sentry held the lamp before him as they made their way down the steps of the lighthouse, the boards creaking beneath their boots. In the courtyard, horses and men were hurtling back and forth in the darkness. At first, the captain thought the encampment itself was under attack but then he heard a soldier shouting about gun smugglers on the beach at Blind Sound. A look-out posted to the beach had spotted the hulk of a dark object that might have been a German submarine breaking through the waves.

Without hesitation, he took the lead, checking the men had their weapons and bayonets drawn. He waved his revolver confidently in the air and marched them along his preferred route to the beach, avoiding roads or laneways. He tried to show them how fearless he was, and he hoped they believed him. In reality, he walked with great wariness, worried that an ambush might spring out of the darkness at any moment.

They felt the Atlantic before they saw it. After the storm, the air was surprisingly quiet, and so still that a thick mist formed around them, soaking their faces and uniforms. Through this aerial sea, they crouched forward. Dogs barked at them from nearby farms, but soon the deafening roar of the Atlantic drowned out all other sounds. By the time their boots sank into the soft sand at Blind Sound, the fog had soaked their tunics, their trousers, even their socks.

Crawling to the top of a dune, the captain stared into the darkness but was unable to see anything. Hesitation now could get him and his men killed, he thought. However, he stayed there, proposing and rejecting various scenarios that might be occurring along the enshrouded coast, waiting for the fog and darkness to peel away and reveal God only knew what. The slow fury of the crashing waves sent shivers down his spine.

In many ways, Captain Thomas Oates felt as though he had run aground on this remote shoreline, marooned for more than a month in a spooky lighthouse with restricted sunshine, food and company and a ramshackle band of men under his command — an unpleasant interlude in his soldierly career. Withdrawn on health grounds from the front line in France, his new posting consisted of inspecting coastal defences and studying sea-charts and timetables to ascertain when and where an invasion or a gun-smuggling operation might occur. There was an added urgency to his work since the interception of Sir Roger Casement the year before on a U-boat stocked with weapons intended for the Easter Rising. Casement, a British consular officer turned Irish Republican, had been subsequently stripped of his knighthood and hanged for attempting to organise aid for the Irish rebellion.

The Admiralty had billeted him to the lighthouse and assigned him a reserve force drawn from the local fishing families. They had not known he was afraid of the sea. Not once had his commanders asked him about his relationship with open water. Ever since his childhood, the sea had been a place of wild creatures, whirlpools and treacherous currents, the coast a final frontier bordering a continual shifting of directionless masses of water. Land was solid, safe, negotiable, while the sea was everything else.

At first, he spent his days in the upper room of the lighthouse poring over sea charts and coastal maps, rather than face the reality of nature. Sometimes he played bridge or wrote letters home. Through the window, he watched the distant sea, the gun-grey waves rising and falling, the surf forming on the strand like the heavy, curling moustaches of the warmongering generals he'd left behind in France, but who still invaded his dreams.

The autumnal storms came, and the sea turned black as tar, flecked with steepening eddies of white. On the clear mornings after the storms had spent themselves, it shone with an exuberant bottle green colour, the breaking waves mutating into sparkling crystals of light.

Eventually loneliness drove him to explore the coast, but despite his best efforts, his solitary trips were always inconclusive. The mist or the rain, the steep cliff precipices and tumbling rock, or the irregular tidal currents would eventually drive him back to the comforts of the lighthouse.

He doubted that if the Germans did arrive in a U-boat he would be able to catch them in time. There was too much sea, and it was always on the move. Keeping even a small patch of the coast under observation was like trying to hold in the mind's eye the twirling movements of a large flock of agitated birds. Nor did he trust the local men in his battalion, the sullen-eyed fishermen and sailors who looked prepared to abandon the lighthouse camp at any moment for a hazardous boating adventure. It was true that they obeyed his orders; they also acknowledged his professional expertise in handling guns and organising patrols, but that was as far as they seemed to trust him. Whenever he joined them for tea or cigarettes, their eyes would fill with suspicion and coldness. Deep down he had the unshakeable conviction that if he went out to sea with them, they would tie him up and tip his struggling body overboard.

His band of men melted in and out of the mist; in the stillness, their disembodied eyes waited, watching his every move. He listened carefully to the Atlantic, fearful of missing a telltale sound amid the booming of the waves. Although last night's squall had long since expended itself, the swell at Blind Sound might continue stubbornly for days. He had learned from his observations that the sea was at its most fickle along this particular part of the coast. Even the fishermen refused to row their boats there, believing that witches and malign spirits haunted the waves.

He had studied the sea's movements in the bay for weeks, and been baffled by the behaviour of the waves. He had walked the beach from end to end, marking the tide levels at different phases of the moon, and following the passage of seaweed on the currents. The closer he observed the sea's behaviour the more confused he became. Sailors and fishermen knew that time and tide were synonymous, and that the year's calendar could be plotted by the familiar rhythm of tidal stages and currents. However, the tides at Blind Sound were labyrinthine in their complexity. At certain times of the day, they seemed to fall under a spell and flow against the direction in which they normally travelled. Sometimes in barely perceptible currents, at other times in very rapid ones. He also noted that when the wind blew from the north, the water in the bay emptied, like bath water suddenly going down a drain. Equally, the time of high-water was vague and changeable, suggesting that the fundamental routines of nature had somehow come unstuck.

One evening his observations were interrupted by the sight of a servant girl from Lissadell House wading out half-naked into the cold sea. He noted how her dark hair unfurled in the water behind her, and that she strode into the waves with an air of confidence rather than discomfort. After half an hour in the water, she returned to the beach, dressed, took out a pocket watch, and wrote for a while in some sort of book, before making her way back along the coast to the winking lights of the estate.

On successive nights, he kept finding her in the same bay, waist deep in the sea, as though trapped in the maze of shifting currents. It sparked his curiosity to see that she, too, seemed fixated by the movement of the tides, exploring their changing ebb and flow, searching for their withheld secret. He watched her make notes and record the time after each of her swims.

He felt a strange sense of ownership over Blind Sound's shifting tides. They were his puzzle, not the servant girl's. What was the reason behind her curiosity? What made her wade out so fearlessly night after night?

It seemed the bay held a mystery neither of them could escape.

A silvery plume rose over the sea, not more mist but the breaking of day. For a few moments, the fog dissolved and the captain had a clear view of the beach, the broad sweep of silver sand, empty of life, and a chain of breaking waves. He took out his field glasses and spied a dark, rectangular object, strangely still in the long swells. It might have been a basking shark, exhausted by its long journey north, or a capsized boat, but an undertow of fear made him worry that he was mistaken and that it was indeed an enemy submarine. He waited for something to happen, but the panorama of ever-breaking surf remained unchanged.

'Have we any reports about a boat sinking?' he asked the sentry.

'No. None at all.'

'The weather has been hellish, and the currents in the bay erratic. It could be an old wreck dredged from the sea-bottom.'

'What shall we do?'

Abruptly, the fog sneaked up behind them again, enclosing them in its frog-spawn greyness. The beach became a hazy blur, and then vanished.

An invisible sense of churning chaos floated before them.

'Let's wait for the fog to clear.'

However, uncertainty gnawed at the captain. He stared at the men but they seemed patient, content to wait. After all, they were fishermen and used to long lonely nights. Through the suspended moisture, their faces looked pale and bloated, like near drownings.

'Are you a reader of poetry, sir?' the sentry asked him.

He hesitated. The literary question had wrong-footed him.

'Yes,' he replied, eventually.

'Then you will have heard of William Butler Yeats. His mother's people were the Pollexfens of Sligo. He used to frequent this beach to compose his poems.'

'I've read *The Lake Isle of Innisfree*.'

One of the younger men spoke up. 'They say Mr Yeats is a magician as well as a poet. And that he can be carried five miles in the winking of an eye.'

Another replied, 'It's also said the Pollexfens' blood is infected with madness.'

'I'd call into question his magical powers,' said the sentry. 'The last time Yeats visited Sligo he took a rowing boat to search for his beloved isle of Innisfree. He rowed the entire day and half the night, but couldn't find any trace of it.'

The men laughed mirthlessly.

The captain turned away and stared at the mist. At first, it seemed to swallow up the daylight, but then the rising sun won through. He lifted his field glasses and surveyed the beach. He watched the sea flicker with breaking surf. It was a view of intensely flickering moments, but at the same time oddly peaceful. The dark outline he could not make out in the fog was now revealed in daylight. It was a black hexagonal shape that could only be a coffin, strangely riding the breaking waves. He paused and saw the men glance anxiously at each other.

'It's going out again,' shouted the sentry. 'The storm must have lifted it from an old wreck.'

The coffin slid back into the waves, a black diamond disappearing from view.

Following the captain's command, the men spilled down the dune and clambered into the sea. They waited for the gathering surge of the next wave to wash over the coffin, and then they circled it. In the slack water it floated towards them, battered and leaking, the dark wood decaying in places. On a heavily rusted brass plate the captain made out some words and a date: Body Unknown, Died at Sea, 1889.

The men began hauling the coffin, but the sea seemed to grow angry at their efforts. It sent a huge wave sweeping over them, dragging the coffin back into its hungry mouth. The men struggled to keep their footing against the pull of the retreating water.

After a few minutes, the coffin broke the surface again as if coming up for air. Unexpectedly, the life went out of the sea. The waves collapsed into a sizzling froth, leaving the coffin floating in a pocket of calm jade. The men waded in, grabbing the coffin and rising as one, heaving it up the beach.

They were barely halfway across the sand when a shout of pain rose from one of the men in front. His boot had caught against a rock. He went down like a sack of spilled rice, tipping his corner of the coffin onto a jagged reef. The worn wood creaked and groaned but held together. The men raised the coffin again, and this time the captain walked behind, checking their progress.

After a few yards, he made them stop. A strange sound came from within the coffin, as though a set of fingernails were scratching the wood. Now that they were beyond the roar of the sea, the sound grew more distinct. He leaned closer to the coffin's damaged corner and listened carefully. He realised the sound was too regular to be that of a living thing. Something mechanical and frail, a gadget of some description, constantly scraping out a message, a code, with the same two sounds. He paused, realising what it was. An icy finger of fear touched his heart. A clock or a pocket watch, he thought. Still ticking, still telling the time. But what was it doing inside a twenty-year-old coffin?

'Set it down and open the lid,' he ordered the men.

Their rifle butts made a dull, sickening noise colliding against the metal clasps, gouging the wood. They kept hitting, harder and harder, until the clasps clattered free. The sentry lifted off the lid and they all stood back in surprise.

The captain smelled a combination of the ocean's salt, rotting sea creatures and a stench of death that drove deep into his nasal passages. The chamber within was lined with disintegrating velvet upon which lay the slim body of a woman in a dress, her face covered in a black hood decorated with a hem of red and black roses. He removed the hood. It was a real face staring lifelessly upwards. Not the face of a nightmare or a decomposed corpse but that of a pretty young woman. From a fold in her dress, a pocket watch slipped out. It had Roman numerals and a moon face on the front. The captain checked his own watch and noted that its time was accurate.

'Dear God,' said one of the men. 'It looks like Rosemary O'Grady. I danced with her two nights ago.'

The sea seemed to move far away, stunned by the sight of the dead girl. The roar of the waves receded. The captain's eyes swam over her body. Blood had seeped from wounds to her hands, dark red rents in her translucent skin. He had also seen her, a few nights previously, wading out with strong strides into the sea. It was the servant girl from Lissadell House. A feeling of deep unease made his stomach queasy. What was he to do now?

Minutes passed. No one moved. The sound of the pocket watch filled the air.

'Suffocated in the coffin or murdered first?' asked the sentry, lifting a perplexed expression to the captain.

'The slash marks to her hands might suggest suicide,' he replied, avoiding looking at the girl's face.

'Suicide or signs of resistance?' The sentry squinted at her bloated hands.

'Suicides and murder victims aren't generally found in coffins.'

'Coffins aren't generally found washed up on beaches.' He glanced at the captain. 'An inexplicable tragedy.'

'We'll have to leave the body here for the police.'

'We can't leave it here like a piece of driftwood.' This time he stared into the captain's eyes. 'We should take her to the priest and have her body blessed.' Gone was any trace of the deference he should show to a superior officer.

'You shall do whatever I say.'

The sentry's dark eyes emptied as the captain pulled out his revolver and levelled it at him.

2

ACE OF RODS

IT was because of an eccentric Irish poet residing in London during the third year of the Great War that I became a ghost-catcher, a post that had me alternating my evenings between titled hostesses' dinner parties in Mayfair and Chelsea, and hushed séances in the grimy parlours of the capital's more humble streets. Both worlds had their own ingrained horror. At that time, London was in the throes of a supernatural paroxysm. While gigantic towers called skyscrapers soared into the air one after another in bright cities on the other side of the Atlantic, across the English capital fantastic energies were equally at work, only on a more ethereal plane. After more than one thousand days of war, grieving wives and mothers were turning in their droves to séances and a host of different spiritualist movements, searching for messages from their lost husbands and sons.

Less than seventy miles away in France, men with grimy uniforms exhaled their final breaths in foxholes and filthy burrows, while back home lights were dimmed in sitting rooms as anxious relatives took up their listening posts. Mediums, mesmerisers and hypnotists emerged from the back-streets with all manner of theatrical props: Ouija boards, moving tables, listening trumpets, mysterious lights, magic lanterns and crystal balls, all to help the population confront its grief and feed an insatiable desire for contact with the otherworld.

London at the dawn of 1918 was a city burdened with grief, while I was a twenty-four-year-old medical student given that rare chance afforded to unhappy youth, the opportunity to follow someone who believed in the extraordinary. After studying the human body and all its known diseases for three years at the city's University College Hospital, I longed for the magical simplicity with which I had seen things at the age of five. I mourned the ignorance I had left behind and all that I had barely understood before my world had been blinded by the rigours of science and all its enshrined explanations of the universe.

The object of my devotion, my leader in this spiritual quest, was a celebrated poet and mystic, who at that time presided over a shambling crowd of artists, spiritualists and mediums that congregated in the dusty halls of the British Library and drab clubs along Kingsway.

I had grown tired of my fellow students and their indifference to the mysteries of life, heartless men who would never learn to see that life was magical, so obsessed were they with their material possessions, their occupations and their expectations of city life. So when this free-thinking genius of an Irishman spoke one evening in a university reading room and described how it was possible for the mind to travel through space without leaving the body, that he had observed dark towers and the bodies of holy men and women adrift in the air, that the stars and the phases of the moon told secret stories of the human heart, and that our spiritual companions floated beside us in an aquamarine sea of ether, I seized the chance to pledge myself to his secret society devoted to the occult. I had witnessed enough bodily suffering. Instead, I wished to feast on the beautiful terrors of the invisible world.

My days at University College had been numbered since the death of my close friend, Issac Wilson, during an end-of-term examination. He had complained to me of nausea beforehand but had dismissed it as indigestion, utterly unaware that it was a warning sign of a heart attack, and that he was about to die. His last memory of this life was of a stuffy university hall, the afternoon light shuttered by heavy curtains, the scratch of pens churning out the lurid horrors of human disease and decay. I wondered how unhappy his dying senses must have felt with what he could still see and hear, and then it struck me that perhaps he had felt the opposite, perhaps he had experienced happiness at his release from this silent suffocation.

For several nights after Issac's funeral, I awoke in a cold sweat to see the figure of my dead friend standing at the foot of my bed, gazing at me with a melancholic smile. In each of the visitations, he raised a glass of wine and toasted the disappointments and defeats of the life that lay ahead of me, the mistakes I would make, and the ignorance of my heart. The note of tenderness in his ghostly voice did not reassure me; in fact, it terrified me. In the weeks that followed, I was afflicted by fainting fits and night terrors. I tried to get a grip on myself, but found it impossible.

I saw the tragedy of the professional life Issac had managed to escape, where everything loses its originality and repeats itself from day to day. From that point on, I began to regard my professors as men who had lost their vitality and curiosity, a school of scientific fanatics, who made their students' lives unnecessarily tedious and dry in the name of intellectual advancement while secretly serving their own vanity and conformity. I began to labour against the taboos that restricted the range of permissible enquiries within their laboratories and tutorial rooms, the institutional inertia that imprisoned our imaginations and stifled creativity.

I stopped going to my lectures and began researching the existence of ghosts, and the possibilities of the human spirit travelling on astral planes. One day in the British Library, I stumbled upon the vast literature that underpinned occult societies such as the Order of the Golden Dawn. My reading of how the Christian Cabbala and Eastern religions had traced the pathways between the individual consciousness and the cosmos appeared to support the ideas that I was developing through my own private experiences. The hunger to explore life's greater mysteries became so intense that it gnawed at my insides, but my professors dismissed my interest in the spiritual world as an excess of youthful morbidity, and an unfortunate waste of my intellectual talent.

'Why do you want to study ghosts, Mr Adams?' they asked. 'Is it to evoke the memories of those you mourn?'

I told them it was to help formulate a theory of life and death, one that might marry scientific research with the latest discoveries of psychic phenomena, but secretly, in my heart, I carried a more selfish desire. I wanted a great adventure, to take a gamble in life, to gain secret knowledge of the universe and the human heart, not by the well-worn path of scientific study, but by walking the bridge that joins the visible world to the invisible.

This was how on the 12 February 1918, I and Edmund Dulac, the painter and fairy tale illustrator, came to be hurrying after the tall, animated figure of William Butler Yeats, as he dissolved into the murky vapours of a freezing London evening. Perhaps it was my overheated imagination, but I believed I could detect the sound of invisible wings beating around us as we hastened along Holborn Street.

A thick fog had descended over the city's great river and its environs. Dimly lit lamp posts loomed before us like the blackened stumps of trees in no-man's-land. The clatter of cantering hooves sounded close by on cobbles, but their source was invisible. Even the dogs we met were huddled together for comfort. I ran ahead of Dulac, anxious that the poet might disappear through a door into a mystical world and leave us behind in a city that in its grief had succumbed not just to fog but to a collective blindness.

However, Yeats walked faster than I had ever seen any person walk, so fast he seemed more a wraith than a man. He did not need to consult a map. He seemed to know the murky side streets of the city the way a boat's navigator knows the backwaters of a river. He knew by instinct where the dark banks of houses twisted left or right or plunged completely from view into rubbled wasteland or rat-infested marsh. For him there was no fog, just a bright sense of his own elation as he hurried towards his destination.

We struggled desperately to stay up with him, especially Dulac, who was neither lean nor tall, but the mist kept congealing around Yeats' shadowy figure.

He stopped repeatedly, but as soon as we caught up with him, he would take off before we had time to catch our breath.

'Stay with me, Charles and Edward,' he shouted.

The frenzy of the supernatural pursuit had entirely consumed his patience. He had the look of a man prepared to knock on every door in the city in search of a portal to the otherworld.

Our eyes led us towards the myriad lights of Regent Street, but out of the darkness, Yeats shouted 'no, not that way', guiding us down through Edgware Road and its rows of trees coiled with fog. He stopped and regarded us with his elegant, gaunt features. Spidery shadows of twigs and branches formed a tapestry on his face. I realised he had left the house in such a haste he had forgotten his hat.

'This is not the time or place for a leisurely stroll', he said, his face wearing a wounded look, as though we had disappointed him.

Dulac complained that Yeats was moving too quickly for his less athletic companions. 'One who is born in mist always feels most at home in it,' he grumbled, referring to the poet's cherished Sligo childhood.

Instantly, Yeats' scowl vanished, and a smile returned to his soft mouth. He stared at us with amusement.

Dulac pleaded with him. 'Talk to us about the joys of married life and give us half a chance to get a breath.'

A few months previously, the poet had married Georgie Hyde-Lees, after a whirlwind romance spurred on by the rejections of his lifelong love and muse Maud Gonne and her twenty-three-year-old French daughter, Iseult Gonne.

'A case of young love,' said Yeats with a glint in his eye. 'Georgie has miraculously helped me recover my youthful bloom.'

A foggy London night can make acquaintances feel as though they have been known to each other since boyhood. The open look in Yeats' eyes gave me courage to pry further.

'But what of your greatest muse, Maud Gonne?'

'Sadly our paths diverged the more I became involved with the occult.'

Something in Yeats' soul seemed to have opened. His face looked suddenly vulnerable, in spite of his superior age and position in society.

Dulac pressed further. 'If it had not been for your spiritual investigations, would she have agreed to marry you?'

'I'm not sure,' replied Yeats. His shoulders slumped a little and his chest shook slightly. 'My worst failing in life has been my timing. When I finally gathered the boldness to propose to Maud, it was already too late. For three decades, I have kept my passions fixated on her classical beauty, in the belief that by limiting the number of women who arouse me, I might eliminate the potential sources of frustration. But Maud's charms have weighed heavily on me, trapping me in a trance of longing. Now I look back on all those years of restraint and wonder why? At the age of fifty-two, am I finally discovering the excesses of youth?' He waved his hands helplessly. 'Maud was right. If we had married, it would never have worked for either of us. We only understand life when we find our true spiritual soulmate.' A volume of condensed air erupted from his mouth in a sigh of frustration. 'Anything can be endured if that is the case.'

'And have you found yours in Georgie?'

'That is a question I mean to ask the spirits tonight,' he said, and then he was off again, lurching into the fog, leaving Dulac and myself surrounded by closing walls of opalescent grey and our own muffled breathing.

The fog instantly absorbed the poet's retreating footsteps. Unable to distinguish much in our surroundings we ran blindly after him.

A few minutes later, the sharp sound of someone knocking at a door brought us back to our bearings and senses. We were at a rundown terrace in a side street somewhere behind the culverts and warehouses of Spitalfields, the sort of street where no gentleman should allow himself to be seen, especially at night.

The fog cleared just enough to reveal Yeats' tall figure standing at a door, a light from within illuminating his face.

'Where is the spirit room?' we heard him ask in an urgent whisper.

'Follow me,' replied a woman standing in the hallway. She was tall, and dressed in a simple black gown. We followed the poet into a hall dominated by a wrought iron stairway. The shadows inside were different from those on the fog-bound streets. Unattached. Transient in the flickering gaslight. They appeared to have a life of their own as we followed the woman up the stairs. The rooms we passed were empty of human life and so quiet we could eavesdrop on the rest of the terrace. Through the walls we heard the voices of defiant children and scolding women running their impoverished households with shouts and slammed doors.

The woman led us into a room on the third floor and sat us at a table lit with candles. She wore no make-up and no jewellery apart from a metal cross with a cluster of red gems in the shape of a rose. Her hair was the colour of polished silver and tied up without a single loose strand.

We followed the sceptic's precautions of not giving our names or asking for any particular spirit. Yeats offered to use his set of mystical cards to clear the room of any negative influences, but the woman declined.

On the table before us lay a case made of Moroccan leather. A set of small phials nestled within, containing, I suspected, laudanum. Dulac leaned forward enthusiastically and drank from one of the bottles.

'You'll find that incense is not the only ingredient essential to supernatural evocations,' he whispered, handing me the phial. I accepted it only because of a hidden fear that if I declined I would somehow reveal myself as an impostor. I tasted a drop before handing it back to Dulac, who looked pleased to be reunited with it.

Yeats sipped from the remaining bottle, and then dabbed his lips with a silk handkerchief, as if feeling for blood. 'My Dublin doctor has advised me to avoid liquid opium,' he explained. 'It brings me out in spots.'

The medium watched us in a direct manner that was not without a measure of scorn. She reminded me of a schoolmistress from my early school days, sitting ready with a ruler to rap the knuckles of a misbehaving attendee.

'It is best not to react to the spirits in any visible way, especially by flinching,' she instructed us. 'If possible keep your face blank and stiff. There is nothing they like more than inflicting fear, and we should deny them that pleasure, whenever possible.'

We stared at her still, sombre face.

She continued: 'Don't be afraid. The spirits may be unpredictable but they possess such a limited range of behaviours they are easy to control and dismiss.'

'I hope you don't mean to toy with our ghostly companions,' complained Yeats. The note of annoyance in his voice stopped her in her tracks.

'Why not? Don't they toy with the living?'

'How do we know you're not toying with us?'

'For the séance to work you must assume the medium is honest.'

'As a psychic investigator I must assume the spirits are telling the truth, but that mediums are prone to lying and fabrication.'

What Yeats said was sadly true. Every new medium was a thorn bush he approached with caution. Drawing on three decades of research into the paranormal, he had concluded that many mediums were charlatans, witting, or not, and that most of the messages they conveyed belonged to the meaningless babble of the subconscious.

'If you are here as an investigator then I have to ask permission,' said the medium. Anger had crept into her voice.

'Permission?' repeated Yeats.

'You will need permission to ask your questions. If you wish to open doors that are not normally opened at séances.'

Yeats acquiesced. 'I thought that was the whole purpose of séances – to ask questions of the dead, but go ahead, if you must.'

Carefully, the woman settled her hands on the table as though
they were ears pressed to the chest of a loved one. A rumbling
voice began not in her throat, but in her body, a humming
growl, like a voice buried deep underground, like the blood I
could hear thumping through my veins. All the time she stared
straight ahead with eyes so lifeless they looked as though they
had been painted on her lids. Yeats lit a cigarette and found
an ashtray. He conveyed the impression that he was bored to
distraction.

After ten minutes the mumbling stopped.

'Do you want to come in?' the medium asked with sudden
animation. The rose of rubies in her necklace glimmered to a
deeper crimson.

The candles flickered and the room was gutted with shadows.

'Do come in,' she urged. 'Enter and tell us how you conquered
Death.' She tilted her head, listening carefully. Something sighed
at the door. It could not have been the wind for there was no wind
that night. Something other than the wind sighed at the keyhole
and blew into the room as though the walls were releasing their
breath. All the candles blew out and the room was plunged in
total darkness. My stomach shrank at the thought of my friend
Issac's weary smile and silent stare.

'I have a message from a spirit,' said the medium. 'But I cannot
hear him properly. He speaks an ancient language.'

Yeats relit the candles and after a whispered consultation with
Dulac, leaned forward and cleared his throat.

'Can you ask the spirit its name?'

The woman mumbled that the name was Bates. Then she
confessed she was not sure what it was.

'Yeats, possibly,' she said.

'But I am Yeats,' countered the poet.

'No you're not,' said the medium in a hoarse voice, as though
the spirit was speaking through her. 'Yeats has left the room.'

Yeats' face grew dark with suspicion. 'You mock me.'

'Why won't you help me?' asked the medium in her altered
voice.

'First you must tell us what they call you.'

'I can't tell you that right now.'

'Then when can you?'

'You'll know when the time is right. Just wait and see.'

'See what?'

'That should be clear to a poet.'

Yeats sighed and reached for his coat.

'Wait,' said the medium in her normal voice. 'Someone else has entered the room. A young woman. Her name is Rosemary. She wishes to speak to Mr Yeats.'

'Can you describe her?' Yeats lowered himself back into his seat.

'Her face is covered in a hood decorated with a hem of red and black roses. She says two men have trapped her in a tiny room with no way out.'

The candles flickered again, hiding the expression on the medium's face, so that none of us could tell what she was thinking. Darkness swung across the room like the shadow of a heavy pendulum. Light and shade, light and shade, as though the entire room was swinging between this world and the next. Someone said something, and I instinctively looked round, expecting to see Issac's ghost, but there was no one there. Yeats shuffled his feet and hummed a little tune under his breath, but his forehead was sweating and his face transfixed with tension.

'Ask the spirit how she knew I would be here tonight. And why has she chosen me?'

'She says only a poet can see what is invisible, the trail of clues that others can't see. Only you hold the magic key, but you must hurry. The waves of water are flooding the room. Already she can no longer feel her feet or legs because of the coldness. She says the waves are about to close about her face.'

'This is a dream of yours,' said Yeats, rising from his seat.

'It is no dream. Her spirit was with you when you entered this room. She was with you all evening. Your life goes on around her.'

'Then tell me why she has attached herself to me.'

The medium stared at Yeats with a mysterious expression. Was it wisdom, sadness or curiosity that shone from her shadowy eyes?

'Mr Yeats, the spirits of the dead pass through this world like bodies falling without a place to land. They search for faces they like, or expressions they can tolerate, people with whom they can identify in some way. They look everywhere, in railway waiting rooms, libraries, concert halls, parks, the crowds milling in the streets. In truth, they are searching for a reflection of themselves, a sign that they are still here, that connects them to the land of the living. But any trace or echo of their former existence is fleeting, because the crowds of humanity are transforming all the time like the clouds in the sky. Every moment they undergo a bewildering set of transformations.'

Yeats nodded in agreement. 'It is the vital connection we seek all our lives. That someone somewhere will remember and love us. But this visitation is a case of lightning hitting the wrong man. I never knew this woman, nor was I responsible for her death.'

'You can't ignore her plight.'

'No.' Yeats voice grew strained. 'I've lost the key. It's out of my reach forever.' He yanked at my sleeve and pointed to the door. We hurried out. In a darkened window, I caught a reflection of our faces, the pale light of panic shining forth.

We ran into the street, none of us speaking until the terrace of houses had blended with the fog-bound darkness.

'Aren't you going to tell us why you are so affected by what she said?' said Dulac, panting to keep up with us.

'No,' replied Yeats.

Dulac sounded disappointed. 'I'm curious.'

'And I am weary, my old friend. It is late, and I want to get home, write up my notes, go to bed and sleep. Mr Adams will see that I get there safely.'

'You look more frightened than weary.'

Yeats said nothing.

'Perhaps it is just weariness,' said Dulac. 'One gets tired attending these sorts of séances, listening to the pitiful wailing of so many frauds. Eventually one feels overwhelmed by their lamentable acting.'

'Promise me one thing,' said Yeats, 'that the events of tonight remain between us, and no one else.'

'I won't say a thing.'

Before parting company and climbing into a hackney cab, the painter apologised. 'I should know better than to press you on personal spiritual matters. If there's anything you need, let me know.'

'You could find me a good exorcist.'

'If I thought one would help you, I would. In the meantime, try and get some rest.'

With Dulac gone, Yeats and I found ourselves on Eastwick Road, an impoverished-looking thoroughfare that smelt of damp cinders. The poet's Bloomsbury rooms were at least a few miles away, and languishing before us lay the black hulk of a Victorian poorhouse, a miserable-looking building covered in soot and surrounded by barbed wire. Like many former poorhouses in the city, it had been recently converted to a makeshift prison to house some of the thousands of Irish insurgents arrested after the failed Easter Rising in 1916.

Outside its gates, a small battalion of women had gathered, banging the gates, singing songs and reciting political chants. Foremost among them were several widows dressed in veils decorated with roses. I took them to be the wives of the rebel leaders executed for their part in the Rising. There was a menacing edge to their grief, like that of women who had hung around too long at the edge of a battlefield. Their faces were gaunt, fanatical. Not for them the special reception given to the widows of men who had fallen gallantly in France. They were the wives of traitors, whose executions the papers had trumpeted, and whose bodies now lay in anonymous quicklime graves.

Yeats stared at the dark, barricaded building and the protesting women. He reached his hand onto my arm, steadying himself.

When the women saw us approach, they swelled towards us with their dark, smouldering faces. They appeared about to pounce upon us when a voice, which seemed to come from behind, drew their attention. A tall stooping woman, dressed in layers of black like an elderly widow, appeared at our side and led the crowd back to their prison gate protest. She shouted above their heads in a voice that sounded more youthful than her appearance: 'Women of Ireland, freedom is never won without the sacrifice of blood. Our chance is coming. The end of the British Empire is at hand and Ireland will rise up from the ashes of the Easter Rising. She has been the land of sorrow long enough.'

The women cheered and returned to banging the gates. At that moment, my attention was caught by the speaker, who was doing something that struck me as odd. She was checking her face in a compact mirror and powdering her cheeks in the manner of an actress preparing for the stage. I tugged at Yeat's coat, but he too had noticed her actions. She snapped the mirror shut and slipped it into a leather purse. She turned her white face towards us and raised her finger to her lips as if we were part of a conspiracy. Her coat opened slightly, revealing the red cape of a Red Cross nurse's uniform. After holding our stare for a moment, she made her way into the throng of protesters. In spite of her stooped posture, I had the impression of a shapely body swaying confidently beneath the layers of black. The effect on Yeats was immediate and dramatic. He reached out with his hand and then sank to his knees.

Across the street, two men cloaked in shadows watched as I helped Yeats move away from the protesters. Their boots rang against the cobbles as they trotted towards us.

'Have you been robbed, sir?' asked one of them. They were dressed in the uniform of London policemen.

'No. Just call us a hack,' said Yeats in a hoarse voice.

They obliged and as soon as the cab pulled alongside, Yeats dropped into the seat. When his colour had returned, he spoke in a whisper, 'What were we thinking walking by such a prison at this time of night? Have we forgotten how dangerous this city has become?'

'We weren't thinking at all, that was the problem.'

Yeats sighed. 'I sometimes fear I've helped drive my country to this perilous brink.'

'You mean England?'

'No. Ireland.' He groaned. 'All my poetry and plays. How have they helped anyone? All they've done is stir arrogant men to violence and bloodshed.'

'Your writing did not start the Easter Rising.'

'But the men who read my words did. I should have tried harder to talk them out of shedding blood for Ireland. I keep going over the past in my mind and wondering if I could have done anything to turn those foolish young men in some other direction.'

Yeats fell silent as if what he had said was a confession that shook even him. He nestled into a moody silence within his high-collared coat. The fog dispersed and the weather got colder to the point of freezing. Yeats nodded off, his head slumped sideways. When the hack drew to a halt, he jerked awake.

'Where are we?' he asked, his eyes blank. He peered through the window and seemed reassured that the street was empty and well-lit.

He gave me a guilty look. 'My wife doesn't know we visited a séance tonight. She thinks I was giving a talk to the Sesame Club on Chichester Street.'

He closed his eyes again. 'The supernatural world is like a beautiful woman, alluring and impossible to resist. Yet it carries so many obligations and hidden dangers.'

'Dangers?' I asked.

He took a deep breath. 'What happened tonight has happened before. Everywhere I seem to go these days I find myself running into the same ghost. Everywhere I look, she invades me with her manifestation. The smell of her perfume constantly overpowers me.'

'Who is she?'

'My black Irish rose. Come to my house and I will explain what I know so far about her mysterious death.'

3

ACE OF SWORDS

IT was just before midnight when we entered the front door of Yeats' home. The rest of the journey had passed in silence, the two of us unwilling or unable to turn our thoughts into words. Georgie, Yeats' wife, was still up when we got in. She had been reading a crime novel and greeted me as though I were a mildly disturbing annoyance, before concentrating her gaze on Yeats, whose pale skin had taken on a bluish translucence from our fog-bound adventures.

The poet's self-possession was soon restored by the attentions of his young wife as she gently helped him out of his coat and poured him a glass of claret.

'You should not be out in such fog,' she scolded him. 'You know how terribly sensitive you are to a heavy atmosphere.'

'Do not burden yourself with worry,' he replied, appearing to take pride in her solicitous manner.

Although a ruddy glow had returned to his cheeks, the shadow of the evening's exertions still lay across his face, and a feverish light shone from his eyes.

'Would you care to join us for a drink?' he asked, laying a hand on her shoulder and glancing at the book she was reading.

'I'd better not,' she replied. 'It's getting late.' She kissed him on the cheek and carefully closed the book.

She glanced reprovingly at me again. Her rising annoyance at my continued presence made me feel like a lost child lingering in her husband's footsteps.

Yeats waved a hand in my direction. 'Mr Adams has come to help me solve a supernatural enigma.'

'Don't tell me you're still searching for that ghost,' she sighed.

'On the contrary, my dear Georgie, that ghost is still searching for me.'

Without further delay, Yeats led me into his library where a fire was flickering in an ornate fireplace. The room was full of books stacked in precarious storeys, and tables of charts and strange diagrams. Shelves lined the walls with an assortment of encyclopaedias, heraldic weapons, crystals, jars of herbs, and implements shaped like quern stones which I had seen him wield to influence the elemental powers.

He sat down at his ebony writing table and proceeded to record his notes for the evening in his customary secret code, his hand shaking slightly. Then he threw down his pen.

'Before we can sum up tonight's events, I must show you what has caused my mind such unrest.'

He began opening drawers in the table, throwing out scrolls written in eastern and ancient languages and various antique ornaments.

Lifting out a heavy old book, he regarded me solemnly. 'I have here a letter that contains the most bizarre proposition ever made to me.'

He allowed for a dramatic pause before opening the book and removing a velvet slipcase from within its yellowing leaves. As painstakingly as if he were handling a wafer of ice, he removed a single-page letter and placed it in front of me. I caught a bleak scent of roses and rain that was redolent of a grand house in a damp country.

'Let me advise you that once you have read what is written here you can never unlearn it,' he warned.

Intrigued, I examined the letter. At first, it seemed to me the hysterical outpourings of a fervent female fan. Addressed to Mr William Butler Yeats, care of the Order of the Golden Dawn,

it began with the outrageous claim that by the time the letter
reached his door, its authoress would be dead. The letter-writer
went on to describe her growing certainty that an unknown
individual was determined to rob her of her life. In the event of
her unexplained death, she begged Yeats to return to Sligo and
investigate her murder, lest the guilty party go unpunished. '*I
shall be all the more powerful in spirit than in flesh,*' she promised
Yeats. '*In return for investigating my murder I will provide for you
admirable proof of the existence of an afterlife, and of your own
psychic skills. It is my plan to return and haunt my murderer in such
a deliberate and powerful manner that his or her identity will become
obvious to your watchful oversight.*'

At the bottom of the letter was the signature of Rosemary
O'Grady, followed by the word Lissadell, which at the time
meant nothing to me. Even taking into consideration the formal
tone of the letter, the writer's words were chilling and dramatic,
made all the more powerful by her affirmative use of the future
tense.

I studied the letter carefully. There was none of the smudging
or ink-blots that suggested it had been written in haste or under
emotional duress. In fact, the letter's neatness suggested she had
rehearsed the lines a hundred times in her mind.

'I have kept it secret this past month,' said Yeats returning
the letter to its slipcase, 'wondering if it was the work of a mad
woman until I came across this in the Sligo Chronicle.' He
handed me the cutting of a newspaper report.

Sinister death on a Sligo beach

On the morning of November 1, the drowned body of a local girl
was washed ashore at Blind Sound beach, near Lissadell. A servant
in the employment of the Gore-Booth family, nineteen-year-old
Rosemary O'Grady was found inside a coffin by Captain Thomas
Oates, who has been stationed at Magheroy Lighthouse since June
under the command of the British Admiralty. According to an

eyewitness report, the dead woman's wrists were slashed and she was wearing a hood decorated with red and black roses. Inspector Derek Grimes of Sligo Royal Irish Constabulary has called for local people to be on the alert for a vagrant or unknown person in the area. On questioning, he refused to rule out suicide as a possible cause for the young woman's untimely death.

'We are on the lookout for any suspicious person or persons,' he told the Chronicle. 'The brutal and tragic nature of this young woman's death has caused deep unease in the local population. We would advise households to refrain from panic but would suggest that husbands and fathers be aware of the whereabouts of their wives and daughters at all times. However, I should add that, at this time, we are still not sure what sort of foul play has occurred.' The Inspector would not be drawn on the police investigation into her death or on the whereabouts of Captain Oates, who, since the gruesome discovery, has taken a leave of absence from his post.

'The letter is hardly proof she was murdered,' I suggested. 'Her death may have been a bizarre suicide, as the newspaper report suggests. In fact, given the letter's unusual proposition it might not be so odd to assume she became the tragic victim of her own irrationality. People who kill themselves have been known to publicise their intentions beforehand. The use of a coffin also suggests a measure of attention seeking.'

'You believe madness overtook her.'

'That might be overstating the case. Perhaps the letter was a melodramatic cry for help.'

I had hardly to remind Yeats that the Order of the Golden Dawn had an unfortunate tendency to attract thrill-seeking females. It was a consequence of the secret society's heavy reliance on daggers, swords and incense, as well as cords and chains in its initiation ceremonies. On more than one occasion, the heady atmosphere of its rituals had drawn the order unwanted publicity and even a sexual scandal involving a false initiation rite performed on a sixteen-year-old girl.

'What about the séance tonight? Does that not provide more evidence? More clues?'

'The supernatural influence certainly compounds the mystery.'

'What puzzles me is why she was dressed in a hood decorated with red and black roses.'

I allowed a pause before replying. 'What might keep me awake at night is wondering why she died and how her body came to be in a coffin in the first place.'

'But why the two colours of roses?'

'Perhaps they're symbols.'

'What do you mean?'

'Emblems chosen by the murderer. A form of signature. A crime as gruesome as murder is sometimes exalted by the killer into a form of ritual.'

'I'm afraid you're mistaken Mr Adams. They're not the killer's symbols. They belong to me, or rather to the Irish literary tradition. Let me explain.'

He stood up with that familiar air of a great poet about to sweep me into his aura, a very special aura that contained secrets capable of changing one's life. 'Rose is the name of a girl with black hair in Irish patriotic poetry; she is Roisin Dubh, or Dark Rosaleen, and personifies Ireland. De Vere wrote on the same theme, "The little black rose shall be red at last". The red rose signifies the flower of love that blossoms from the cross of sacrifice. Which is why the Golden Dawn, like the Rosicrucians, has adopted the symbols of the rose and the cross as its emblems.' He stared at me. 'Now do you understand why I am so fixated on the red and black roses?'

'I suppose so.'

If Yeats was fixated on the symbol of the rose, then so were substantial sections of the esoteric communities of London and Paris, where interest in occult societies dedicated to such imagery was gaining rapidly by the day.

'Don't suppose it. Understand it.'

Although I did not possess Yeats' crystalline insight into

literary symbolism, I could see he needed assistance. If I could not offer pearls of poetic wisdom, I could at least guide him down the practical path of commonsense.

'Let's concentrate on the facts,' I suggested. 'The red and black roses may be nothing more than an incidental detail in this macabre saga. However, it's possible that whoever placed the hood on her head was trying to communicate something hidden in the same way you use the symbol of the rose in your poetry, or any symbol for that manner.'

'You mean the embroidered hem carries a secret message?'

'I believe it is possible.'

'But for whom? The killer or the victim? Or the person who discovers the body?'

'Or someone else. Perhaps the message was meant for you.'

Yeats appeared to discount my proposition. 'You are suggesting we have a murderer who thinks and behaves like a poet writing for an indeterminate and invisible audience. God help us all.'

He began to pace the room.

'The truth is this dead woman has me in a terrible grip,' he said. 'Her letter is too provocative to be ignored.'

'Yet it is tantalisingly bereft of clues,' I replied. 'For instance, she doesn't mention how her suspicions were aroused in the first place.'

'But something has made her morbidly suspicious. Perhaps it was just a vague dread. We'll never know.'

'I wonder if she shared her fears with anyone else.'

'The letter suggests she kept them secret.'

'Why would she have kept them secret?'

'Because she did not want the person to find out, and that suggests the killer, if there was one, was close to her, or in a position of power and influence.'

'Unfortunately, there are no instruments of science to tell us with any degree of certainty whether the voice we heard tonight was the letter-writer speaking from beyond the grave.'

Yeats had grown pale again, and he was perspiring.

'What is certain is that we know nothing about this woman,

apart from what is contained in this letter and the newspaper report. Nevertheless, she has appealed to the society of the Golden Dawn for assistance.'

I detected a slight shift in Yeats' expression, as though he had come to an important point in our discussion. He looked at me out of the corner of his eye.

'Unfortunately I cannot return to Ireland in the present circumstances,' he said. 'Dublin has become too political and Sligo is too damp at this time of year. Besides, I have important spiritual work to conclude in London. And I'm unable to drop my literary engagements at such short notice.' He stared at me without blinking. 'The simple matter is I'm not equipped to cope with such a gruesome incident. You, Mr Adams, however, must have experienced this sort of thing in your medical studies.'

'My course did not include training in how to deal with dead bodies mysteriously found in coffins.'

Yeats shuffled through his papers, as if he could not be bothered to listen. He handed me the newspaper report and the letter. 'Mr Adams, I want you to summon all your talent and commit yourself mind and soul to investigating this young woman's death.'

I stared at the evidence in my hands. 'I don't know what you expect me to be able to do.'

'Naturally, the society of the Golden Dawn will be very keen to hear your findings, and you will receive from its members all the assistance you require.'

I hesitated to refuse. To perform a task under the behest of the Order of the Golden Dawn was to participate in a grand and secret tradition that was interwoven with the destiny of European civilisation, a tradition maintained by daring avant-garde figures such as the flamboyant mystic Aleister Crowley, who had himself described the cult society as the Hidden Church of the Holy Grail.

At that moment, my host stood up abruptly, remembering that he had to catch an early train to Oxford to perform a poetry reading at one of the women's colleges.

'I suggest we leave it at that for tonight,' he said. Then with profuse apologies for his sudden lack of hospitability, he rushed me out of the house.

'I am very tired and have a great longing for order,' he whispered as he closed the front door.

PAGE OF WANDS

THE smell of dinner drifted from the kitchens of the Strand Hotel, a rich meat-heavy smell that provided no comfort to the hungry pedestrians on the street; the grey city-workers, the shop-girls, the servants and tradesmen, most of whom had been surviving for the past three years on meagre rations and what they could extemporise from their depleted larders.

The previous year, Winston Churchill, Minister of Munitions, had requisitioned the hotel for the duration and set up offices for the Air and Naval departments in the Strand's former ballrooms and bedrooms. Major Charles Rogers had spent nine months sitting in a deep leather armchair at a desk in Section M studying maps and reams of intelligence reports on Europe's Atlantic seaboard. When his work was finished, he dined every evening dressed in a dinner jacket under the splendour of crystal chandeliers caressed by clouds of the finest cigar smoke.

In spite of his elegant surroundings, Rogers found his daily tasks – the allocation of aircraft alongside the various squadrons and shipping convoys to counter the U-boat menace – frustratingly mundane.

It upset him that military airplanes were still being used by the Admiralty solely as a tactical weapon, in support of naval activities, rather than as a separate fighting arm. Invariably, the planes were grounded. It soon became apparent to Rogers that in the North Sea, when the moon was right for flying, the weather was probably not. Finding the long periods of desk-bound inactivity almost unbearable, Rogers had applied for a transfer to flying duties himself, but Churchill had little faith in the new-fangled aircraft and was not prepared to waste a first-class intelligence officer on one of them.

When Rogers had pestered Churchill for a post more suited to his temperament and experience, one a little closer to the action, he was rewarded for his persistence with the additional task of monitoring the movements of Irish Republicans and their sympathisers in London. Principally he was to target the activities of secret societies devoted to the occult, which had been infiltrated by undesirable rebel elements.

Rogers studied the file that had been handed to him.

'Mystics and Irish folklorists?' he asked Churchill with incredulity. 'What has the war effort got to do with this ragtag band of misfits?' He tried to make his point as forcibly as possible. The Easter Rising might have caused a little local trouble in Dublin, unnecessarily prolonged because the rebels had the bad form to kick-start their revolution on a public holiday, but surely the Admiralty had more pressing problems on its mind. What about the German U-boat campaign and the threat posed by the Kaiser's High Seas Fleet?

Churchill grunted and eyed him coldly.

'The Admiralty has learned that the Irish rebels have sent representation to the German high command, urging them to invade along the country's western seaboard. At the same time, their sympathisers are raising funds and support for Irish independence in this very country. Ignoring them would be akin to falling asleep in a crime-ridden city and leaving the back door wide open. Your task is simple. Here is the list of a very busy little network of rebel supporters. I want you to stop them in their tracks before they can commit treason.'

Rogers licked his lips and tried to generate some enthusiasm in his voice.

'Sounds straightforward.'

'Of course it is. And remember, our country is engaged abroad in a war to end all wars, but right here, at home in this city, there are dangerous elements just as potent lurking in the shadows, and they are hell-bent on achieving their ghastly aims.'

Rogers nodded curtly, and Churchill sighed contentedly. 'By the way, they're serving Beef Wellington tonight,' he said. 'The Admiralty never forgets that it is the stomach that governs the world, rather than the head or heart.'

By the time Rogers had finished dining on the evening of 12 February, a fog had risen from the stagnant Thames and was pressing down upon the darkened city. He raised his lit cigar to his mouth and savoured the aroma of tobacco as he stood on the steps of the hotel. In the darkness, he heard the sound of someone coughing belligerently.

Unexpectedly, the figure of one of his spies, a tall, lean Irishman known as Wolfe Marley, emerged from the corpse-white fog. On spotting Rogers, the spy removed his black cap. His crown of thick grey hair bristled in the dripping air, making him resemble a badger that had aggressively poked its head from its lair. He bounded up the steps and joined Rogers.

'Just passing by in the course of my patriotic duty, sir,' said the Irishman.

Rogers felt a flicker of annoyance at being approached in such a familiar manner by one of his underlings. He had the impression that Marley had been waiting close by in the fog for some time. For what? For him to emerge from the hotel? The warmth of the Strand and the cigar's aroma quickly evaporated. The night air tasted damp and cold.

'Do you know where you are, Marley?' Rogers' hushed voice emanated hostility. Majors and generals in white shirts and black suits accompanied by women in glittering dresses cautiously manoeuvred around them. Marley was wearing a nondescript coat, held up by a worn-looking leather belt.

'Of course I do. The stench of money and arrogance helped me navigate my way.' He dipped his bare head in mock respect.

'Unfortunately, growing up in Ireland has ruined my relationship with the upper classes. I see that they exist in their cocoon of wealth, but I can never seriously respect them, or see a reason for their existence. If all this were taken away by a German bomb should anyone care?'

Rogers felt tension tug on his face. He grimaced.

'Are you just going to stand here? You look like a tramp.'

'I thought I'd accompany you this evening.'

'Accompany me? Haven't you other duties?'

Marley flashed a crooked smile at Rogers, who glared back. The Irishman represented the world of subterfuge and violence, which he tried to sweep from his mind every evening on leaving the hotel. He had assigned Marley the task of watching the movements of Madame Maud Gonne MacBride, the former actress, and the widow of Major John MacBride, one of the executed leaders of the 1916 Rising. Rogers' department had served her with a notice under the Defence of the Realm Act, placing her under house arrest in Balfour Street. The authorities did not want the charismatic widow to return to Ireland, fearful that once set loose she might stir up the embers of rebellion like a modern day Joan of Arc.

'I hope our grieving widow is keeping you busy,' said Rogers.

Marley's head darted about, taking in the windows of the hotel and the enormous span of the brightly lit dining room. He stared with fierce interest at the departing staff. Compared to their well-fed faces glowing with alcohol, he looked much too gaunt and starved. There was no excess left to his face or body. His eyes were like those of a ravenous fish swimming in a lifeless pool.

'I've been searching for her all week,' said Marley.

'Searching?' Rogers' voice grew more clipped. 'The woman's under house arrest. And you're meant to be watching her.'

'Somehow she's got wind of the hunting dogs following her. Unbeknownst to us, she's been slipping in and out of her house in the disguise of a Red Cross nurse. The black widow has lost none of her theatrical skills. In fact, now that she has a secret audience they are flourishing.'

Rogers frowned at Marley. 'Gonne is an actress. A lover of disguises and masks. What's so important about this that it couldn't wait until our next scheduled meeting?'

Marley flexed his tongue and licked his lips. 'Last night, I followed her to a house off Edgware Street. There was a séance taking place upstairs.'

'Have you come to warn me that the widow is recruiting ghosts?' interrupted Rogers. 'Or perhaps you're worried she's using a medium to take commands from her executed husband?'

'William Butler Yeats was in attendance at the séance.'

A distant horn throbbed from the direction of the Thames. In the fog, it felt like a ghostly vibration.

'So? Everyone knows that Ireland's most famous living poet is obsessed with ghosts.'

'I believe revolution is starting to interfere with his ghost-hunting. The house he visited was a former safe house for Irish rebels on the run. It's currently being rented by a man called Theodore Havel, who used to be one of the most successful weapon smugglers in Europe. This is about more than an obsession with the supernatural.'

'Gonne is part of Yeats' hobby, too. No one has a greater personal interest in that woman. He would go to the ends of the earth to catch a glimpse of her.'

'He's not that servile or a fool.' Marley bared his teeth. A look of excitement came over his features. 'My informants tell me that a plot to bring Gonne back to Ireland is at an advanced stage. Along with a large consignment of weapons from Germany. I believe she poses a very dangerous threat to the nation's security.'

'And what part does Yeats play in all this?' Rogers inspected him over his cigar.

'I'm short of information in that regard. We should not forget that Yeats was a member of the Irish Republican Brotherhood in his youth. He also had links with several of the traitors behind the Easter Rising. Yeats likes to think of himself as a great benefactor to the Irish nationalist cause. It's part of his mystical persona.'

'There is no such thing as the Irish Republican Brotherhood

anymore. At least not in any form we're familiar with. That's the problem with these hot-headed revolutionaries and literary types. Always rowing and forming splinter groups. If Yeats is still involved politically then it's with the splinter of a splinter group.'

'Yet he's there in the background. Pulling the strings, I suspect.'

'Nonsense. I know Yeats from the Dorchester Club, and he's a typical Irishman. There's no real harm in him. He just can't choose carefully enough. Not his lovers nor his friends. Nor where his national allegiance lies.'

'Yeats wants it both ways. He wants his English friends to treat him like a fellow Englishman, while Gonne and her Irish rebel friends expect him to behave like a passionate nationalist.'

Rogers stubbed out his cigar. 'The department are more interested in watching Gonne. The idea of that mad woman roaming London at large would give my commanders nightmares. Remember she's meant to be under house arrest.'

'She knows she's being watched and she's enjoying it. She abhors anonymity. You could say she's conducted her whole life in front of an audience.'

'You knew her professionally, didn't you?' Rogers' face sharpened.

'A little. Before the war.' Marley's accent changed to that of an actor in a music hall sketch 'When the 'Oirish theatre was in its heyday, I treaded the stage day and night at the Abbey.'

'An actor and a spy. Quite a combination. And there was me thinking you were just a second-rate informer.'

'Deception is my game now.'

'I'm as keen on subterfuge as the next man in this business, but you must remember intelligence is my game. I deal in facts. Hard evidence. What proof do you have that Gonne is at the centre of this conspiracy? All this talk of gunsmuggling, séances and London's most famous poet, it all sounds so mysterious and far-fetched to me.'

A siren sounded in the street warning of a possible Zeppelin bombing raid. Dogs began yelping from back alleyways. Rogers took advantage of the distraction and called a hackney cab.

'You have to remember,' he continued, 'that we have Gonne's passport, which means she can't return to Ireland or escape to France. She's a refugee in a city hostile to her cause. I want you to keep her in your sights. Perhaps you'll have something more interesting to tell me next week at our briefing.'

Rogers put on his hat and made to leave, but Marley reached out and gripped him by the arm. The siren grew louder.

'You should stay and hear me out.' Marley's teeth were clenched. 'Gonne is a doomed woman, and that's what makes her so dangerous. Doomed and ruthless. The perfect combination for treason.'

'Let go of my arm.'

'I want her arrested.'

'I can't grant you that.'

'Then what is the purpose of my following her and reporting my suspicions to you?'

'There is no purpose. Other than letting her know we are watching her.'

A half-smile froze on Marley's lips and his eyes went cold and still. Rogers glared indignantly at him. The Irishman was a night-wanderer, a double-crosser, a violent and shadowy creature of instinct. What was his motivation in helping the British? Not the fine dining at the hotel Rogers had just left, nor the warm sitting room tended to by the rosy-cheeked wife where he was headed. The Irish were the untamed animals of Europe, whatever their allegiances. Rogers was beginning to understand why so many of them ended up in the carnage of the trenches in Flanders, blindly pursuing a political ideal and the promise of nationhood. He looked back at the hotel, into the dining room filled with overweight middle-aged men who preferred their dinner rounded off with light conversation and a gentle doze.

'I've done my duty. I've informed you of my suspicions,' said Marley tensely. 'I've pinpointed potential troublemakers. It's your job to negate their potential for violence. If you relay my suspicions to your superiors I'm sure they'll act upon them.'

'I wouldn't count on it. In the military, devotion to routine and duty very often replaces intelligence.'

'Can't you see how dangerous Gonne is?' Marley's face dripped with ice-cold moisture. 'Half of Ireland hangs on her every word and regards her as the widow of a martyr. She's the living, breathing personification of Mother Ireland, the incarnation of Roisin Dubh. With the Republican leadership gone there is no one else who can unify the militant nationalist movement.'

Rogers leaned against the railing of the steps and drummed his fingers nervously. Marley's restlessness had taken seed in him. 'In unity there is strength, a truism no less valid for all its triteness,' he remarked. 'A coalition of these splinter groups led by Gonne could be a dangerous step towards an Irish revolution.'

'And if Gonne returns to Ireland with a consignment of weapons, you'll be the one held responsible.'

'But what else can be done to deter this, other than throwing Gonne and every Irish Republican into gaol?'

'I have a plan to discredit Gonne. I believe a more malleable figurehead can be persuaded to take her place, someone who would provide a focus for the disaffected Irish population, but who could be counted on not to cross certain lines.'

'Who do you have in mind?' Some of the caution had left Rogers' voice

'A poet with a penchant for spooks and stately homes – Mr William Butler Yeats. The rebels are a bunch of felons and diehards. They would embrace a figurehead like Yeats because without him they will seem a disorderly rabble to the Irish population. Nothing more than a gang of misfits and murderers. A man of letters like Yeats would make them appear civilised and principled.'

Rogers nodded. 'Yeats is in receipt of a pension from the King. A sum of money that is vital to his livelihood. We should remind him of where his priorities lie.'

Marley grinned and winked. 'I have a few acquaintances,

rough fellows who could persuade Mr Yeats to cool his passions for Irish independence. A little skirmish on a darkened street would be enough to convince him he should keep his creative energies focused on wine, women and song.'

'You're speaking metaphorically of course.'

'Naturally. Poetry is the language of the street.'

Rogers thought aloud. 'And in the meantime, Gonne must be discredited to the Catholic population of Ireland. Not only the responsible citizens of that country but also those harbouring revolutionary sympathies.'

'Most importantly of all, she must be discredited in the eyes of the radicals,' added Marley. 'This last area requires entirely different tactics from the first two.'

'What are you proposing?'

'A series of letters to the British and Irish press, ridiculing Gonne for her Anglo-Irish descent, and her illegitimate daughter. The letters would point out that her father was an English soldier and that she was born in Surrey, which would make her membership of revolutionary organisations such as the Daughters of Ireland invalid. An erroneous reference to how she still receives her father's war pension should also be included.'

Rogers' eyes glowed with enthusiasm.

Marley continued. 'And if we could hatch a plot identifying her as an informant, this would ruin her reputation in the eyes of dangerous radicals.'

'Very well. You must concentrate on exposing this conspiracy and negating Gonne's role as a figurehead.' A touch of friendliness crept into Rogers' voice. 'I will make more men available to you and funds, of course. Use whatever means you deem as necessary. And get in touch with me day or night if there are any developments.'

'And what about Yeats?'

'Tread carefully, to paraphrase one of his poems. He has connections in high places. In the meantime, I want you to make ghost-hunting your hobby, too.'

Marley nodded. His face was without expression.

'What goes on in the afterlife will soon be the least of Mr Yeats' worries.'

He pulled on his black cap and disappeared into the fog.

5

O

QUEEN OF WANDS

WHILE Yeats was busy talking to his apprentice magician in the study, Georgie waited anxiously for a signal from her new accomplice and former love rival. She was unable to sit and resume reading her crime novel, so with her sleeves rolled up, she brushed out the rugs in the sitting room and then dusted the shelves. When she heard the secret code of knocks they had devised, she rushed to answer the door, but there was no one there. The view from the doorstep was as cold and dark as an empty grave.

She was about to shut the door, when a woman in a Red Cross uniform appeared from behind a tree and ran up the steps. With the breathless haste of a nurse attending a medical emergency, the tall, red-haired figure of Maud Gonne brushed by Georgie into the hallway.

'I met a policeman at the end of the street,' she said between breaths. 'I thought he was going to arrest me but instead I think he followed me here.'

'I'm not surprised,' said Georgie. 'You look like some sort of vision.'

Maud's hair lay in bright red ringlets and her face was powdered white. Her cheeks were pale as candles.

Georgie embraced her and drew back. 'You're shivering,' she said.

'So are you,' replied Maud, and the two women broke into nervous laughter.

'Is the uniform real?' asked Georgie, helping her off with the blood-red cape.

'No,' said Maud. 'Just a stage costume. But what a joy it is to wear with so much gloom in the air. Would you like to try it on?'

Georgie blushed slightly. Before falling under Yeats' spell, she had been about to start a good job at the Foreign Office. She was regarded as sensible and level-headed, if not a little dull, and it had been hoped by London's literary circles that she might steer Yeats away from his spookiness and personal melodrama.

'It's a little late for dressing up,' she said.

Behind them, a floorboard creaked, and they both started.

'If the authorities find me here, they'll have me arrested, and Willie, too,' said Maud.

Although what she said was probably true, Georgie found her manner a little over-posed. There was something searching about her gaze as she spoke, as though she were playing to an invisible audience. Georgie ushered her into the comfort of the sitting room where they sat by the crackling fire.

'Willie never appeared at the Sesame Club tonight,' said Maud.

'I guessed as much.' Georgie's voice tightened.

'What state was he in when he came home?'

'Distracted. Definitely.' Georgie paused. 'I'm not worried that he might be unfaithful. It's his detachment from reality that frightens me. Sometimes he appears to completely forget where he is.'

Gonne smiled. 'Poor Willie, always the dreaming adolescent.'

'I feel I'm married to a man who's already attached.' She stared at Maud. 'Doubly attached.'

'I followed him from a séance near Edgware Street. He looked frightened. There was something strange about his behaviour. Perhaps his silly occult games have become too real for him.'

'No, there's something else. Since our wedding, he's become more and more obsessed with his supernatural investigations.

Every evening, he returns home after midnight, exhausted, his hair in disarray, as though he's been wrestling demons all evening.'

Georgie was still trembling. Maud hugged her, and the younger woman placed her head upon her shoulder, as if they were mother and daughter rather than love rivals. They stayed like that for a while until Georgie broke the silence.

'I don't know how this madness will end,' she whispered.

'Don't confuse madness with a loss of control,' said Maud. 'Willie might be a great poet, but it doesn't mean he can do whatever he wants, or subject you to these fears. He's a husband as well as a poet, and someday soon he will be a father.'

For the first time a genuine smile appeared on Georgie's lips.

'It might be a good idea if the two of you were to leave London,' continued Maud. 'Remove yourselves from this circle of madness. A couple of months in Ireland would clear his head. His imagination is not the problem. It's the forces that are preying upon it.'

'But I fear that a trip to Ireland would make him worse. I don't want to hear anything more about his ghosts, or ancient legends, or lost truths hidden in dusty libraries. All I want is for our marriage to work, and Willie not to be destroyed by this mad obsession with ghosts.'

'Do you scold him?'

'No.'

'Good. To keep Willie's attention a woman must either elevate herself to the role of an ethereal presence, or become his surrogate mother. You must learn to quell your temper.'

Georgie's face coloured slightly with anger. 'I won't be an accomplice to my own subjugation,' she said defiantly.

'And that is good, also,' said Maud soothingly.

'Women have a place of honour and respect in his poetry, and the same should be true in his domestic arrangements. The same above as below, as he has written on numerous occasions.'

Maud nodded. She watched Georgie's eyes glance around the room, her youthful mouth curled in dismay. She was too young to understand the quiet suffering and countless daily sacrifices that underpinned many apparently happy marriages.

'I love him all the same,' said Georgie, staring earnestly into Maud's eyes.

'And what about him? Does he love you?'

'I believe he does.' Georgie lowered her eyes, determined to hide whatever doubt might be revealed by them. 'I'm not a mind-reader.' She looked up at Maud again. 'He walked past me in the sitting-room this afternoon and didn't seem to recognise me. He looked lost. Dazzled, even. I've noticed other changes in his demeanour. He frowns a lot. Not the frown of someone vexed with his surroundings, but a frown at himself, the way a man might frown in a room full of blind people, certain that no one can detect his irritation.'

Maud regarded her with one of those soft full looks that melted the heart of Yeats in his youth. 'I'm afraid that Willie has become a slave to his own vanity,' she said. 'This belief that the otherworld is eager to communicate its secrets with him.'

'It's more than vanity. Since our wedding, I can feel his growing despair. As if he's had to finally give up the hopes and dreams of his youth. Embracing the spirit world has become a way of sublimating his desires.'

'If that is the case, you must cut him off from his occult societies and these dreadful mediums he keeps visiting. Catch his attention when he starts babbling on about his ghosts.'

'But how do I manage that?' Georgie felt like an apprentice in the presence of a great master. She was more than twenty years younger than Gonne, and as well as youth, she had intelligence on her side, but her deference bordered on submissiveness. Gonne belonged to what was already regarded as a legendary age of Irish politics and theatricality.

'You should live like Scheherazade and find a way to captivate your master with tall tales.' Maud stared at her intensely. 'Don't be afraid of hoodwinking him in order to distract him from these infatuations. Remember, I speak from experience. For nearly thirty years, I have held his unwavering attention during all kinds of personal scandals and political upheavals.'

The sound of Yeats' raised voice in the study distracted them.

'I must go now,' said Maud.

Georgie sprang up to hug her but Maud broke away like an actress returning to a demanding stage role.

Before she stepped into the street, she delivered one final piece of advice to Georgie.

'Remember what I said. Look out for a new ghost for Willie. A good ghost. One that will take your side and keep him in check.'

Georgie watched her flowing figure disappear into the night. She thought how nice it would be to live like Maud and dress up in such lovely theatrical clothes, the opposite of the dowdy and virtuous garments in her own wardrobe. But then she dismissed the thought from her mind as mere attention-seeking vanity.

SIX OF SWORDS

THE morning after I received my assignment from Yeats, I briskly made my way to the bookshops on Charing Cross Road, and amid their dusty recesses acquainted myself with the latest texts on criminology. I placed a large order for books by the French author Alexandre Lacassagne, a specialist in the field of deviant behaviour, and a pioneer regarding scientific detection techniques, as well as Galton's guide to the classification of fingerprints, and charged them to the account of the Order of the Golden Dawn.

The question of whether one succumbs to the irrational and its emotional storms is usually a conscious one, at least at the beginning. Recalling the events of the night before, I felt uncomfortable and anxious. I had given myself over to another world, a universe of strange spirits and haunting obligations that were beyond my understanding, blotting out the faculties of reason and common sense. Somehow, I had moved away from the role of impersonal weigher of facts, a trained investigator of the paranormal, to that of an unwilling participant in Yeats' personal melodramas.

It was with relief that I leafed through the latest detective manuals. I felt the breath of new ideas and opinions. The fog had lifted overnight, and the city was drenched with spring sunlight, the rays untangling even the gloom of the Thames, and the raggle-taggle shadows of the run-down streets. A breeze picked up. I tucked my bundle of books under my arm and felt the freshening wind of science blow alongside me, wafting away the cobwebs of superstition and fear. I thought of my friend's dismal ghost, and realised that I now had the opportunity and tools to gather evidence that the soul lived on after the death of the body. My mission would require effort and careful observation, as well as dangerous lines of investigation, but for the first time in months, I felt the glow of intellectual excitement. In the clear reality of a bustling city morning, the enchantment of the previous evening dissolved and I was left with the image of a coffin washed up on a stormy beach and a restless sense of curiosity.

A week later, I boarded the mail boat at Holyhead, bound for Sligo. Among the other passengers in the first-class cabins were an invalid soldier in a wheelchair helped on board by a red-haired nurse, an army major, called Blemings, accompanied by his young wife, and a tall gaunt man, wearing a black belt and cap, who stood smoking against the railings, watching everything with half-closed, inquisitive eyes.

A watch bell tolled on the upper deck, a cold iron jangle that chimed with the rattling shackles of dozens of Irish prisoners who were being lined up on the docks with martial impersonality. A row of prison guards made the men stand in falling sleet as the passengers in steerage boarded. From the first-class deck, I watched the guards prevent the paraded men from squatting or kneeling. The prisoners were Republicans, many of them barely out of their teens. Unlike their executed leaders, they had played minor roles in the Easter Rising, and were now being deported back to their homeland where they were to be freed at Dublin port.

Major Blemings wore a pained smile. 'I don't understand why the authorities can't keep them locked up,' he complained. 'My advice to everyone is watch your possessions and hope the bloodthirsty ruffians don't creep into your cabin at night to slit your throat.'

The man in the black cap mournfully agreed in a soft Irish accent. 'Times like these no one is safe,' he said. The glowing ember of his cigarette was reflected briefly in his dark eyes.

The slur of rubber knocking against the deck made everyone turn to stare at the tall figure of the Red Cross nurse, pushing the invalid soldier in his wheelchair. She was middle-aged with burnished red hair tied up in a bun, which when released must have extended to the full Celtic mane. There was an exhilarated look to her features, which were oddly familiar. Her eyes were bright, and a long strand of hair hung loose. She gazed around the cabin with a challenging look, and then wheeled the soldier to the shelter of a bulkhead. She wrapped him tightly in blankets and joined us at the railings.

'How is your patient?' asked the major.

'Not in any immediate danger. Though he's gravely ill from his wounds.'

'Then he'll not survive a rough passage,' said the man in the black cap a little brutally. He tossed his cigarette into the dark waters below.

'My patient has vowed to return to his birthplace should he shuffle there on his knees.'

'Then it will be more penance than pilgrimage.'

Although the nurse looked composed, I could see the sinews in her neck muscles stretching with anger. She breathed heavily as though the air on deck had grown scarce. Then she walked back to the invalid soldier.

After the paying passengers had boarded, the ship was loaded with its cargo. The prisoners on the docks linked their arms, less a gesture of solidarity and more an attempt to remain upright and resist the rolling waves of exhaustion that passed through their ranks. After another hour had passed, the guards finally led them onto the boat. Unwashed, bedraggled and soaking wet, they dragged themselves up the gangway in the shambling crouch used by miners underground.

From my vantage point, I did not see any traitors or heroes among them, just a lot of humiliated young men, some rather scared, some isolated and lonely looking, all of them lacking any sign of tenacity or allegiance to a die-hard cause. Perhaps the government had deprived them of their moment of heroism and that was why they looked so hollow and defeated.

Eventually, the boat steamed out of the harbour, and the men were left to find whatever shelter or comfort they could on the quarter deck. The Red Cross nurse emerged from the cabin next to mine and walked among the prisoners, tending to the ones who appeared to be suffering the most. Their eyes lit up at her red-haired presence, as though something bright and warm was being brandished before them. She seemed perfectly at ease in the company of these down-hearted men, many of whom spoke only in Irish. It was as though she had known them all their lives. There were no signs of awkwardness or strain on her part, and her soothing words appeared to revive them.

It was a rough passage overnight to Dublin, the boat's first stop. With no lights allowed anywhere on board because of the blackout, the deck of prisoners became a chaotic dormitory. To add to their discomfort, the weather was freezing cold. I had not imagined such a large boat could be gripped by frost while rocking from wave to wave in the middle of the Irish Sea. Snow began to fall, forming a pale coagulating slush on the decks. The boat drifted through the slowly descending flakes.

Unable to sleep with the rocking motion of the boat and its creaking timbers, I sat up and stared through the porthole at the gathering snow. From the cabin next door, I heard a door open and close gently. Pulling on a coat with deep pockets, I left my cabin and followed a single track of footsteps around the bridge and down to the lower decks.

A dark layer of greasy ice covered the wooden boards where the prisoners slept on the quarter deck. I walked along the dark edge of their bodies. Strangely, in that oppressive environment, a feeling of expansiveness overcame me so strongly that it circumvented the bonds of loyalty to country and King. I found myself giving cigarettes and some of the bread and cheese I had crammed into my pockets to one of the men, a mad-eyed, bearded young fellow. His hands were eager, and they were joined by a circle of other outstretched hands.

A figure carrying an oil lamp moved from behind a bulkhead at the far end of the cavernous deck. Its only identifying feature was a red cloak. The Red Cross nurse turned, her red curls falling about her pale face. She moved through the men on some mysterious wave of self-confidence, as though she were testing her middle-aged beauty on the soon-to-be-freed prisoners. They cleared a space for her, giving the impression they were expecting a stage performance. She spoke in a low angry whisper, which the creaking of the ship disguised, but I caught a phrase now and again. She was talking about patriotism and a coming war, and there was a raw energy in her voice. I stared at her and suddenly saw her in the right light. It was the same woman who had addressed the protesting widows outside the converted poorhouse.

'Ho! What's your name,' whispered one of the prisoners.

'Charles Adams.'

'Well, Mr Adams would you mind feeding me, too.'

I handed him a hunk of dry bread and a slightly damp cigarette.

'How do you cope with these conditions?' I asked.

'What conditions?'

'The overcrowding. The cold and the hunger.'

'We're Irishmen. We're used to these things.'

He hunched forward and lit the cigarette. A haggard look of exhaustion was thrown into sharp relief across his youthful features.

'Officially, we're not meant to be here,' he said. 'We're the ghosts of the Easter Rising.'

'What do you mean?'

'The British government sentenced us to death by firing squad, but fortunately for us, they grew tired of executing rebels.' He snorted out two jets of smoke and jerked his head back defiantly. 'Their offer was to go back home and give up the struggle or languish in gaol. But damn them, we're not going to give up now.'

It struck me that the ship was a symbol of England's relationship with its oldest colony, a union drifting in the dark towards a terrible new dawn, a hold of mutinous men trapped below decks.

'I'm a law student, not a soldier,' confided the young prisoner. 'I didn't even know the Rising was going to take place on Easter Sunday. I happened to be passing Boland's Mill when I saw the rebels take up their positions. When I get back to Dublin I shall continue the struggle, only this time in the courtroom.'

The nurse drew her cape over her head and climbed a set of steps at the other end of the boat. In her absence, an agitated current seemed to stir the bodies of the prisoners. Someone coughed. A voice rasped from the darkness. A controlled, anonymous voice. 'Don't get carried away with your charity, Mr Adams. Ye and the nurse are only paying back England's debts to Ireland. They're six hundred years old and fathomless.'

I turned in the direction of the voice but there were only bodies slouching in various stages of sleep.

The next morning, before the sun rose, I got my first sight of Ireland. The rattle of the anchor chain woke me from a disturbed sleep. The engines slowed and the deck was full of footsteps. Through the porthole, I could see bonfires blazing on the wild hillsides of a subdued-looking coast. Under a blanket of feathery falling snow, the natives had gathered, determined to celebrate the return of their glorious rebels.

At Dublin port, the prisoners disembarked, free men now, to a crowd of cheering well-wishers. The gangplank was their last connection with grim reality before their feet temporarily touched dry land, and then they were lifted off as returning heroes by their supporters and carried away into the darkness of a winter morning.

The mail boat ploughed back into the Irish Sea. I went up to the bow deck with my books but was distracted by the sight of the waves rising higher and higher. A storm had been brooding behind the snow. The boat seemed to gather speed, as if plunging downhill. The deck tilted sharply with the surges, and I held on to the railings for dear life.

One of the passengers from first class had followed me to the bow. It was the tall man with the black cap and the hungry look to his face. I had caught his eye earlier that morning, and from then on, I seemed to become a focus for his attention. He stood at the opposite railing and watched me, his face darkening with angry curiosity as the boat toppled from wave to wave, and the sky grew warped and heavy with storm clouds. He seemed indifferent to the rolling pitch of the sea. I retreated below, but his presence stalked me as I wandered from deck to deck.

The storm reached its peak when we passed Belfast, prompting a recital of the rosary from the passengers in steerage. I had no clear recollection of the ship's passage along the circuit of cliffs and silver strands that make up the Antrim coastline, other than that it felt like a grim descent down the course of a steepening cascade. Struck down with seasickness, I passed my time staggering from my cabin to the deck railings, where on several occasions I emptied my stomach into the whirlpool of the sea until there was nothing left to retch but bile. Like the sea, the nausea came in waves, lifting me from crest to crest of violent self-purges, then reducing me to a state of exhaustion in between.

At one point in my ordeal, my stalker joined me on the railings.

'No one ever died of seasickness,' he reassured me.

However, there was nothing kind or comforting about his facial expression. He grinned at me like a hangman at the gallows.

I was reluctant to open my mouth, afraid I would vomit again. The scorch of stomach acid hitting my throat reduced me to a coughing fit.

'Drink this,' he said, taking a small medicine bottle out of his pocket. With shaking hands, I tipped its contents into my mouth and swallowed them in a single gulp. He peered closely at me, his grin slowly sinking back into his skull. It crossed my mind that he might be a scoundrel, intent on robbing me. A large wave struck the side of the boat, and his silhouette was briefly wreathed in a halo of sea spray.

'Just lie there,' he said sitting down beside me. 'I'll keep you company until the sickness wears off.'

Another wave of nausea made me sweat all over.

'Tell me, Sir,' he asked in a slow, almost absent-minded voice, 'why aren't you fighting in France?'

I explained that I had failed the army medical due to fainting fits.

'Then are you a supporter of the Crown?'

I stared at him. 'What do you mean?' I could feel the hairs on the back of my neck prickle.

'Do you hold the King and his loyal forces in contempt?'

'Of course not.'

'Then what were you doing tending to the prisoners below deck last night?'

'They were starving and nearly freezing to death.'

He aped astonishment. 'Starving? Almost freezing to death? I wasn't aware that those bloodthirsty rebels were suffering to that extent. You should have reported your discovery immediately to the captain of the boat.'

'Why are we discussing this matter?' I asked.

'Orders, Sir.'

'Whose orders?'

'Winston Churchill's. My name is Wolfe Marley; I'm an agent of the British War Office.'

I tried to read his features, but his expression was dark and inward.

'What did the prisoners say to you?'

I found myself unable to reply. My mind contracted with suspicion. His questions were surely an attempt to make me incriminate myself.

'Did any of them try to engage you in conversation regarding future acts of treason?' Again his empty gaze.

'No,' I said. 'Why is this important?'

'Spies, Sir. I'm hunting for spies. Infiltrators, agent provocateurs hiding in the hold. You've read the newspaper reports, I'm sure. The whole of Ireland is a powder keg waiting to be set off by the meddling of naive Englishmen and vengeful Germans.'

Sweat trickled down my neck.

'Were there any other passengers from first class in the hold?'

'No.' My lie was too quick and it made him pause.

'What are you reading?' A faint contempt threaded through his voice. 'William Butler Yeats? Now there's an extraordinary poet.'

'What do you mean?'

'Not many poets take an annual pension from the King, and then campaign to have his kingdom overthrown.'

'Mr Yeats' political beliefs aren't that simple,' I endeavoured to explain. 'He has told me he doesn't know which lies heaviest on his heart. The tragedy of Ireland, or the tragedy of England.'

'And is that because of his poetic soul, or is he just muddle-headed?'

'You're trying to needle me. Mr Yeats is a friend of mine and a confidant.'

'I'm only needling to find the truth. If Mr Yeats is your confidant, then what has he confided in you?'

A darkness squirmed in his eyes. A pitch-black, wriggling darkness.

'You're travelling to Sligo?' he asked.

'Yes.'

'Why?'

'To visit a paternal aunt,' I lied.

'You've been there before?'

'First time.'

'I'm baffled.'

'Why?'

'Why a young Englishman would suddenly decide to make his first trip to Ireland at the most dangerous point in six hundred years of occupation.'

'I'm not interested in history.'

'Then you're not equipped to visit Ireland. History will surround you. And the hatred it has spawned. When this storm abates, you should take a good look at the coast. What civilisation exists is centred on the estates of English landlords, and even their substantial mansions and castles face out to sea, away from the forbidding land. The sea is their point of contact with the rest of the Empire, their all-important escape route.'

He lifted the book of Yeats' poems, and felt its heft.

'I'm not a literary critic, just a fellow Irishman. But tell Mr Yeats he should have the good sense of his compatriots Wilde and Shaw, who wear their nationality lightly, and dramatise the world they know, rather than spinning one out of their boyhood imaginations.'

When I did not reply, he stared at me.

'You'll find out soon enough that the real Ireland is nothing like Yeats' portrayal. It has grown cruel and savage beyond belief.'

He handed me back the book. It fell from my grasp onto the deck, spilling its contents across the wet boards.

'What do we have here?' said Marley, lifting Rosemary O'Grady's letter and the newspaper clipping. He gave them a furtive caress and read their contents with growing interest.

'This is not my province at all,' he murmured. He examined me closely. 'I take it you are going to bring this letter to the attention of the Sligo police?'

Before I could reply, water came surging over the bow of the boat, forcing us to retreat below deck. The momentum of the waves rocked the boat back and forth in steep, sickening arcs. Overcome with seasickness, I slumped against a bulkhead. My stalker swung himself alongside.

'Tell me, what are you doing with this letter?'

I felt my stomach dangle above the bottomless depths of the ocean, and then the motion of the boat hitting a sudden swell hurled it upwards again.

'It was given to me,' I said weakly, 'by the Order of the Golden Dawn. The society has sent me to investigate her death.'

He handed me back the letter and news report. We took advantage of a brief lull in the boat's pitching and staggered to the dining cabin, where the major, his wife and the Red Cross nurse were deep in conversation. I sat on a bench and pressed my head against the cold porthole. They were discussing English perceptions of Sligo, and my ears pricked at the mention of Yeats' name. I tried to quell the surges of nausea sufficiently to concentrate on what they were saying.

'Sleuth Wood, Glencar's waterfall, Rosses Point, none of them are worth the detour,' sniffed the major. 'Their names rouse the fancy but Mr Yeats has romanticised them out of all proportion. When his readers think of Sligo, they see gaunt cliffs, wild woods and crystal cascades. His image of Ireland might delight English readers but it hides a grim truth. The disquiet that pervades the country. Houses ablaze and men with guns everywhere. If Mr Yeats visited Sligo today none of it would feel familiar or safe.'

'Is it true they've started assassinating English people?' asked the major's young wife, who had yet to visit the country.

'Only those who have lived there for hundreds of years,' replied the nurse with a glint in her eye.

'Tell me about Sligo,' the major's wife asked the nurse. 'I've heard the landscape is impressive.'

The major grunted. 'The rain is impressive.'

'I've been that long in France I'm homesick even for the rain,' said the nurse, a soft dreamy look filling her features, as though she were the queen of bad weather returning to her kingdom of rain.

'The Irish seasons,' said the major gruffly, 'can only be distinguished by the temperature of the downpours. The cottages there and many of the big houses are so damp you could wash your face in the water streaming down the walls. The peasants and servants collect the drips in pots and pans and pour them into the rivers, which sweep the water out to sea where great clouds sweep it all back again. It's an endless cycle of misery.'

'But Sligo can be wonderful, in spite of the rain,' said the nurse.

'Thanks to its prosperous Protestant merchants and the great Anglo-Irish families who built it up from a muddy hovel,' replied the major.

I felt another convulsion heave my stomach. I rushed from my seat and burst forth onto the deck. When I returned to the dining cabin, the mood of the conversation had darkened. Marley had joined in the discussion.

'They're all leaving you know,' he said.

'Who?' asked the major's wife.

'The Burkes, the Butlers, the Gibsons and the Montgomerys. One by one, they're going away. They're forsaking their mildewy mansions and leaving in trains and boats and automobiles. Before the rebellious mobs take their estates apart.'

'It's true,' said the major. 'We were in Liverpool last week and the place resembled an aristocratic refugee camp. They even have their own solicitors and clergymen in tow.' His voice took on a low grumbling tone. 'This rising is nothing more than the whim of a lunatic population. Ireland has had countless rebellions in the past. Its peasants don't know how to react from one day to the next except to oppose everything England affirms. The landlords will return with their entourages when the mood changes.'

The nurse interrupted. 'This time it's different. The Rising wasn't a stray event. It marked a distinct stage in the development of the Irish nation. Everything has changed utterly.'

A silence greeted the vehemence of her words.

'Shouldn't you be tending to your patient,' asked Marley, 'rather than trying to justify an act of treason?'

The nurse's jaw was clenched as she fought to control her annoyance.

'What are you? A doctor? Whatever you are you're not a gentleman.'

'And what are you? A nurse or a revolutionary? Haven't you grown tired of cradling the heads of dying Irishmen in France? Or do you wish to spend your days dressing the wounds of Irish men on Irish soil?'

'One can be sick in peacetime, too,' she replied. 'An entire nation might be dying on its feet and not a drop of blood shed.'

The ship tilted and the door of the cabin flew open with an unseen force and then slammed shut again. No one spoke, and the tension in the cabin rose. Marley lit a cigarette and put his feet up on the bench opposite, right next to where I was sitting. He stared at me and blew out a long trail of smoke.

'My young friend here has an interesting tale to share with us,' he announced to the cabin. The walls began shaking with the reverberations of the rising waves; the glass lantern swung on its beam, and the glasses slid on the table, but all the passengers' eyes were fixed upon me.

'He tells me that he's a ghost-feeler,' continued Marley. 'Do you know he's travelling to Sligo in the hope of communicating with the spirit of a dead girl?'

The passengers looked amused. I turned away, suddenly shy at his mocking camaraderie and his careless revelation of my secret mission.

'A ghost?' asked the major's wife.

'Quite. Mr Adams is investigating the death of Rosemary O'Grady.'

'The girl in the coffin?'

'Yes.'

The major exploded with laughter and slapped me on the shoulder. 'You go to Sligo at grave risk,' he said. 'The people there are sufficiently medieval to have you burnt at the stake.'

I felt a flush of humiliation.

'You'll have a job finding your ghost,' continued the major. 'The entire country is possessed. Banshees, ghosts, fairies, everyone is haunted by something.'

'The Irish peasants have two things that can never be taken from them,' said the nurse. 'One is their hunger for justice. The other is their belief in the supernatural.'

There was a note of tension in her voice, but, fortunately, the subject of the occult proved a safer topic of conversation for her and her fellow passengers. Intrigued, they began to discuss what they knew of the case.

'I gather this young woman's body was found in mysterious circumstances, in a manner that cannot be explained by logic or common sense,' said the major. 'Then there's the puzzling development concerning Captain Thomas Oates, the man who found her body. Apparently, the event so jolted his mind, he abandoned his posting and went into hiding.'

'And what are Mr Adams' thoughts on this?'

'He believes we should look to the otherworld for guidance,' said Marley.

The nurse's eyebrow arched. 'I believe Mr Adams is correct. No man or woman can claim omniscience in such dreadful matters.'

I was sensitive to every shade and nuance in their conversation and every flicker of expression on their faces, but my unwavering interest was undermined by another bout of sickness. I felt the room and their faces turn round and round, slowly at first, then quickening as though a wind had taken hold of them, spinning them further and further away.

'Lie down.' I heard the nurse's voice suddenly beside me, magnified in my ear. 'Take no heed of their contempt.' Her voice was cracked with emotion. 'Ghosts are our friends. They can tell us what we cannot see. They are our spies. I want you to listen carefully to what this ghost tells you, and record it carefully.'

She slipped a rolled blanket beneath my head, the first comfort I had received on the voyage. I felt that under her tender care, I might make slow but steady progress back towards good health, and lulled by her presence I drifted off to sleep.

When I came round, she had left the cabin. The attentions of Marley and the major, who leaned grimly towards me, destroyed whatever sense of ease I had gained. Relentlessly, they continued their interrogation.

'Do you understand the political situation in Ireland?' asked Marley staring at me eagerly.

'Does anyone?'

'I mean are you familiar with the pattern of the Irish rebellion?'

'I've read the newspaper reports.'

'You need to be careful with your English accent,' advised the major. 'The natives will instinctively feel something sinister is afoot when you start asking questions. And watch out for the

Irish Constabulary. They're a rum lot. They might decide you're a troublemaker and fling you in gaol before you can cause them bother.'

'Or give you a kicking just for the fun of it,' added Marley. 'Of course, you can always take refuge on the Isle of Innisfree. You'll be out of harm's way there.'

I tried to convey an expression of indignation rather than fear. It was what my education had taught me to do. As though a show of pluck might encourage them to desist.

'We're only warning you to be on the look-out,' said Marley.

'I don't need a protector,' I said, as a large wave struck the side of the boat. Through the porthole, I could see the sea, the dark horizon and the storm clouds boiling together. 'And if you're trying to frighten me it's not working.'

He shrugged. 'If you're not afraid then that tells me two important things.'

'What?'

'That you don't believe in the ghost of a murdered girl, and the Order of the Golden Dawn has sent the wrong man.'

At this point I shuffled off to my cabin. I was perspiring but my skin felt as icy as a corpse's. The storm eventually blew itself out, and for the rest of the passage, I avoided association of any kind. I had heard enough about Ireland and its people, or at least the exaggerated tales of my fellow passengers, to make me want to shun their company. I saw Marley several times moping along the railings, his face set in a suspicious frown. Of the nurse and her invalid, I saw nothing more until we disembarked.

It was late evening when we docked at Sligo. It seemed a gloomy place, the wild and bleak shoreline leading to a humdrum town hunkering under the sombre silhouette of Ben Bulben, Sligo's familiar mountain landmark. A pair of Royal Irish Constabulary officers made their way up the landing ramp to stop some of the passengers in steerage. They wore a distinctive dark green uniform with black buttons and insignia reminiscent of the British Army rifle brigade. They searched through baggage and inspected papers with the air of men who found the very smell of sea air suspicious.

The nurse pushed to the front of the queue. She seemed in a hurry to be off the boat. With scant regard for safety, she propelled her invalid down the landing ramp, his wheelchair squawking horribly, the hood of his army coat pulled low over his head, his eyes covered like those of a condemned man. The only parts of him visible was his mouth, which was stretched into a contorted ecstatic smile, and his large hands. Throughout the voyage, they had dangled lifelessly from his thin wrists like dying plants, but now they gripped the armrests with restored vigour. A rare triumphant smile also broke out on the nurse's face. Then she caught the wary gaze of the policemen, and a look of proud disdain flashed in her eyes, as though she was angry at being caught in a secret moment of delight.

One of the officers approached her and she roared, 'What are you doing? Can't you see you're in my way?'

Deftly, she steered the wheelchair around him and down the ramp at speed, driving the grinning invalid like a demented demon onto Irish soil. The thought crossed my mind that the roar of her voice and the sweep of her formidable figure through the disembarking crowds were like a call to war.

7

KNIGHT OF WANDS

AFTER several days of sensory deprivation on the grey seas, the colour of early spring flowers seemed to me as intense as gemstones. I was riding a four-year-old gelding through the Gulf Stream warmed forests of Lissadell Estate. The trees were already in bud, a glimmering screen of tantalising green, and the wind that sifted through them felt mild and fresh. Ahead of me rode Richard Denver, the estate manager, whom Yeats had arranged to be my guide.

I had spent my first night in Ireland in the estate's gatehouse, a small block of granite stone, with peace and solitude its only comforts. It had been previously occupied by a pair of Church of Ireland clergymen from Dublin who had come for a holiday on their bicycles. But that had been the previous autumn, and over the winter, the place had grown mildewy and damp.

Denver knocked on my door shortly after seven o'clock and offered to take me on a tour of the estate, before visiting Rosemary O'Grady's former cottage, which lay on the periphery of the three hundred acre grounds. An Irish draught horse was waiting for me.

'I'm putting you on Cromwell,' he said. 'A good horse for the inexperienced. Keep your hands down, elbows in, a firm rein and gripping knees. Remember you must be the master and not the horse, else it might take the bit between its teeth and throw you off a cliff.'

The estate manager had the dark locks and eyes and the swashbuckling manner of one of Yeats' wild Irish horsemen. He watched with a wary look as I scrambled onto the gelding's back. It broke into a trot with barely a kick and I felt the exciting power of landed wealth carry me down a lane overgrown with elderberry bushes and ferns. The pleasure of a pleasant early spring morning was tinged with the barely suppressed panic of being in charge of such an impressive beast. Therefore, it was with a jittery sense of elation that I followed Denver's larger chestnut mare. I was hardly an accomplished rider and I fervently hoped my horse was a forgiving and gentle beast.

The broad flat leaves of rhododendron and laurel trees slapped against the horses' sides as we made our way down gravelled avenues. I caught a glimpse of the over-sized Lissadell mansion and its irredeemably barren face of granite, and in the east, the flat top of Ben Bulben, which in the morning light looked as solemn as an altar. Whatever the menacing nature of the changes the country was undergoing, and the atrocities being committed in the name of freedom, the grounds at Lissadell appeared to be steeped contentedly in the glory days of the Protestant Ascendancy.

The horses were used to the estate, leaping with ease over stone walls and thorny hollows. We skimmed a blackthorn hedge and squeezed through thickets of oak and ash. We crossed a field wall running westward, and rode to within a few yards of a cliff. Denver pointed to a remote silver strand, and ten minutes later, we were racing along the breaking waves, the horses' hooves adding to the leaping sea spray. Bursts of rain tracked us across the seaweedy shore, and then we were back on forest paths.

Denver turned his horse and trotted alongside me. So far he had been inscrutable, neither obviously friendly nor downright hostile.

'I'm duty bound to give you all the assistance you require,' he said. 'However, first, I want to know why you are so interested in Rosemary O'Grady.'

My reply was cagey. 'Mr Yeats sent me to Ireland on a personal matter. Which naturally I will not divulge to anyone.'

Denver gave a hoot of laughter, which unsettled my horse. 'I know perfectly well why you are here. Yeats has sent you to seek out Rosemary's ghost on behalf of his mystical society.'

He gave my animal a crack of his whip, which sent it off into a kidney-jarring bolt. I bounced about on its broad back, unable to return to a trot.

Denver cantered at ease beside me. 'Don't worry if you fall off,' he said. 'It might knock some sense into you.'

I fought to regain control of the animal until Denver leaned over and took hold of its reins. He grinned at me. 'I fear that Yeats has sent you on a folly of his over-heated imagination.'

'All I know is that a young woman has died and no one knows why.'

In truth, however, I feared he was right. I had arrived in Sligo, but still did not know what Yeats expected me to do.

'You be straight with me and I'll be straight with you,' said Denver.

'Of course.'

'You've come to a land of exiles, gypsies and thieves to chase the ghost of a servant girl. Anyone who knew anything about her death will have gone to ground like rabbits. Besides, the police have already followed all lines of enquiry and exhausted them.'

'What about you? What do you know about her life?'

'To be honest, I know more about her death than her life. But first I want to show you what is happening to the Ireland Yeats once knew and loved.'

He backed his horse away, swung it round in a tight circle and galloped off. My horse took after his, propelling me over bramble traps and deep ditches of mud. More than once, I lost his trail and had to shout until he returned. He regarded me with a mixture of amusement and wariness. My city-bound sense of orientation told me we were riding in spirals through a labyrinth of leafy corridors, without really going anywhere. It occurred to me that by placing me on such a powerful horse, Denver had succeeded in turning me into a captive audience, one that he could keep his eye on and intimidate at will.

Soon we had left behind the boundary walls of Lissadell Estate. We rode on for several hours until my legs ached. Through iron-wrought gates and overgrown hedges, I caught glimpses of castle-like mansions that seemed enchanted by the wildness of their overgrown gardens.

'What happened to the people who lived here? Did they run out of money?'

'Not money,' replied Denver. 'Time.'

The glory and fortune of Ireland's landed gentry languished in neglect, a collapsing graveyard lavishly decorated with entangled statues, fountains, courtyards, and the dark towers of chapels and follies. Denver listed the family names as we passed each abandoned estate, like an executioner in a corridor of condemned cells.

'When one family departs, so do a string of others, in extremely rapid succession,' he said. 'These were once the best managed estates in Ireland, or anywhere in the empire. We built tennis courts and walled gardens and taught our tenants about soil and hygiene. We encouraged them to change their primitive farming methods and ancient superstitions. We weaned them off their reliance on disease-ridden potatoes. But all that has stopped now. Ireland's heyday is over for good.' His voice was tinged with disgust, and there was a self-justifying tone to his anger.

We trotted in the direction of a stone tower jutting through the trees. The horses pulled up to a set of broken gates weighed down by thorns. Denver explained that they marked the entrance to Burke's estate, which had been abandoned shortly after the Rising. It had already fallen into a state of irreparable neglect. He dismounted and pushed the gates open. A shower of rust fell from the massive groaning hinges. The horses' ears shot forward and they began whinnying. I squeezed my animal's sides and pushed it through its fear. Ahead of us lay another mansion enclosed in a plantation of rhododendron and laurel.

'Great people lived and died in houses like these,' he said. 'Magistrates, colonels, members of parliament, captains and governors. These peasant rebels are killing our great houses. To kill a good house where great men lived, married and died should be declared a capital offence.'

He broke a birch branch from the hedge and smacked it against the trailing brambles. The resiny smell of leaves hung in the air. He then expounded on the important Anglo-Irish families of Sligo, speaking at length on the part they played in making Ireland's wealth and social fabric. Throughout he made repeated references to the connections with his own family name, making it clear that he was the inheritor of the same nation-building stock and the beneficiary of first-class breeding.

I followed my walking history lesson and his horse through a dense grove of yew trees. The wind breathed through the unmoving branches. From what I could see of the estate, the only thing on the move was nature, in its grandest sense, flowing along its own mutating course. In the rose gardens, a vegetal panic had broken out. Weeds welled up and drowned the bushes and shrubs. The house itself had become a prisoner of its former horticultural glories. Jasmine and clematis netted the bay windows, the panes of which had been broken, presumably by vandals or thieves. Birds had whitened the pavements beneath the roof eaves with their droppings. For all its tons of marble and granite, the mansion looked impotent, a gaping shell surrounded by encroaching wildness.

'We are at war with the Germans,' said Denver. 'This is a time when you should look to your countrymen for kinship and allegiance. The last thing you expect is insurrection and betrayal, vandalism and attacks in the night. Who are the people who have banded together to overthrow us? A few small farmers, labourers and national schoolmasters. That's all they are.'

He then kicked his horse into a gallop along the avenue in a show-off burst of exultant muscle that spooked my gelding and had him wheeling in tight circles as though he were under attack from the motionless yews.

When the horse had settled, I wondered about the background to Rosemary's life as a Catholic servant girl working at one of the few remaining Protestant estates. Perhaps with so much violence surrounding her she had felt disinclined to report her fears that someone was trying to kill her. Why would she, when the threat of murder hung over every one?

'These are anxious times,' I said when I caught up with Denver. 'What part does Rosemary's unexplained death play in all this?'

'Everyone is saying she was murdered.'

'And was she?'

'Murdered? Yes. But the girl had been inviting trouble.'

'What do you mean?'

'Rosemary was bewitchingly pretty, with a confidence bordering on the brazen. She wasn't shy and she wasn't a giggler. She had a lot more going on in her life than the other servants. The rumour was she had joined the Daughters of Erin, a secret Republican sisterhood devoted to the destruction of Ireland.'

'You knew her personally?'

'I can't remember ever having a proper conversation with her, if that's what you mean.'

'But you knew her.'

Denver removed his riding gloves and took out a pocket flask of whiskey. 'I danced with her a few times.' He knocked back a mouthful. 'But then everyone danced with Rosemary.'

'Really?'

'No. I'm being mischievous. More truthful to say that everyone wanted to dance with her.' He offered me a drink but I declined.

'When was the last time you saw her?'

'At a Céilidh for Lissadell staff. A few nights before she was killed. She teased me for making a botch of the three-hand reel. That was the last time I spoke to her.'

'But not the last time you saw her.'

'Correct.' Denver hesitated and chose his words carefully. 'I'm a middle-class Protestant and she was a peasant Catholic girl. Even though we worked on the same estate, we were unlikely to have many opportunities for social interaction. My life and hers ran parallel for most of the time, but it astonished me how difficult it was to contrive a private meeting with her. In other words, I saw as much of her as I could, which was not enough.'

'Where did you last see her?'

'She left the dance early and walked home along the beach at Blind Sound.' He took another mouthful of whiskey and put the flask back in his pocket. 'I saw her wade out into the sea. The water was much too cold for bathing.'

'You weren't alarmed by her behaviour?'

'No. I had seen her wade out before, and she always came in.'

'Yet a day later she was found dead on the same beach?'

'The truth is if she hadn't always been dashing off to subversive meetings, nothing would have happened to her.'

'Who organised the meetings?'

'The Daughters of Erin. Or *Inghinidhe na hÉireann*, as they call themselves.'

'And that is why she was killed?'

'Why else would anyone murder her?'

'That's not an answer. It's another question.'

'It's the truth.'

'Perhaps it was reason enough to arrest her. But why kill her? What sort of threat did a girl of nineteen pose to British Rule?'

'There is more than one war going on in Ireland at this present time. Women of all classes are rebelling, and some people don't like that. They think it's wrong for women to wear the same clothes and rise to the same level as men. They put the keeping of order above everything else. Political and social order.

'Someone has to take control, but should that mean killing people?'

'In a state of emergency, yes.'

The wind rattled the open windows of the mansion. The tinkling of glass breaking echoed from within. The horses grew agitated like two clairvoyants about to see a ghost.

Denver was distracted. 'I think we have one of them,' he said. 'This is very fortunate. These vandals think they can break into our great houses and plunder as they wish. It is time they were taught a lesson.'

A splashing sound from the side of the house made Denver kick off his horse. Cautiously we moved through the undergrowth. Someone had pulled tapestries and curtains half-way through a broken window. The figure of a young man was bent over them, emptying the contents of a tin of paraffin.

'There he is,' whispered Denver. 'The enemy is in sight.' He pulled an oily rag from his pocket and unwrapped a revolver. He balanced the weapon in the palm of his hand, stretched his arm out and squinted down the sight.

'You can't go shooting people for trespassing,' I whispered back.

Denver bristled like a thwarted hero. 'Can't you smell the paraffin? He's trying to set the place alight.'

'I didn't realise I was riding with the local militia.' My voice was tense.

'Someone must uphold law and order,' he said regarding me with scorn.

He then took aim and squeezed the trigger. At the last moment, the horse stepped sideways. Denver's arm swayed and the gun went off in the wrong direction.

The would-be arsonist turned round and saw Denver take aim again. He dropped the paraffin and leapt through the shrubbery. In one effortless bound, he had jumped onto a piebald pony. A crack reverberated through the air as he struck the animal furiously on its haunches, and the pony bolted off in a burst of mud and leaves. It took the measure of a garden path in one stride and crashed through the trees on the other side. Although the rider was hunched low, I could see he was small and slight, little more than a boy. Denver's horse barrelled after him, and my horse took off in pursuit, a volley of bent branches whipping against us.

We chased him for half a mile or so, ducking branches and sweeping over ditches, leaning the horses one way and then the other, and then the forest ran out and I could smell the Atlantic. We were on faster, bigger horses, but our quarry was a better rider. He took chances on his pony not even Denver would have attempted in a sane mood. We followed him leap for leap until we were within earshot of crashing waves.

A seemingly insurmountable hedge of wild hawthorn separated us from the sea. The rider turned his animal towards the sound of the crashing waves, slowing a little to size up the hedge. He glanced back at us. A black scarf covered his mouth and a cap was pulled low over his head. Steam rising from the pony's body hid his features. Nevertheless, I caught a glimpse of a pale, youthful face that resembled the ghost of a truant schoolboy. The rider sped his animal up, leaned out of his saddle, and cleared the hedge as neatly as a salmon leaping upstream. He gave a high-pitched whoop of delight and disappeared across the sand.

My horse faltered back, half-kneeling, its eyes twisting behind. I glanced at Denver's face as his beast reared into the air. The veneer of arrogance had split, revealing a darker more troubled look.

'I'm not going to force the horses on,' he shouted. 'Something about this beach spooks them to the core.'

We dismounted and picked our way through a gap in the hedge onto a sandy cove. The rider was long gone. Only his hoof marks in the sand remained, and the action of the waves was already erasing them.

We walked to the sea's edge. The air was explosive with the sound of the ocean. The wind roared, and the surf pounded and sucked back against rocks that were so overgrown with seaweed they resembled neglected tropical gardens.

'This is where they found the body,' shouted Denver.

The din of the crowding waves was magnified by the shape of the cove, which curved deeply into a set of cliffs. I could make out the dark mouths of caves, which looked accessible only by thin terraces of rock.

'The cove is known as *An Sunda Caoch*, which means Blind Sound. It's always been a haunted place. Several boats have overturned here and drowned the fishermen as they tried to come ashore. They say that at twilight you can see the apparitions of boats battling the waves, as well as strange lights shining from the cliffs.'

I stared at the forward rush of each breaking wave, mesmerised by the sight and sound of their violent crashing. The tang of salt and crackling seaweed stung the air. I thought of Rosemary's coffin lifted in the palm of those powerful waves, carried high like a boat towards heaven.

'Come,' shouted Denver. 'You haven't travelled seven hundred miles just to watch waves breaking on a beach.'

KING OF WANDS

AFTER working from his bed all morning on his latest manuscript, Yeats rose shortly before noon and lunched on cold beef, cheese and claret. Keeping in mind his doctor's warning that his body, like a singer's, was an instrument of his art and needed to be rested accordingly, he returned to his bed for an afternoon nap.

He woke again in the early evening. Confident that he had built up enough strength to see him through the coming ordeal, he slowly pushed himself further up in his bed. With his head supported by a pillow, he began his breathing exercises. Then he rotated his feet clockwise and anti-clockwise, and did the same to his wrists. The final ritual of his daily resurrection involved consulting an astrologer's chart. When he had reassured himself that the omens were favourable, he climbed tentatively out of bed.

He dressed in a soft green jacket with a yellow shirt and dark bow-tie that were colourfully out of fashion, and with a sense of gathering urgency, said goodbye to Georgie at the front door. A few months ago, she would have embraced him but now she merely offered him a cheek to kiss.

'Promise me you won't stay out after midnight,' she pleaded.

Yeats stooped to kiss her. 'You worry too much, my darling.'

A hackney cab brought him from his door to a terrace house in a quiet part of East London. A mongrel dog lapping from a puddle was the only sign of life in the street, half of whose buildings were boarded over or crumbling into rubble and weeds. The sweetish smell of horse dung hung in the air. The dog regarded him warily before padding down a side alley.

Yeats opened a gate into an empty, grass-filled courtyard, which looked to be a nightly haven for vagrants. At the opposite end was a weathered black door leading to a shuttered house. The most secretive meetings of the Golden Dawn were sometimes held in this anonymous building, although they were never called meetings. The society's occult rituals and rules made its gatherings very different from the conventional social meetings of gentlemen's clubs and literary circles. The Golden Dawn had been formed in London in 1888 as a secret society of mystics devoted to the practice of medieval and Eastern rituals of magic. Through carefully guided steps, divided into nine sections of three degrees or orders each, its members were encouraged to advance to the highest levels of wisdom, from the earthly to the heavenly, where the darkness disappears and the golden light of understanding shines through.

The order's origins were linked to the discovery of a coded manuscript, claimed to have been lost for centuries, which turned up on a bookseller's barrow in Farringdon Road, London, in 1884. Yeats was particularly captivated by the idea of a powerful lost book, as well as the order's cabalistic, Masonic and astrological symbolism. He had successfully progressed to the highest inner levels of the order, and hoped to attain the title of magus or priest, which would recognise him as a human conduit of wisdom from the supernatural to the natural.

A man dressed in the uniform of a butler ushered Yeats upstairs into a room on the third floor. The five men seated within were used to assembling in more luxurious environments, in plush sitting-rooms overlooking the Houses of Parliament, or fine manors in the countryside where the extensive parkland provided a necessary buffer against prying eyes, and the more adventurous members of the Order could entertain the society's female novitiates.

The room in which they had gathered was so secretive only a handful of elders within the Golden Dawn had ever set eyes upon it. The library shelves and walls were masked in dark tapestries embroidered with iridescent symbols and Latin words woven into Celtic knots. A series of allegorical pictures ran the length of the room, depicting a man torn in two by an eagle, wild beasts, hunchbacks and jesters with gaping smiles. The central tapestry depicted a large diagram in the shape of a wheel where the phases of the moon were intertwined with a golden apple, an acorn, a silver cup and a wooden wand. Upon the ceiling was an immense rose wrought in mosaic and coloured with red and black petals.

The five men were seated on a platform lit by candles in the middle of the room. At the centre was a hollow, in which an opened coffin lay. When Yeats entered, the men were muttering together. The mood was not good-humoured.

The eldest of the men, who went under the title Ruling Chief, rose with the help of a walking cane, and greeted Yeats. He had a trimmed white beard and shining eyes, and his hand gripped the ornate ebony head of his cane. He seemed eager for the poet's company, while his companions remained in the shadows cast by the bright oval candle flames.

'My dear Willie, we were beginning to worry you had been kidnapped.' A smile played upon his lips.

'Why would that cross your mind?' asked Yeats.

'These are dangerous times, you know. Troublemakers and spies have overtaken the city, while abroad good men are dying in their thousands. Killing on such a grand scale is very contaminating and strenuous on the collective consciousness.' He tapped the cane on the floor. 'Are you ready for the ceremony?'

'Ready enough.'

The leaders of this occult movement set their own rules of conduct, devised their own rituals, but sometimes they went a step too far. The last ceremony Yeats had taken part in, the enactment of a fake hanging, had left him so overwrought that afterwards he had to rest in a chair for two days without reading or trying his mind in any manner.

'Enacting one's death is hardly an experience one looks forward to,' murmured Yeats.

'You should think of Lazarus who was four days dead before being miraculously raised.'

Very slowly, because beginnings are more difficult than endings, Yeats undressed the upper half of his body. The old man slipped a hood over his head, and with the help of the butler, Yeats laid himself out in the coffin. A bell tinkled, and a stiff curtain of tapestry that had been concealing an inner door shifted and into the room slipped a young woman wearing a white dress bordered with a hem of red roses.

'I hope you are not afraid of ghosts, my dearest,' said the elderly man.

She smiled weakly in the flickering candlelight.

'More afraid of flesh and blood,' she whispered.

The Ruling Chief understood her comment as a reference to the fate of the last handmaiden, a sixteen-year-old girl called Celestine.

The old man's voice sank. 'That was an unfortunate accident. Caused by an excess of zeal from a member who has since been banished from the society.'

The girl moved to the centre of the room. Her dress was bound tightly around her body, hiding her legs in a long winding fishtail.

'This is the last time I shall say this,' said the elderly man, addressing both Yeats and the girl. 'You may leave now if you wish, but not afterwards.'

Yeats remained silent.

'I don't wish to leave,' said the girl. 'I only wish to understand.'

'There is little to understand, only the pleasure in forgetting. All you have to do is surrender yourself to the mysteries of the Golden Dawn.'

If the girl felt any fear, it was hidden by the look of devotion that fell across her face. She picked up a dagger that lay beside the coffin.

'I am not a coward,' she said.

'And neither is Mr Yeats, our new guardian and resident of the coffin.'

The girl's face was flushed with concentration. Wielding the dagger, she traced the sign of a pentagram in the air above the coffin. The room was hushed as she drew the shape of a cabalistic cross on Yeats' torso, and then covered his upper body in a white sheet. Her eyes were glazed yet still in touch with what was happening in the room. She wore the gaze of someone simultaneously exhilarated and admired, afloat on desire and reverence. The intensity of her face made her seem full of light, while the men in the armchairs looked drained, opaque in the shadowy darkness. For a moment, the roles were reversed. Now she was the master of the ceremony.

'You are the angel wielding a flaming sword,' breathed the old man. 'You have been entrusted with the closing of the lid.'

It made a heavy creaking sound as she brought it down over Yeats' body. Shaking slightly, she climbed on top of the coffin and stretched her slender form along its length. She stared at the ceiling and its rose mosaic.

The old man stepped towards the centre of the room and raised his hands over her body.

'Mr Yeats has climbed the Order's ladder of knowledge,' he intoned. 'He has mastered the alchemical principals of sulphur, mercury and salt, the suits of the tarot pack, and the symbolism of the Cabala. He has applied himself with distinction and diligence, extending our knowledge of the pre-Christian hermetic rituals of swords, passwords and paces.' He paused dramatically. 'Let him arise again.'

A bell chimed, and the girl rose and lifted the coffin lid.

Once Yeats was out of the coffin, he was made to stand with the hood still on his head, while the girl tied three strands of golden rope around his waist.

Guided by the old man, Yeats intoned the oath.

'I solemnly promise to persevere with courage and determination in the labours of the Divine Science. If I break this, my magical obligation, I submit myself, by my own consent, to a stream of power, set in motion by the divine guardians of this order.'

The girl dipped the dagger in wine, and held it before Yeats, as he swore to keep his role as guardian secret all of his life, and never to reveal any of the Order's teachings to a non-initiate.

The old man rose and kissed the girl's hand. 'You were marvellous my dear,' he said. 'You may return to the inner sanctum. The Order wishes to welcome its new Frater and Adept Major.'

He removed Yeats' hood and helped him to an empty seat in the shadows, where the four men surrounded him. A judge, an admiral, a doctor and a professor; each of them representing the highest levels of their professions.

The Ruling Chief handed a glass of brandy to Yeats, who took a drink with a trembling hand. The Chief raised his glass and proposed a toast to the newest guardian of the Golden Dawn. The men clinked their glasses and waited for the colour to return to Yeats' face.

'What message do you have for us?' asked the professor.

All five believed that Yeats was a world-master at fantastical imaginings. Their experiences had taught them that messages and images could well up from a source deeper than the individual memory or subconscious, from a universal store they called the *Anima Mundi*, the soul of the world. The pool of wisdom offered guidance toward resolving personal dilemmas, as well as bestowing a rich source of imagery for poets, writers and painters.

'The spirits revealed an image to me,' replied Yeats. 'A man whipping his own shadow while a blood-dimmed tide advanced towards him.'

'What does it signify?'

'The imminent destruction of civilisation.' Yeats' words were hushed but they filled the tapestry-lined room.

The others fell silent.

'What do you mean?' asked the professor.

'Isn't it obvious what is happening to society? Last night,

for instance, I was set upon by two vagabonds. Only the quick assistance of a passing policeman saved me from a violent attack. Further afield the situation is worse. Much worse. Europe is reeling from the effects of war, while in Russia the threat of Bolshevism is on the rise. War has broken out between the sexes. Not only are women doing the jobs of men, but millions will never have husbands. Ireland is on the brink of rebellion and the Protestant Ascendancy has lost its grip. Civilisation and the old order are dying.'

The five men remained silent. Yeats was a poet, respected for the intensity of his vision. Sometimes, however, the fervour of his words verged on intellectual intimidation. They studied the poet as he sat slumped in his chair. His face was still very white and his eyes had a look of dark desperation. Perhaps the initiation rite had taken its toll on his delicate sensibilities, they decided.

The professor changed the topic of conversation. 'We have read your essay on the dissensions of the Greeks and Romans, and we have made our corrections and amplifications.'

'Then you should understand the threat posed by the coming chaos,' replied Yeats. 'All civilisations come to an end when they have given their light like burned-out wicks.'

'Forgive me,' said the admiral. 'But what does a poet know of the modern age and these threats to society.'

'Poets can see things others can't. Elements falling into place. A design. A shape in the chaos of the age.'

'And what have you discerned?'

'That after an age of truth, mechanism, science and peace comes an age of freedom, fiction, evil and war. Our age has burned itself to the wick.'

'What do you propose we do?' asked the judge.

'That is a question I keep asking myself.' Yeats' eyes glazed over as his thoughts turned inward.

'Perhaps Mr Yeats is correct,' said the Ruling Chief. 'Perhaps we should consider the terror that is to come.'

The doctor interrupted. 'I fear that we are too timid at wielding our influence and embracing these unfolding events.

Like a deferential husband reluctant to consummate his marriage.' He glanced pointedly at Yeats. 'What I see in society is not an end but a transformation. This is no accidental pattern. We are witnessing the growing pains of democracy and social conscience. The Order should support these changes, such as the cry for political reform, rather than oppose them. We must join the modern world rather than hark to a dim and glorious past.'

'I'm afraid you are mistaken,' replied Yeats.

'Enlighten me – how?' The doctor appraised him with troubled eyes.

'England has become the victim of powerful forces. Accumulated over centuries.' Yeats' voice was strained, strident almost. 'Civilisation does not progress from stage to stage, guided by reason and truth. First we had the outbreak of war with Germany, then the Easter Rising and the execution of its leaders. The whole of Ireland seethes with rebellion, threatening the very fabric of the British Empire. This is no orderly descent from level to level. No waterfall but a whirlpool. A gyre.'

A brooding silence settled on the gathering. The doctor found himself fixated by Yeats' haunted-looking eyes. A light sheen of perspiration had formed on the poet's brow, and his long, delicate fingers still shook slightly as he held his glass. He wondered whether Yeats was ill or suffering from a mental imbalance. It seemed clear that he needed some form of retreat or recuperation.

'Willie, you look drained,' said the Chief. 'Is something else preying on your mind? Perhaps it's this business with the dead girl's letter?'

'I don't know.' Yeats voice fell to a whisper. 'I've hardly slept since I learned of its contents. Last night I barely got a wink.'

'That doesn't surprise me. But there is no need to feel anxious about the matter. As long as we proceed with caution. Where is Mr Adams, our ghost-catcher?'

'At Lissadell House. A safe vantage point on the Sligo coast. One where he won't be bothered by sinister elements.'

'He has agreed to carry out our instructions?'

'He believes devoutly in the principles of the Golden Dawn.'

'And what about Maud Gonne? Will she obey our instructions?'

'Most definitely not.' Yeats managed a weak smile.

'She is no longer a believer?'

'Correct.'

'An atheist?'

'A Catholic.'

'What a pity.'

The admiral joined in. 'If Mr Adams manages to make contact with this ghost, there will be dramatic consequences for the Golden Dawn.'

'Do you mean an upsurge in spiritual fervour?' asked the doctor.

'Precisely. Think of the excitement it will cause, not only among members of the Order, but in the hearts of all people who want to believe in an afterlife. We will have thousands knocking on our doors to help them make contact with their loved ones. Mr Adams might soon find his services in great demand.'

'But what if he fails?' asked the judge.

'We would be open to ridicule and the foundations of the Order undermined.'

'Which is why we must control the situation at its source,' said the chief, clutching his glass of brandy tightly.

'Whether we like it or not, the news will spread rapidly,' said the judge. 'I dread to think of the sensation the press will make of this, if they ever get wind of it.'

'It is vital they don't. We have had too much criticism from them already. We should not offer them any encouragement.'

'Of course not.'

'What age is Mr Adams?' inquired the judge.

'Twenty-four.'

'Isn't he rather young to be pursuing the secrets of the dead?'

Yeats seemed to shrink into himself. 'If he was learning the piano he'd be considered too old already,' he said.

'But shouldn't he have a senior member of the Order to guide him?'

The men whispered among themselves.

The Chief gripped his walking cane, and spoke, ignoring the look of rising distress on Yeats' face. 'Mr Yeats, the Order has decided to entrust you with taking charge of this task. You must return to Ireland and direct Mr Adams as he unravels this mystery.'

The poet said nothing. He simply rubbed his hand across his temple and eyes.

'A piece of advice, Mr Yeats,' added the admiral. 'Be sure not to hand yourself over to the first mob you encounter there.'

Before Yeats could reply, a gentle knock on the door interrupted the proceedings.

'Yes?' said the Chief.

The butler peered around the door. 'There is a gentleman below behaving in a very insistent manner,' he said in a worried voice. 'I'm afraid he won't go away. He's from the *Daily Telegraph*.'

Everyone in the room stiffened to attention. Even the shimmering figures on the tapestries seemed to rouse themselves from the walls and lean into the chamber.

The butler's voice was grave. 'The newspaper would like a statement about claims that members of the Order have become entangled in a murder scandal in Ireland.'

The Ruling Chief of the Golden Dawn clenched the arms of his chair so tightly his pale knuckles showed right through the skin.

9

ACE OF CUPS

'THIS squalid mud terrace once housed a dozen families,' declared Denver, flicking his whip at what seemed to be the decaying end of a long dunghill. 'Rosemary lived with her father in one of the last fragments of a hundred-year-old village.'

It was raining steadily as we made our way along the back roads to Lissadell House, and my horse kept slithering on patches of wet ground. If Denver had not pointed out the squat cottage I would have mistaken it for a straw-covered hummock and not given it a second glance.

I dismounted and followed the estate manager as he pushed back clumps of witch hazel and sauntered up a weed-grown path to a half door. The low walls of the cottage had been whitewashed once, but not much had survived the Atlantic winters. The only sign of life was a whisper of smoke rising from a chimney pot sitting half-collapsed in the rotten thatch. The cottage itself was little more than a hovel, hidden from the rest of the estate as though thrust to the back of its consciousness. Briars grappled the lopsided walls, threatening to pull them into a deeper oblivion.

Denver opened the door without knocking. He did not bother with the usual formalities of an introduction or an apology for arriving unannounced. A voice from within warned us to be aware of the step. We entered a main room barely lit by a turf fire, which flickered and hissed with drops of rain skittering down the wide chimney. I peered into the darkness at what seemed to be the blackened carcasses of ancient furniture.

'Are you sick, Mr O'Grady?' asked Denver.

A shape moved by the fire. The springs creaked on a dilapidated chair and an old man rose to his feet.

'No,' he answered. He watched us silently. I could sense his body stiffen beneath his ragged shirt. A visit from the estate manager was hardly an occasion to be greeted warmly.

'Perhaps we've come at a wrong time,' I said.

'No,' he replied again. 'You haven't come at a wrong time.' There was a further silence.

Denver walked in and poked at the fire until the dark red embers lit up the dingy cell. Sparks rifled up the chimney and were snuffed out in the thick smoke. The walls hung bare, apart from a calendar showing the shortest month of the year, and a picture of the Sacred Heart, mantled in gloom. Mildewed potato skins covered a wooden table. The only noise was the mindless fidgeting of birds and small creatures in the thatch. I got the impression that the cottage's one treasure had been forcibly removed and was gone forever.

'I've brought you a visitor,' said Denver.

Mr O'Grady croaked a few words of muffled welcome and backed away.

'This is Mr Charles Adams from London,' said Denver. 'He is conducting an investigation into your daughter's death.' His voice was cold and matter-of-fact, as though our visit was a routine piece of business, like a livestock inspection.

The old man stared at me. 'What do people from London care about my daughter?' His voice was edged with soot and damp. He sat down again and watched me from the vantage point of a dark corner, silent, unblinking. Smoke wafted in threads through the thatch and sneaked back into the room, hiding his face.

'Fire away with your questions, Mr Adams,' said Denver.

'I'll just stay a moment to warm up.' He stood with his broad back against the fire. 'I'll be on my way when the rain eases.'

I told O'Grady that my visit was personal rather than part of any official investigation.

'A couple of months ago, your daughter sent a letter to an associate of mine, claiming that she was living in mortal fear for her life. I need your help to shed light on the letter.'

'How do you think I can help?' He looked genuinely mystified. He seemed unsure if I had come to tease him, or prolong his agony, or whether I really wanted to help solve the mystery of his daughter's death.

A clamour of caws echoed down the chimney. Denver and the old man started. I realised I was sharing a room with two tense people. I could understand the old man's unease but what was making Denver so tense?

'Rosemary was a private girl,' her father explained, with a hint of agitation in his voice. 'She kept herself to herself.'

'You could have fooled me,' whispered Denver, loud enough to be heard.

The old man fell silent again. Denver studied us for a long moment, and then the sound of the horses whinnying distracted him. 'I'll be outside,' he said.

As soon as Denver had closed the door, the old man extracted a few lumps of crumbling turf from a bucket and crammed them onto the fire. Abruptly, the light in the room was extinguished.

'Are you one of them?' he asked.

'One of whom?'

I could sense his eyes scrutinising me intensely, searching for a faltering, a shift of the gaze, a nervous tic.

'I can see you're probably not,' he said eventually. 'I have to keep a watch for them.'

'For whom?' Slowly my eyes adjusted to the gloom.

'Agents of the British Admiralty. I was warned to be on my guard.' He stared at me with more than a flicker of interest. 'I never heard of a letter. What did it say?'

'She was concerned someone was trying to murder her. Does that surprise you?'

'No.'

'Why not?'

'How much do you know of what is going on in this country?'

'Practically nothing.'

'Then you have no starting point for your investigation.'

'My starting point is your daughter's personal life, the people she knew, the things she did.'

'Her private life is not your concern.'

'I only want to know about her private life because she had an inkling that a murderer was targeting her. She's not the guilty party.'

He did not take his eyes off me. He watched me warily as though convinced I had been sent to bring him fresh suffering.

'Nothing you tell me will be shared with another soul,' I reassured him.

He paused. His black-rimmed eyes stared at me through the turf-smoke.

'Mr Adams, you're too late. There is nothing left of my daughter's life to talk about or show you.'

'What do you mean?'

'I burned everything she owned.'

'Why?'

'I was under orders.' His eyes drifted away.

'Whose?'

'A woman came to my house the day after they found her body. She rode a black horse and said she was from the Daughters of Erin. She was very forceful in her instructions. She warned me that the police might find treasonable material in her bedroom.'

'What did you burn?'

'Pamphlets. Letters. Notebooks of her writing. I didn't make a list. But the woman was right to warn me.'

'Why?'

'Because my daughter was a revolutionary. She was prepared to defy British Rule by whatever means necessary.'

He spoke with pride, not aggressively, but with a shade of excitement in his heavy eyes. I wondered how did a servant girl become a revolutionary. Did she join a club, or pay a subscription?

Or was she part of a secret society with rituals and a code of silence?

'What treasonable material did you find?' I asked.

He considered my question in wary silence. I could understand why the Daughters of Erin might want to hamper an investigation into Rosemary's death. They were obviously fearful of what stories and names might come to the surface, but why would her father go along with their wishes? There was something both suffocating and confusing about the old man's grief.

'Rosemary got pulled into politics while working at Lissadell House,' he explained. 'She was Constance Gore-Booth's favourite servant. She accompanied her on all the political rallies. Every day there was a new pamphlet or book to read. The mistress spoiled her with education. Taught her to read and write, and compose letters. I could see the changes in my daughter. She grew hard-headed and serious. A wave of bitterness washed over her heart. Life isn't as simple as a political pamphlet, but it was pointless telling her so. With every passing week, she grew angrier, until all she could talk about was the rebellion.'

'What do you know of this group, the Daughters of Erin?'

'Only some gossip. I heard rumours of unusual relationships among its members.' His eyes darted away. 'Their leaders cut their hair and wear their dresses short, showing their legs right up to the calf. Sometimes they put on trousers and ride horses in twos and threes like the men I used to see riding on the slopes of Ben Bulben with their swords swinging.'

He leaned forward and poked the fire, setting off a creaking noise that might have been his joints or the chair. Smoke spiralled from the turf and the darkness in the room expanded.

'I asked Rosemary why she should devote herself to a group run by upper-class English women. But she told me that God had chosen them to free Ireland from British Rule.'

'Was there anything missing from her room before you cleared it out? Something that should have been there but wasn't?'

'Nothing I can think of.'

'What about the police investigation? Did the Constabulary tell you who their suspects were?'

'They rounded up half a dozen men who had danced with her the previous night. Then the police found out about her political allegiances. An Inspector came calling from Dublin Castle, and everything changed. The men were released without charge.'

'What do you think happened that night?'

His eyes went dark. 'I think a lot of things.'

'Had your daughter shown any signs of fear or worry?

'Not at all.' He regarded me closely. 'If you believe she took her own life you're wrong.'

'I'm not suggesting that. But sometimes our nearest and dearest are good at hiding their feelings.'

'Rosemary would never hurt herself. She was nineteen years old. She had everything to live for.'

'But had she ever harmed herself in the past?'

He shook his head in silence.

'Ever attempted to drown herself?'

He seemed to sink into a deep loneliness. Again he shook his head and sighed.

'Staff at the estate saw her wade out at night into the sea when it was freezing cold,' I pressed on.

The creases on his perplexed brow deepened.

'I've had enough talking. Feel free to look in her bedroom, if that is what you wish. Maybe you'll find something to satisfy your curiosity there.'

He slumped over the turf embers like a man condemned to toil over a fire that would never give enough heat or light.

I stepped beneath the lintel into her bedroom, feeling more than a twinge of embarrassment. For the first time I experienced the secret thrill of a witness observing the scene of a tragedy. I stood in the centre of the room without making a sound. I took a slow look around. The room was bare and clean. Like an empty shell on a beach. Far removed from the life and soul of a nineteen-year-old rebel girl. I peered into the shadows hoping to find some trace of her, but the distempered walls were blank, and there were no ornaments or books on the windowsill, or on the shelves and bedside cabinet. A jug and basin sat on a table, next to a cracked bar of soap in a dish. The neat bed with its folded blankets looked innocent of nightmares; the naked light of day was all that lay upon it. Somehow, it did not look like the bed of a dangerous revolutionary.

I realised that if I were going to uncover any clues, I would need some assistance. I decided to test Mr Galton's new theory of fingerprint detection with a little practical application. I removed a tiny phial containing iodine crystals from my pocket and emptied them onto the soap dish. A fine brown vapour rose into the air. According to Galton, the fumes emitted by the crystals should attach themselves to the oily substances of a fingerprint, making them visible to the naked eye. I moved the soap dish around the room, wafting the vapour across the few pieces of furniture, but everything drew a blank. Not a fingerprint in sight. The room had been thoroughly cleaned. I checked the walls, again nothing, apart from a partial hand-print that appeared at an odd angle above her bed like a welcoming signal from the spirit world. My pulse quickened. I had found my first trace of Rosemary O'Grady. I stood on the bed and placed my hand over the fading outline. She had put her hand there for balance. I looked up at the ceiling rafter. I ran the burner along its length and found a concentration of fingerprints appearing like phantoms at one particular spot. I reached up and felt around the timber. My fingers found an old tin biscuit box amid the dusty cobwebs and husks of dead insects. It was the closest thing to a treasure chest in that miserable abode.

Inside the box were an old fountain pen, a leather notebook, fragrant petals of flowers and herbs, and some old scraps of newspaper. I opened the notebook. It was damp and smelled of the sea. The smudged pages were filled with an indecipherable stream of numbers and words. A cryptic code written in a delicate hand.

Frothy 16B 4th *Phase* 42 11
Cheerful Charlie 23B 2nd *Phase* 42 12
Comte de Chombard 14B 13th *Phase* 42 9
Invincible 18B 13th *Phase* 41 9
May Queen 16B 28th *Phase* 42 9

1-12y, 2-14y, 3-15y, 4-13y, 5-17y, 6-18y, 7-20y, 8-21y,
9-21y, 10-23y, 11-23y, 12-24y, 13-21y, 14-24y, 15-24y,
16-22y, 17-22y, 18-21y, 19-19y, 20-19y, 21-17y, 22-17y,
23-15y, 24-15y, 25-13y, 26-13y, 27-13y, 28-12y

And on it continued for about a dozen pages, including a series
of charts, each of them divided into twenty-eight segments with
more reams of numbers. A photograph slipped out of the back.
It showed a tall, captivating woman with an exquisitely pale
face and darkened eyes staring to the side of the camera with a
fierce look, as though poised for battle. She was dressed in layers
of black wool and silk with a mannequin's waist. The face was
strangely familiar in spite of the heavy make-up. It was a woman
I had seen not so long ago, someone who wore more than one
disguise, had more than one role. The Red Cross nurse on the
mail boat. Below the photograph ran the caption: 'Maud Gonne
playing Cathleen Ni Houlihan on the Abbey stage'. Followed by
a date: *1902*. I placed the notebook in my pocket and returned
the tin box to its hiding place.

I glanced into the main room. Rosemary's father was still
tending to the fire with pointless Napoleonic effort. His poker
stirred the embers, raising little more than a few writhing rags
of smoke. Through the tiny back window, I caught a glimpse of
a field riddled with hummocks of weeds and stone, and in the
distance, the spectral forms thrown up by waves breaking on the
Atlantic coast. Denver had yet to return, and it occurred to me
that this might be the perfect opportunity to probe the invisible
world.

Taking care that the old man would not disturb me, I locked the
bedroom door and prepared myself for a spiritual vigil. Drawing

my legs underneath in the Hindu style, I sat in the dead centre of the room. From a coat pocket, I took out Rosemary's letter and on a sheet of paper drew out the letters and numbers of a Ouija board, a ghost-hunter's first tool of investigation. I placed a coin on the piece of paper and lightly rested my fingertips upon it. Where was her ghost hiding? I wondered. What messages might she wish to communicate? I closed my eyes and cleared my mind. The coin moved slightly. I felt a sudden infusion of confidence mingled with excitement. I had the notion that it might be within my grasp to solve this mystery before the day was over and triumphantly bring my findings back to London, to the rapturous attention of Yeats and the guardians of the Golden Dawn.

I opened my eyes, closed them again, shivered, and groaned slightly. I concentrated with all my might. 'What secrets do you wish to communicate?' I murmured aloud. The coin slid across the paper. I followed its movements as it glided from one corner of the paper to the other. The hairs on the back of my neck stirred. The coin twisted and changed direction, lively as an eel, barely resting a moment on any particular letter or number. My mind struggled to spell out the frenzied message.

My concentration was irretrievably broken by a sudden rasping that shook the bedroom door. I watched the coin spin back and forth between the letters 'O' and 'S'. 'SOS' I spelled out. Save our Souls. The key rattled in the lock as someone frantically tried to work it. The handle turned this way and that, the hinges groaned, and at last the door flew open. To my surprise, in rushed Wolfe Marley accompanied by Denver and a middle-aged policeman with a haggard moustache and a panting red face.

I stood up immediately. 'Shouldn't you knock first?' I said indignantly.

'We were hoping to catch you by surprise, Mr Adams,' said Marley, 'that is if it's possible to catch a ghost-hunter by surprise.' He looked around the room as if searching for a hidden spirit. 'Well,' he said cynically, 'are you having any luck?'

I glanced at the wall behind the bed and was relieved to see the hand-print had faded from view.

'What are you up to?' asked Denver, staring at the piece of paper in front of me. 'Learning the alphabet?'

I explained that it was a Ouija board, a device invented for ghosts to send signals to the living.

'I didn't realise it was necessary for ghosts to spell.' A look of curiosity enlivened Marley's features. 'Must they?'

'The ghosts send their messages through the subconscious forces of the medium,' I explained.

'What language do they communicate in then? Latin, Greek or the mother tongue? I suppose you're going to say the language of the particular place.'

'They no longer inhabit any particular place, or speak any particular language. The board is simply a means to leave behind patterns for the medium to decipher.'

Marley renewed his sceptical mien. If anything, he inhabited it more fully than before.

'Tell me, Mr Adams, aren't all your ghosts anonymous?'

'What do you mean?'

'I mean if all they have to communicate with is an alphabet on a piece of paper, how can you be sure of their identity, of who they say they are?'

I shrugged. 'Sometimes the message is more important than the ghost.'

'If I were a medium being guided by a ghost, I'd want to be very sure of whom I was dealing with.'

'You're a cynical man, Mr Marley,' said Denver. 'Not even the dead escape your suspicions.'

'I've dealt with countless criminals, traitors and spies since the war broke out,' replied Marley. 'And I've been an Irishman all my life.'

The policeman coughed. He raised himself onto his toes to assert his presence in the room.

'By the way, Mr Adams,' said Marley. 'This is Inspector Derek Grimes, head of Sligo's Royal Irish Constabulary. Your presence here has aroused his curiosity.'

I leaned forward and shook his hand.

The Inspector sniffed, pulled out a handkerchief from his cuff and blew his nose. Through the material, he said, 'Rosemary's death was a sad business, make no mistake about that.' He stuffed the hanky into a pocket of his crumpled-looking uniform and wagged a finger at me. 'But, whatever the circumstances of her death, Sligo policemen are in charge of the case. No one else.'

'That is as it should be,' I replied.

'Then what are you doing prying into her affairs?' he snapped. His expression was both surly and superior.

I stared at him closely. Something lay slumped at the back of his yellowish eyes. Something hungry and suspicious. Perhaps it was a fear that his incompetence might be exposed by a strange Englishman who believed he could communicate with a dead girl.

'You have to excuse Mr Adams,' said Marley soothingly. 'He's a ghost fanatic who wants to turn a crime scene into a séance. I also fear he's been reading too many detective books.'

'I was sent to make some inquiries into Rosemary's death,' I replied. 'After I have done so I'll be on my way.'

'That's the boy,' said Marley with mock enthusiasm.

'And what about you, Mr Marley?' I asked. 'You're a real detective, I suppose.'

Marley grinned. 'I wear so many uniforms; it's hard to remember what I am.' He circled the room. 'My interest in the case is based purely on my fascination with what you are doing here, stirring up old ghosts, so to speak.' He lifted the letter from the floor and handed it to the Inspector. 'Mr Adams has a new lead for you, Inspector.'

The Inspector read the letter quickly. I got the impression he had already been appraised of its contents.

'Running after ghosts is not a job for His Majesty's police force,' he sniffed. 'We tend to gather evidence we can bring to court.' He handed the letter back to me with a dismissive gesture. 'How did this come to be in your possession?'

'It was sent to the office of the Golden Dawn.'

'Then it must have been hand delivered rather than posted.'

'How can you be so sure?'

A slightly sheepish expression came over him. 'We had some men following Rosemary for the past few months. Checking her movements and correspondence. None of them reported her posting a letter of that nature.'

'Maybe she knew she was being followed and went to considerable lengths to keep the letter secret.'

'That is possible.'

A messenger then, I thought. We should be looking for whoever delivered the letter. They might know something of its contents and the nature of Rosemary's suspicions. Perhaps a fellow member of the Daughters of Erin. The fact that the letter had successfully reached its destination meant that Rosemary had either known she was being watched, or suspected she was, or was naturally cautious.

'Why were your men following her?'

'She had some brushes with the law.'

'What sort of brushes?'

'She was a member of the Daughters of Erin. The organisation behind the vandalism and arson on local estates. Moreover, we believe its members are hatching a plot to bring German weapons to Ireland. One of their leaders is Maud Gonne, a fanatical woman who preaches violence and is intent on raising hell.'

I felt Marley's eyes watch me closely. I was acutely aware of the notebook in my pocket with the picture of Gonne dressed as Mother Ireland. I began to wish the room were a little less claustrophobic. I tried to change the tack of the conversation.

'Out of curiosity, Inspector, have you interviewed Captain Oates?'

'The captain is difficult to reach.'

'I hear that after the body was found, he deserted his post and went into hiding. Does that not arouse your suspicions?'

'Captain Oates appears to have suffered some sort of mental

breakdown,' said Denver. 'According to the locals he is away.'

'Away?'

'Away with the faeries. The sight of apparitions has him frightened out of his wits.'

'Madness does not necessarily infer guilt,' warned Marley.

'But it should at least encourage the police to interview him. Especially since Miss O'Grady vowed to haunt her killer.'

'I have to warn you,' said the Inspector, 'that you are fouling the name of a better man.'

'What have the RIC done so far? Have you found the murder scene?'

'We've yet to locate evidence that a murder was committed, if that's what you mean.'

'What about an autopsy?'

'We examined the corpse,' he grimaced. 'We were satisfied she died by drowning.'

'But what were the circumstances of her drowning?'

'Perhaps it was an accident, or some sort of ghoulish game that went wrong,' he suggested.

It struck me why Grimes might be at pains to explain away Rosemary's death as an apparent suicide or an accident. Suicides and accidents did not demand patient investigation or attract a lot of political attention. On the other hand, a murder might expose shoddy police work and stir up sectarian tensions.

'I'd like to know what made her so careless that she climbed into the coffin and allowed herself to be pushed into the sea in the first place.'

'What do you propose we do, Mr Adams?' The Inspector's eyes were cool and patient but his mouth was twisted into a sneer. 'Dig up her corpse and shake it by its ankles to see what falls out.'

'I gather that the body was soaked through with sea water,' said Marley. 'Cleansed of all its clues. The ocean is renowned for its superhuman purity. Perhaps her killers were counting on it.'

'If there was a murderer, the only mistake he made was placing the body in the coffin.' Grimes' voice carried a note of professional disapproval. 'He should have dumped her corpse in the sea and passed it off as an accidental drowning.'

'I suspect the murderer had no intention of passing it off as an accident,' I said.

'What are you implying?'

'He was sending a message. A warning to others.'

'What others?'

'Her comrades in Daughters of Erin.'

'Why use a coffin?'

I was unable to make a rational reply. The silence was broken by Marley.

'I happen to have a theory to explain precisely that. Mr Adams, how familiar are you with initiation rites to secret societies?'

I gave him a puzzled look.

His eyes taunted me back. 'My understanding is that initiates of the Golden Dawn are placed in a coffin with a hood over their head. A ritual known as the ceremony of re-birth. The belief is that the participant is born again into the Order, and that his or her life is transformed thereafter.'

I struggled to keep my face a blank.

'I have a theory that Rosemary's death was just such an initiation ceremony,' he continued. 'One that went horribly wrong.'

I stayed silent, but alert. I could see what Marley was hinting at. With such a theory, Rosemary's death might place the entire Order of the Golden Dawn under a cloud of suspicion.

'Any reason why you appear to have lost your tongue?' pressed Marley. 'Perhaps you are bound by a code of silence? The Golden Dawn is rumoured to punish severely any member who betrays its secrets. Did the society wreak such a vengeance upon Rosemary?'

I had the impression of a razor-sharp inquisitor pushing for a confession. He was correct about the order's oath of secrecy. The Golden Dawn threatened those who divulged its secrets with what it called a deadly and hostile Current of Will by which the oath-breaker would fall slain or paralysed without visible weapon.

'Admit it, Mr Adams. The handprints of the Golden Dawn are all over her death.'

I kept my silence.

'The Order has already drawn unwanted publicity from a rape scandal. If memory serves correct, it involved a teenage girl and just such a botched initiation rite.'

'That was a splinter group masquerading in the Golden Dawn's name,' I muttered.

'Perhaps this was a splinter of that splinter.'

Grimes cut in aggressively. 'Mr Adams, are you a Satanist or a Christian?' He leaned so close I could smell his sweat. I backed away and held my tongue. His lips and eyes grew agitated in his overheated face.

'Why won't you answer?' insisted Marley. 'Are you a Christian?'

'If you mean born again,' I stammered, 'then yes I am.'

Grimes seemed satisfied with my answer but Marley's face was still dark with suspicion. A part of me felt sick with dread. I was beginning to realise that I had stepped into a labyrinth, a twilight world of secret societies and revolutionaries, dangerous rituals involving young women and mysterious messages left behind by the dead.

Some kind of night bird screeched nearby. Darkness was advancing. We stood silently and listened. The bird called again.

'Perhaps that's Rosemary's ghost enjoying the night air,' said Denver with a smirk.

'Take your pick,' replied Marley. 'Faeries, goblins, witches, or Captain Oates changed into a wolf.'

'What is there to believe or not to believe?' said Denver.

Grimes turned to me. 'I'm getting worried for you, Mr Adams. I have this foreboding.'

'What sort of foreboding?'

'This is not part of the normal society you know. You must be the first Englishman to visit Sligo armed with nothing more than a hastily scribbled alphabet.'

'I have an obligation that I must fulfil.'

'You're still intent on continuing to pry?'

'I only want to find out what happened to Miss O'Grady.'

'It's time to start considering what will happen to you,' said Marley. 'You have no legal authority to be in this cottage. You don't know the people of this country. You don't even pretend to understand the dangerous political situation, which is a relief. You can't investigate. All you can do is become entangled.'

'Entangled with what?'

'Ireland. Which is darker and more complicated than even Mr Yeats' poetry suggests.'

I took back Rosemary's letter and left the room.

'Be careful with your ghost hunt, Mr Adams,' called Marley. 'In my experience spirits are created, not discovered. We the living are but transient shadows. Never for a moment can we trouble the nothingness of the dead.'

10

TWO OF CUPS

WE threaded the horses through dripping trees as an evening mist descended. I could feel the salty warm breath of the sea change instantly to water droplets as it encountered the colder air of the forest. Denver followed well-trodden paths that were recognizable even when shrouded in mist. He seemed to know the forest intimately. A solitary oak loomed in the fog, its frame bare as winter, followed by a thicket of willows furred with spring blossom. A blackbird scolded us from a tier of ivy that threatened to pull down a stately elm. Its gnarled bough made Denver suddenly veer left. He sat proudly on his mare, avoiding conversation or eye contact, as though he were accompanying a prisoner back to his cell. I began to worry that a fog-bound forest might prove an easy place for a ghost-catcher to vanish.

The prod of his whip in my chest stirred me from my thoughts.

'Hold your horse and be still,' he said. 'Look over your right shoulder. Between the branches of the hornbeam.'

I turned my head as slowly as possible and examined the puffs of vapour swirling like smoke into the hungry void of the forest. The mist snagged around the shape of what appeared to be a skeletal tree, and then I realised I was staring at the thin figure of a man. Sweat banded my forehead, in spite of the cold air. The stranger seemed unaware of our proximity, transfixed by something floating before him in the nothingness. He was dressed in a full military uniform that was black with mud and the decomposing leaves of the forest. The scene was so quiet I could hear the breathing of the horses and the squelching of mud sticking to the man's boots as he began arranging invisible objects on a mossy tree stump. He held out his hands as if he were inviting a guest to a dinner table. Then he sat down and mimed the actions of serving food.

He spoke in a clipped English accent. 'We're both a bit dishevelled but that can be fixed up later.' His eyes followed the sinuous movements of a wraith of mist as though it were a warm, living body.

'After we've finished eating we could go for a stroll along the beach,' he added. For several moments, he busied himself at his phantom table, and then he sighed.

'Can't you talk about anything else,' he chided. 'You've been wandering endlessly but now it's time to enjoy the meal and chat about ordinary matters.'

A look of distress flickered on his pale face. He listened intently, nodding from time to time, until his attention was distracted by the sound of a branch snapping deeper in the forest. He crouched, and, whipping out a pistol, pointed it in random directions. He crept off, disappearing silently into the mist like a submerging sea-creature.

Denver blew out a relieved sigh. 'There is proof, if any were needed, that Captain Oates' wits are out.'

'What do you think he was doing?' I inquired.

'Dining with the faeries. The locals say anyone who eats their food and drinks their drink is bewitched forever.'

When we arrived at Lissadell, the house was no longer a stately mansion but a grey wedge shrouded in mist. I glanced up at the looming flank of the west wing. Electric lights were blazing from the conservatory, where a dinner party was in full swing. The effect was as though the walls of mist had creaked open, revealing a fantastical world of immaculately groomed men and women being served glasses of champagne and canapés under sparkling chandeliers. In the distance, the sea churned endlessly. I felt as though I was staring at an illusion, like Oates' dinner scene, an image invented from the subconscious to fill the murky void.

'You've been invited to the dance,' said Denver abruptly. 'The Gore-Booths want to meet with you.'

'I have no other plans.'

'This is an invitation you can't refuse.'

I followed him with the strong suspicion the summons might be a means to continue keeping me under close observation. Red-stockinged doormen greeted us as we mounted the steps to the marbled entrance hall. Denver looked as though he relished the grandeur of his surroundings.

'Count yourself lucky the Gore-Booths are running out of guests to fill their great halls,' he whispered. 'In the current climate, they'd throw a ball for a new litter of pups.'

Gilded full-length mirrors along the walls ensured I could view more of myself than I had seen in a month.

'Before the war they used to book an entire orchestra for these dances,' said Denver.

Strains of gramophone music greeted us as we strolled into a conservatory filled with people moving about and conversing with an exalted air, like figures trapped in a perfect bubble. I recognised the tune from Verdi's *Nabucco*. Groups of people turned to stare at me, and I felt like a Hebrew slave marched before Babylonian royalty. I could sense a breathless state of anticipation from the women, while the men regarded me over their trimmed beards and moustaches with suspicion. Slowly, they resumed their conversations.

'That's it, Mr Ghost-catcher,' hissed Denver, 'you're on your own now.'

The leading families of the Protestant Ascendancy were gathered before me, still desperately trying to prove they were the country's finest. They gave off a volatile aroma of power, money and fear. However, Denver's tour of the abandoned estates had brought home to me the abnormality of their existence in this troubled land. A butler turned up the gramophone, as though the music were a blunt instrument to blot out the sound of something unnerving in the distance, the sound of looming danger. Laced curtains dangled at the side of cracked and boarded up windows. Young women in crisp dresses ran to greet each other with relieved smiles to find they were not the only ones to have stayed behind.

My nose winced at the odour of damp wood and sour cloth not quite smothered by an artificial fragrance of flowers, and something more sinister, the acrid smell of paraffin. I sensed how important it was to act as though I did not notice the smell. It was the smell of destruction and decay, and no one in the room wanted to be reminded of it. If the pretence that all was fine and normal broke, then many more would be swept away on boats to England. An elderly couple bravely took to the empty floor. As long as the music played and the champagne flowed, death and destruction might assume an elegant shape, one that they could all bear. More couples joined them on the floor.

I turned to look for Denver, and found that a pretty, dark-haired woman had grasped him by the arm. He introduced me to Clarissa Carty, his fiancée. Her eyes fully engaged with mine, as she ran her hand along her cheek and throat. She was wearing a white lace blouse, opened at the neck to reveal a necklace with a silver crucifix and a cluster of red gems in the shape of a rose. I had seen a similar necklace before but could not recall precisely where.

A figure tore itself away from one of the chatting groups. A man in a white dinner jacket with glassy eyes and a slightly brutal mouth stepped towards me with the air of someone about to evict a troublesome tenant. At the last second, he flashed a grin and introduced himself as the sixth Baronet of Lissadell, Sir Josslyn Richard Gore-Booth. Denver had informed me that Sir Josslyn was the first landlord in Ireland to sell his land to his tenants after the Land Act, a decision which explained why the mansion was still intact when so many others had fallen into ruin.

'Glad to see you've joined us, Mr Adams,' said the Baronet. 'Wouldn't want you to miss out on the fun.'

Women in décolleté gowns and men in tuxedos glided behind
him. The party might have been in full swing but the crowd
seemed distracted. I shook the Baronet's hand and could not
help but notice the sidelong glances and whispers.

'Mr Yeats has informed me you're here on behalf of his
occult society,' he said. A woman dressed in a sparkling gown
of chiffon, who I took to be his wife, appeared at his shoulder.
Denver spotted us and hovered at the edge of our company. I
kept catching the gaze of his fiancée. At one point, she wrinkled
her nose at me.

'You've come to the right place,' said the Baronet. 'This part
of Sligo is the British Empire's greatest centre for wandering
spirits and séances.'

'Sounds more like London at the current time,' I remarked.
'One hundred thousand grieving widows have triggered a major
upheaval in terms of supernatural agitation.'

'Then why bother to come here if you're searching for ghosts?'

A small, attentive group had assembled around the Baronet.

'I've come to search for one ghost in particular. That of
Rosemary O'Grady.'

The group fell silent, and I had the uncomfortable sensation
of enclosure. There was so much suspicion amongst the guests;
I felt it float above their transfixed faces like a battalion of little
Zeppelins. The music stopped and the only sound in the room
was the clicking of ladies' shoes deserting the dance floor.

'I hope you haven't come to cause us trouble,' said one of the
men in tuxedos. He lit a cigar and relaxed into a nearby chair.
His tuxedo climbed up his ample belly. 'I have to warn you that
I have a licence to employ twenty emergency men to round up
any agitators.'

'Forgive us, Mr Adams,' said the Baronet's wife. 'We are wary
of every newcomer to Sligo.'

'We keep a sharp look-out,' continued the man in the seat, 'for
subversives bent on stirring up the locals. I'll bet your friend is
mixed up in this rebellion.'

'Who?'

'The poet that draws the King's pension yet dreams of Irish independence.' A row of sharp teeth appeared in his beard. His eyes were humourless, alert.

'Mr Yeats skedaddled to London when things got too hot for him in Dublin,' said Denver. 'He ran like a rabbit. That's proof he's a coward, not a subversive.'

Sir Josslyn's wife fluttered her arms in a cloud of chiffon. 'Come now, let's hear no more of these serious matters.' She grabbed her husband by the arm. 'You haven't said hello yet to Uncle Montgomery.'

Sir Josslyn politely nodded in my direction. 'I hope you have a successful stay here, Mr Adams,' he said. 'Duty calls.'

The circle dissolved and I was on my own again. I spent the next half hour hovering at the fringes of the swaying crowd, until Denver's fiancée took pity on me. She sidled up alongside.

'I'm wondering why you keep glancing at me,' she said with a straight face. 'Do you think I'm a ghost?'

I returned her gaze. Stately looking couples danced by us with a minimum of movement and speech.

'I could not be more dazzled if you were.'

She leaned towards my ear as if confiding a secret. 'This is the last ballroom at the edge of Europe. At the western-most edge of the Empire. All the other ballrooms in this part of the country are empty of everything but ghosts.'

'I thought the environs were lacking in *joie de vivre*.'

She grabbed me by the arm. 'Would you care for a dance?'

I barely had time to nod. She was quick and lively, holding my left arm with her right, guiding me onto the floor. We locked in with the other dancing couples.

'People are calling you a meddling fool, Mr Adams,' she said. 'They're taking bets that you will be on the next mail boat to the mainland.'

Her accent was more musical than the upper-class tones that filled the ballroom. It was pure lilting Irish. Somehow, she did not feel the need to anglicise her voice.

'If I were less a fool, I'd be booking my passage now.'

'You're not a quitter, Mr Adams, are you?'

'I haven't come on holiday, if that's what you mean.' I looked into her eyes, which shone with a fearless light.

'I know someone who's desperate to meet you tonight,' she whispered, glancing over her shoulder. I followed the line of her gaze and found Denver's glaring figure standing at a table of drinks. Something about her behaviour suggested he might be more her enemy than her lover. 'Someone who wants to talk to you about the murdered girl.'

I tried not to flinch. 'I'm all ears,' I said.

'Meet me in half an hour at Lissadell beach,' she whispered.

It was almost midnight, the mist had lifted and a thin beam of moonlight was enough to guide me to the beach. I stood at the edge of the sea and waited. The only sound was the continual wash and hiss of the waves.

A soft scuffling sound in the sand made me spin round. A horse and rider appeared out of the night and drew to a halt. The rider's hand reached down and a cold but courteous voice beckoned me to climb on behind. I stepped backwards, half-stumbling. I had the chilling sensation that what was happening was all wrong, that bearing down upon me was the rider Denver had chased that afternoon. But now, up close, I could see the feminine shape of the rider's hand, and the outline of a delicate neck. It was a young woman, not a boy. The rider had hidden her hair under a cap, and wrapped a scarf around her mouth, but I recognised the voice of Clarissa Carty.

'We've several miles to ride, Mr Adams. Climb up!' Her cheeks were flushed pink with excitement.

'I'd rather walk.'

'Be reasonable.' The scarf slipped and I saw a patient smile like that of a mother rebuking an unruly child. 'We can't wait about.'

'Where do you propose to take me?'

She sighed. 'To a circle of friends. In this country, it's important to know exactly who one's friends are. Trust me on this.'

I clambered onto the horse. I could feel a slick of warm sweat on its flanks. It had been riding for some time. Clarissa slipped her boots out of the stirrups and I felt them dangle by my shins. With her encouragement, I stepped into the stirrups. Then she handed me a hood to wear.

'I'd rather see where I'm going,' I said.

'It's in your interests to be ignorant of your destination.'

'People will think you've kidnapped me.'

'That is the intention. The Admiralty's spies are everywhere.'

Reluctantly, I pulled on the hood and adjusted my seat. No sooner had the stirrups taken my weight, than Clarissa pushed into the horse's undercarriage with her free heels and the animal set off at a brisk canter.

I remembered the feeling I'd had earlier that afternoon, the thrill of the chase along overgrown paths. The thrill returned, only this time it was undercut by an incipient panic. In my mind's eye, the horse's gallop took us on a terrifying journey past crashing waves full of drowning girls, trees haunted by ghosts and mad soldiers, spies skulking behind shadows. When the branches of a thorn bush whipped my hood, I mistook them for sharp, grabbing fingers threatening to pull me into a bottomless grave.

11

QUEEN OF SWORDS

After an hour of swift and reckless riding, we reached our destination. I pulled off my hood. We had drawn up to a building that was like a small church or schoolhouse. The windows were blacked out with heavy cloth. My eyes, made keen by the darkness of the hood, picked out the small fluttering passage of bats against a gauzy moon. A bell rang out one o'clock from somewhere nearby.

'Make the most of this visit, Mr Adams,' said Clarissa. 'It will certainly open your eyes.'

She led me to a red door with a heavy brass handle. 'Wait here,' she advised, while leading the horses to a stable at the side of the building.

After several minutes, the door opened to the sound of women singing. 'Ah, my English sorcerer,' said a voice with a slight hint of mockery. 'Don't be shy, Mr Adams. We're not going to cook you.' She waved me into a hallway. 'Men usually feel a little nervous when I introduce them to my handmaidens, the Daughters of Erin.'

My hostess had recognised me first. She had exchanged her Red Cross uniform for a handsome black velveteen cloak and a more theatrical look, her make-up showing to strongest effect her seductive eyes. It suddenly dawned on me that the tall figure framing the doorway was none other than Maud Gonne. She moved back a little but her eyes invited me closer. What I found most disconcerting about her gaze was the confidence that blazed from within. I stepped into the hallway. Her presence seemed to swell and fill the narrow space.

'What role are you playing tonight,' I enquired. 'Devoted nurse, Cathleen Ni Houlihan, poet's muse or a martyr's widow?'

'A woman has many parts to play, many masks to hide behind,' she replied with a smile.

When she stepped to the side, the first thing I noticed was the communal air that pervaded the building. Young women sat gossiping on the stairs and corridor. In the large room beyond, more girls were seated at a long table, engaged in some sort of embroidery work. I detected a look of wariness on a few of their faces. Not for the first time since my arrival in Ireland, I felt like an outsider.

Gonne clapped her hands as if calling a meeting to order. 'Girls, we have a visitor,' she announced.

The Daughters of Erin stopped their conversations, put down their needles, and turned to watch me with mute, questioning looks. In terms of their cosmetics and accoutrement, they were dowdier than their middle-aged mistress, who was dressed and made up, it seemed, to strike a series of breathtakingly heroic poses. By contrast, they wore no make-up and their hair was brushed in simple styles or cut short like members of the Suffragette movement. Their faces were natural-looking, full of youth and untainted, shining with innocence. With their pastel-coloured loose-fitting smocks, they almost looked like prisoners or members of a grim workhouse. The place certainly smelt of one; a mixed aroma of polish and disinfectant filled the air. On the wall above, a large portrait of Padraig Pearse, the executed rebel leader, glared down upon the proceedings.

'Daughters of Erin,' said Gonne at the top of her voice. 'Why do we believe in an Irish Republic?'

'Because we believe in God,' chanted the room, 'and the message of the glorious martyrs he has sent us.'

'What must we serve at all costs?'

'The will of the Irish people, who are struggling for freedom.'

'Daughters of Erin, I say that freedom is never won without the sacrifice of blood. Our chance is coming. Your motherland calls you; she has been the land of suffering long enough.'

Then they launched into a round of prayers.

'Good,' said Gonne when they had finished. 'Now, return to your tasks.'

'What happened to your invalid soldier?' I asked as she led me on a tour past the table of seamstresses.

My question disconcerted her. 'That was my son, Sean,' she replied. 'In disguise. The War Office had barred us from returning to Ireland. Sean's in Dublin now, training with the Fianna, the Republican brigade for young men.' The note of maternal concern in her voice sounded genuine.

'Is that why you're back? To start a war?'

'I came back because of politics. Irish politics. Which pulls you in, bit by bit. Until you forget everything else.' She spaced out the words for dramatic emphasis, back in performance mode. 'Look around you, Mr Adams. The Fenian leaders had no idea how popular our movement would be among the women of Ireland.'

Like a drilled regiment, the girls bowed their heads before us and picked up their cloths. Their fingers were on the move again. Needles dipped and glinted in the gaslight. Thimbled thumbs moved across the grain of the emerging embroidery. I watched transfixed as a wrinkle of thread seemed to veer off from the round nimble fingers of a young girl and grow into the shape of a rose.

'The men of the Easter Rising thought it impossible to convince the fairer sex that bloodshed was necessary,' she continued. 'When I started the society, I thought it would take at least a generation but the thing was a runaway success from the start. For the first time, we had the scent of power in our nostrils. It has made us fanatics.'

A sinister quiet fell over the room. Staring at the obedient rows of pallid-faced young women, it struck me that Maud's society seemed twenty years out of date, redolent of the Celtic twilight, rather than the new dawn of women's liberation and political revolution. I wasn't sure if the Daughters of Erin were political pioneers or reactionaries, living in the past or the future.

'We know our strength now,' declared Maud. 'Our soul has grown large, and it will continue growing. We've discovered our courage, and that will be enough.'

'Your rebels are producing very pretty embroidery.' I tried to keep the sarcasm out of my voice. In spite of the concentrated effort of the seamstresses, I had the impression that the gathering was more about performance than industry.

'This is only a very small part of our operation,' explained Maud. 'I have forty girls here. Most of them are farmers' daughters, or servants at the big houses. We get the odd retired schoolteacher volunteering to take classes. The girls start in the crafts room, making gifts and artefacts to raise funds at our shop in Dublin. Then they move on to intelligence work, devising coded letters and signals.'

She escorted me into another room, where a magic lantern show was projecting images of evictions and tenant persecutions. An audience of young women watched bailiffs set light to thatch roofs while shabbily dressed survivors with grimy faces huddled like families of scarecrows in lanes and hedgerows.

'The photographs were taken in Donegal at the end of 1894,' Maud informed me. 'I witnessed the persecutions personally while on a riding tour with my cousin and my faithful great Dane, Dagda. The weather was cruel and the going hard for two young women and their pet dog. Poor Dagda's paws were cut to pieces by the sharp stones.'

The projector made a crackling sound as the images flitted across a gauze screen. From a gramophone, a voice, thin and faraway sounding, recounted the miserable statistics of Ireland's brutal landlord system. I could detect a wave of rage building within the audience. Their dresses rustled as they shifted with agitation, like the sound of a dry wind rising to fan a fire. I had seen charlatans use magic lanterns containing photographs of dead people to imitate ghosts and induce terror in unsuspecting relatives, but I had yet to see one used so dramatically for political purposes. The lantern was initiating a new battalion of recruits, one that might not be content organising rummage sales and knitting uniforms for their male counterparts.

Maud led me out of the room and into a drawing room where a frugal tea was being served. She turned her head towards me and a smile floated across her face. Her eyes shimmered. Our tour of the building was not as tricky as the terrain we were about to negotiate in words. Maud was using her charm like a serene beam of light to steer me across both. She was a political activist and a self-styled rebel leader, but it was clear she had learned all her posing on the theatre stage.

'Do you approve of what we are trying to create, Mr Adams?' she asked. 'The revolutionary changes in Irish society?'

'Only if they work,' I replied. 'But that's the problem with revolutions. They often fail, don't they?'

'Only because they are sabotaged by the opponents of change.' She examined my face with a frown. 'I fear you feel no sympathy for our struggle.'

I was now certain that this was more than a propaganda visit, and that Gonne wanted something from me, something that she herself realised might be difficult to extract.

'As far as Irish politics is concerned I'm impartially curious,' I told her. I wondered in what possible way she believed I might serve the interests of a women's militia.

'If you're planning to stay in Ireland, you must choose a side. Or do you have the modern compulsion that demands you should please everyone?' She was so close I could feel the heat of her face.

'If I take sides, I'm less likely to discover the truth.'

'What do you mean?'

'Political activists are easy to cheat and fool. They've already bought into a cause, a fixed set of heroes and villains. Their objectivity is blown. For instance, they cannot afford to believe that one of their own might be a murderer. A neutral doesn't care one way or another.'

'How can we trust you then if you won't take sides?'

'You wouldn't have brought me here if you thought I was untrustworthy.'

She bit her lip. Before she could come up with a response, I pressed on. 'I need the Daughters of Erin to furnish me with some important answers.'

'What sort of answers?' For a brief moment, a cloudiness appeared in her eyes, like the first roughening of the horizon at the approach of a storm.

'Was Rosemary on a rebel mission the night she was killed?'

She gave me a cold glance. 'You are forgetting the terms of your instructions.'

'What do you mean?'

'Willie didn't send you to Sligo to pry like a common detective. It's your role to make contact with Rosemary's ghost. To follow the clues she has left you and identify her murderer.'

'If you're concealing information as to what she was doing that night surely that's obstructing the wheels of justice?'

'I wouldn't go that far, Mr Adams.' She smiled thinly. 'It's not up to me to pass sensitive information to you or the police, who are, after all, the agents of the Crown. The RIC is a military force armed with rifle, bayonet, and revolver, and trained to act as an army. They are taught skirmishes, volley firing and defence against cavalry, exactly like an infantry battalion. It's a matter for the Daughters of Erin to decide what information is released on its operations to the enemy.'

I held my tongue. It struck me how easily a murderer might find shelter within her organisation.

'Rosemary was as much a martyr as the leaders of the Rising,' said Maud. 'That is all you need to know about that matter. She was an important member of our movement. She ran great risks to advance the cause. We believe she was betrayed.'

'Are you suggesting she was informed on and murdered by the Crown forces?'

'We can't be sure.' Her tone grew less overbearing. 'But, in the circumstances, there is no other satisfactory explanation.'

'Who could it have been?'

'We're hoping you will help us find out.'

'The Daughters of Erin is a secret society with rules. Who makes them?'

'Some are mine. Some were devised by Countess Markievicz. But not all of them. The rules are dependent upon our members. We're organised along democratic lines.'

The countess had been born Constance Georgine Gore-Booth. A close friend of Gonne, she had been arrested as a sniper during the Easter Rising, and saved from execution by her aristocratic connections.

'What about initiation rites?' I asked.

'We took some advice from the Golden Dawn. From Willie, in particular. He was interested in what we were doing and made some suggestions.'

'What sort of suggestions?'

'Oh, impractical stuff. Passwords and swords and ancient symbols of goddesses.' She eyed me warily. 'All nonsense, of course. The sort of thing that has become the hobby of a certain type of educated Englishman. A means to hide their nondescript dullness. I used to attend the meetings of the Golden Dawn. I found it comical watching all those drab middle-class men dress up in cloaks with daggers. Then I discovered that their passwords were the same as the Freemasons, and I washed my hands of them completely.'

'There's a theory going round that Rosemary was killed during a botched initiation ritual.'

'Complete claptrap.'

'You can't shed any light on the possibility?'

'Why on earth would the Daughters of Erin put one of its members in a coffin?' She gave a half-hearted laugh. 'What would be the point?' She turned to a tea stove and began preparing a tray. 'Added to that, if such a ritual took place, nothing would have persuaded a girl like Rosemary to allow herself, consciously, to be mixed up with it.'

'You said consciously. Perhaps that's the point.'

A small cyclonic disturbance in the stove distracted Maud's attention. The hot water began to steam. She busied herself with pouring it into a teapot. I took advantage of the interlude and explored the darker confines of the adjoining rooms.

My attention was snagged by a long diamond-shaped box sitting on a table in the shadows. Sweat trickled down my spine. I felt disbelief give way to shock as I approached the table. It was a closed coffin of pale pinewood. I ran my fingers along the side and felt something drip, sticky, like congealing blood. The lid hung slightly ajar. I barely pressed it and it fell away, hitting the floor with a crash that made Gonne spin round. I stared into the coffin's dark cavity. The rough shape of a uniformed soldier lay crammed within its narrow confines. Before I had time to examine further, Gonne was at my side.

'Don't be alarmed, Mr Adams,' she said. 'The corpse is not real, but the paint is quite fresh.' She flashed a smooth smile and lifted a lamp to show where the words 'British Empire' had been daubed on the sides. My fingers had smudged some of the lettering.

'What sort of prank is this?' I asked.

Her eyes narrowed and her mouth grew taut. 'This is not a prank. We are arranging a mock funeral for the British Empire. This is another element of our resistance. A little piece of theatre to drum up support for our cause.'

In the lamplight, I saw that the body was an old uniform stuffed with straw. The coffin itself looked as though it had endured a long journey. A dank smell of salt rose from the weathered wood.

'It's a pauper's coffin,' said Gonne. She rubbed the side with the flat of her hand. 'You can tell from the pinewood.'

'Where did it come from?'

'The sea.'

I raised my eyebrows.

'It was washed ashore a few nights ago.'

'Aren't you curious as to how it got there?'

There was a slight wrinkling on her elegant brow. 'The sea washes up all sorts of debris.' She shrugged.

'Two coffins washed ashore seems more than a macabre coincidence. I think it would be a good idea to find out where exactly it came from.'

'And how do you propose we do that? Advertise in the *Sligo Chronicle* for its rightful owner to step forward. In the first place no right-thinking corpse would want to claim a pauper's coffin.'

The lips of her firm mouth were pursed in scorn. Her voice had grown tense. I sensed her dilemma. Part of her wanted to be a good hostess, but my constant questioning was irritating the rest of her. She went back to the stove and busied herself with preparing tea for her female coven.

'Thank you for your visit, Mr Adams,' she said. 'At least now I know what sort of mission you are on. Before you go, promise to do me one thing.'

'And what is that?'

'I want you to send Willie a telegram. Tell him he should be here in Ireland, rather than hiding in London.'

'Why?'

'Because he's a free Irishman. Free in spirit and imagination, while the rest of his compatriots labour in chains. This country needs its poets and academics. It needs its core of wise men and women to form the political movement that will save us from ruin and civil war.'

'I'm beginning to agree with you. By the way, I promise that all I have seen and heard here tonight will be locked away in my confidence.'

She shook my hand and gave it a little push. 'Very good, Mr Adams. Your horse and rider await you.'

12

O

TWO OF SWORDS

THE crash of a hidden wave sent me stumbling backwards, soaking my feet and bringing me to my senses. Cold drops of water fell on my face and down my neck as Clarissa removed the hood. We had returned to the moonlit strand at Lissadell. The roar of perpetually charging waves surrounded us, and my exposed eyes wept in the salty, biting wind.

'This is the most beautiful piece of no-man's-land in all of Ireland,' shouted Clarissa, retreating from the water's edge. 'Only ghosts and seagulls haunt it.'

'I don't doubt it, but I should leave. Denver might be looking for me.'

Since dismounting from the horse, I had felt curiously light, as though my spirit was still riding while my body remained motionless. I tottered slightly, overcome with the sensation that the sand was moving, hurtling me towards a dangerous brink. I grew worried that one of my fainting fits was about to strike.

'How did you become a ghost-catcher?' asked Clarissa suddenly.

I had been asking myself the same question since arriving in Sligo. 'I wanted to be a doctor, but grew tired of examining dying bodies,' I explained. 'I became secretary to the Golden Dawn and increasingly the spiritual world drew me in. I had some strange occult experiences and now I find myself hunting the ghost of a dead girl on a strange shore.'

'I was Rosemary's comrade. And her friend. What questions do you need to ask?'

Intuition warned me I should be on my way, but her invitation seemed too promising to ignore. We pulled back further from the breaking surf and found a quiet spot in the shelter of a sand dune. Clarissa's face was half-hidden by the high collars of her coat.

'Which of the men at the barracks was Rosemary seeing?'

'How do you know she was seeing anyone?'

'I'm told she danced with every man in the parish. There were twelve soldiers stationed up there. She must have danced with at least one of them.'

She raised her pointed chin in anger.

'Rosemary was too busy for men, but that didn't stop them from chasing her.'

'I heard she was more than happy to respond to their advances.'

'Why don't you try searching for her murderer instead of poking around in her private life?'

'The last time you were together what did you talk about?'

'I can't answer that question.'

'Because you're not allowed to?'

She stepped away, afraid of confiding a secret. I felt a twinge of sympathy. I too was a member of a clandestine society, and understood how difficult it was not being allowed to reveal secrets.

'Why did Rosemary wade out into the bays along this coast? Was she trying to drown herself?'

She snorted. 'She was collecting shells for our art classes.'

'Even at night?'

'She took a lamp. We often went in pairs.'

'In case one got into trouble?'

'Of course. Especially at night.'

'What about the night she died?'

'We were supposed to meet up at Raghly Harbour. When I got to the pier there was no sign of Rosemary, but I saw a group of fishermen loading barrels onto a horse and cart. A man was watching over them, writing in a big ledger. He was wearing some sort of uniform, like a soldier or sailor.'

'Smugglers?'

'Who knows? This part of the coast is famous for them.'

'What was the weather like that night?'

'Moonless. With patches of thick fog. Perfect conditions for smuggling. Is that a part of your investigation now?'

'I'm just curious.'

'Why? I thought you were only interested in the invisible world.'

'I'm dedicated to finding Rosemary's murderer, and I doubt that he's invisible.'

'This place is smothered with murderers,' she replied. 'They hide in their grand mansions and behind the uniforms of the Royal Irish Constabulary.' I glimpsed a flash of contempt in her eyes but her voice maintained its amiable tone. 'By the way, you can have these back now.' She handed me Rosemary's letter and a small loosely tied brown parcel. 'I removed them from your coat before you mounted the horse.' She watched as I stuffed them into an inner pocket. 'I thought the parcel contained some sort of poison or explosive chemical. However, Maud says it is edible hashish. A drug used by poets to summon visions. She told me Mr Yeats takes it so he can watch the leopards play on the moon.'

'I use it for purely medical reasons,' I said quickly. 'To fight off fainting fits.'

'Well it looks and smells disgusting.' She stepped towards me. 'Tell me, Mr Adams, what sort of creatures do you look for on the moon?' She stared at me with an insolent smile, watching closely how I took this carefully administered dose of indignity.

I tried to answer the question, but the proximity of her slender body left me groping for an answer. The moon's luminous face seemed to grow closer, sharpening her inquisitive features.

'Why aren't you looking at me? You've avoided looking at me all night.'

I hesitated at telling her the truth, that I had been imagining what the contours of her body looked like during the entire blind horse ride through forests and along surf-pounded beaches, absorbing every physical movement of her lithe body with the concentrated avarice of a man finding himself unexpectedly in the middle of a room full of treasure.

'I want you to stop looking for invisible things like ghosts and creatures on the moon. I want you to imagine me. Look at my face. Remember my features.'

The wind carried the churn of the distant surf in snatches. I wondered had I heard her correctly.

'You don't see me.' She looked at me sadly, as one looks at the mad or afflicted. 'Tell me the colour of my eyes.'

'I'm not sure,' I mumbled.

The top buttons of her mannish-looking coat had come undone. I could see the tender boundary of skin between where her hair ended and her dress began. A few drops of sea spray glistened on her slender collarbone. Behind her, the tabular shape of Ben Bulben was the deepest possible shade of violet. Its darkness seemed immune to the silver tint of the moon and the misty light of the sea. A mysterious darkness to be penetrated. I thought of how far I was from London, and how different and constrained city life was to this strange territory of ghosts and gunmen and alluring women dressed in disguises. A whole minute passed before either of us said anything. From the horse came a low jingle, and a glint of metal. Along the shore, wraith-like shapes dissolved in the sea-spray.

'My eyes are green as the sea,' she said. 'Now, I want you to look for a birth-mark on my shoulder.'

The moon glided through a corona of cloud. Its light rippled across the waves and surged across her face in a silver stream. She struck a pose and smiled coquettishly. I stepped backwards.

Her voice hardened. 'These are instructions from Maud Gonne,' she said, pressing herself closer to me. 'Your continued freedom in this country will depend upon on them.' Her dark hair fell around her cheeks, which were slightly flushed with anger.

'I don't understand why my life might be dependent upon a birthmark.'

'You're so dense.' The coldness of her response was like a blow to my face. 'If the police find out you were with the Daughters of Erin tonight, your presence in this country will no longer be tolerated. They'll throw you onto the next boat, or worse, lock you up in their darkest cell. If they interrogate you, tell them you spent the evening with me on this beach. I have a strawberry shaped birthmark on my left shoulder. You tried to take off my blouse but I scratched your face and ran off.'

I glanced into her eyes, but felt overwhelmed, as though I had stepped up to a treacherous brink. Like the face of every other woman I had stared at, her features became a mirror for looking inwardly at myself. I saw ghosts of my own vanity and anxiety, arrogance and lust, all springing from the bewitching light of her sea-green eyes.

'What are you searching for?' she asked.

At that moment, the moon disappeared behind a cloud and her face was hooded in darkness.

'Don't you know it's a waste of time trying to prove the existence of something that cannot be seen or touched?' Her voice floated in the night. 'Trust only what your fingers tell you is real.' Her body, tense and supple, brushed against mine.

I lifted my hands and felt the sharp point of her chin. My fingers kept moving, committing to memory the curve of her lips, the snub of her nose, the soft lines of her eyelids. I saw her face, but this time in the world of the imagination. My fingers burned with desire. I knew that as soon as the moon reappeared the picture in my mind would disappear and my fingers lose their sensitive feeling. My hand dropped to her neck and slender shoulders. Immediately, her body tightened and a sharp set of fingernails raked the skin of my cheek.

The moon returned. The patch of sand in front of me lay empty. She had jumped onto her horse.

'I came to Sligo to help,' I told her. 'I'm not your enemy.'

'The person who summoned you is beyond helping,' she replied.

'That is true. Will you contact me again?'

'It depends. Perhaps the Daughters of Erin will need help from you in the future.' She swung her horse around. 'Don't take my rebuke personally. I liked it when you touched my face.'

'I haven't forgiven you for pick-pocketing me,' I shouted, but already her horse was galloping off across the beach and into the breaking surf.

I walked back to my accommodation, deep in thought. I found myself in a situation for which few could adequately prepare themselves. Little of what I had learned in my studies, secular or occult, or from my own upbringing and family, was of any use. I certainly did not feel like a ghost-catcher, or a sorcerer, or a spy, or proficient in any role requiring subterfuge and guile. I was just the same person as ever. A confused young Englishman, valiantly searching for evidence that there might be an afterlife, who now found himself straggling after the ghost of a dead woman and meddling in the dark tinderbox of Irish politics.

In the doorway of the gatehouse, a man stood smoking a cigarette. With surprise, I found myself staring into Denver's interrogating eyes. He frowned without speaking, devoid of the casual ease which he usually emanated. His eyes sparked with a dangerous light as though he was about to lash out in anger.

'I thought you'd be in your bed after such a tiring day,' he said. His jaw moved slightly and his neck muscles strained. His nose wrinkled. 'Is that you?' He was talking about the smell. My clothes reeked of horse sweat.

'I was in the stables. Checking on the horses.'

He pushed his belligerent unblinking face into mine.

'Where's Clarissa?'

I told him I had no idea where she was.

'Are you sure?'

'I've already told you. I've just returned from the stables.'

'That's right. You reek of horses.'

'Why do you ask? Is she missing?'

'I don't know. All I know is that I no longer care what happens to her.' Now it was his turn to lie. He seemed to struggle with something inside himself. To regain control he pulled a newspaper from inside his coat and thrust it into my hands like a baton.

'Have you read the news?' he said with a smirk. He was slowly regaining his superior manner.

'Is this what you've been waiting in the dark to show me?'

A small smile tugged at his lips. 'Some newspapers will stop at nothing to widen their circulation. Read it and see.'

It was the previous day's edition of *The London Times*. The front page was dominated by stories about the aftermath of the Bolshevik uprising in Russia and the progress of British troops in France. On the third page, my eye caught the headline: 'Mr Yeats' Ghost-catcher Arrives in Sligo under a Magical Obligation'. The article boasted an exclusive interview with myself, which I deduced had been cobbled together from scraps of conversation overheard on the mail boat to Sligo. It also carried a misleading explanation of occultism and a scandalous history of the Golden Dawn. I felt a rising heat colour my cheeks as I read on.

'Expressing contempt for Christian justice and the efforts of His Majesty's police force in Ireland, Mr Adams has declared he intends to secure a full confession from the still-at-large murderer by employing his paranormal powers. However, in spite of his magical gifts, he spent most of the sea journey to Sligo languishing with sickness, and appeared so queerly dazed as to have little cognizance of his surroundings or company.'

'You should avoid any further publicity in this matter,' warned Denver.

'And how do you suggest I manage that?'

He gave me a cold stare. 'By dropping your investigation. Completely. You're attracting trouble the way a magnet attracts iron filings.'

'You pay me such compliments.'

'Only because you have such special talents.' He stepped backwards revealing a broken door. 'While you were away, your bedroom was burgled.'

'Did you see who it was?'

He grew hesitant. 'Yes.' A pained look fell over his features. 'I followed Clarissa after you left the dance. I thought there might be something going on between the two of you. I saw the way she looked at you in the conservatory. She came here and forced her way through the front door.'

'This is the last place I would expect to find her,' I said truthfully.

'She was in your bedroom going through your suitcase. When I confronted her, she told me the truth. That she belonged to the Daughters of Erin. They've instructed her to keep an eye on you.' He glared at me as if I had been responsible for bringing out the worst in his fiancée. 'For months, I had been discounting the rumours about her. However wilful and selfish my fiancée was, I could not believe she would betray her country, her own people.' His voice lowered to a confidential level. 'Which is why I have broken off our engagement.'

'Perhaps you never took the trouble to find out who she really was.'

His face grew pale. He tried to speak but failed.

'What are you going to do?'

'Report her to the police. Don't worry, she won't be back to disturb you. At least not tonight.'

The door of the gatehouse lay slightly ajar. I stepped inside and locked the door behind me. I felt uneasy. I stood in the hallway and looked into the rooms, listening as if the burglary might still be in progress. The distant sound of crows settling down to roost formed an unruly backdrop to the silence of the house. I went into the bedroom and saw that my suitcase had been emptied. Clothes and books lay strewn across the floor.

By the time I settled to bed my mouth was dry and my chest hurt. To quell my excitement, I unwrapped the bitter cake of

hashish and ingested a sizeable amount with a greediness that
was completely alien to pleasure. I slid under the covers and
heard the restless sound of the sea return. I fell asleep like a
shell creature dropping off a rock into a churning ocean, falling
through an underwater darkness that flared with a thousand
fluttering shapes. The face of Issac gazed up at me with vacant,
billiard-ball eyes, and mouthed something, but his words were
lost in my ceaseless tumbling.

13

THREE OF CUPS

CAPTAIN Oates experienced his flight from terror as a dreamless passage through derelict mansions, rocky cliffs and gurgling tides, with the dead girl's haunting breath always on his neck. He spent wild mornings stumbling over rock pools and under steep cliffs, or in the hinterland of overgrown estates, searching for a new hiding place. He still had his wits about him, whatever people thought, but his mental apparatus had served him poorly. He realised that now. Straightforward military intelligence was useless against the adversary he faced. God might have been of assistance, but he had turned his back on Him, after witnessing the sight of soldiers' bodies stacked like countless sandbags in the trenches of Verdun and the Somme.

Nevertheless, he had almost cried out in prayer when he first saw the ghostly figure of Rosemary O'Grady, gasping and struggling as if she were drowning in air. From the start, he had tried to rationalise what was happening. The spirits are people like ourselves, a housemaid with the second sight had once told him. Earthbound souls who believe they are still alive, but are condemned to repeat over and over again the painful moments of their death. They should be treated like guests and offered hospitality and sympathy.

He had grown used to the ghost's presence, and that of her companion spirits, the swaying forms of their bodies, their

anguished cries, and the wailing drift of their voices as they cried
out his name, driving him out each morning to the sea-whipped
extremities of the Sligo coastline. There his mind took refuge in
the sound of the drowning surf.

It frightened him greatly that he was able to feel their deathly
cold hands. He had run up against them in his panic the previous
night; light, delicate hands, but substantial all the same, and ice-
cold, pushing him to the side as he tore through the darkness.
That night had been the worst in a succession of cruel hauntings
that seemed designed to test his fragile sanity. It had finally
dispelled the lingering possibility that the whole thing might be
taking place inside his head.

He had sat huddled over a fire in a single room cabin at the back
end of an overgrown estate, when, shortly after midnight, the
wind picked up and rattled through the cabin with the sound
of rotten bones knocking together. And then something fragrant
and sweet hung in the air, along with the laughing sound of
young women's voices. But what women would be abroad at such
a time in the night, or in such a place? He sidled to the left of
the fire, where an angled mirror gave him a view of the door,
allowing him to see who was entering without them noticing
him. Immediately, he pulled his head back. The ghostly faces of
several young women had appeared upon the mirror's surface,
their eyes darting in all directions, as though they too were using
it as a window to peer into the room.

He lay down and pretended to be asleep, watching with
apprehension through his half-closed eyes.

Slowly, a group of cloaked figures filled the room like vapours,
hovering over his prone body. The sound of their whispering
made his blood chill.

'If he's guilty, he must be punished.'

'Rosemary must be avenged.'

'Dear Captain, do not resist.'

'Is he trying to hide from us in his sleep?'

'He dare not run again.'

'He is wicked to the core. I can see it in his face. Wicked and guilty.'

'Then let's trap him in this nightmare. Paralyse him in his sleep.'

'Make him one of us.'

'Let's take him now. Sweet man, it is time to come with us.'

He was so overwhelmed with fear that he dared not draw a breath. Their voices were low and seductive, but cruelty rang through their sweetness with the harsh clang of metal. He thought helplessly of escape but at the same time the tenderness of their voices made him burn to stay.

Their whispering stopped, and then he heard a commotion in the air, a frantic beating of sticks and something softer like feathered wings, closing in around his head. Then the prodding began, so sharp it felt like a series of bites. On his head, and then his limbs and chest. He heard the sound of laughter, female and exultant. Half-mad with fear, he squirmed on the floor. When the prodding became too intense to bear, he jumped to his feet and brushed by their soft forms, feeling their cold hands propel him out into the darkness. He fled into the night, running for his life and his reason.

'Give me the sea as a hiding-place,' he kept saying to himself as the darkness enclosed him. How else was he going to survive these haunted nights?

14

KING OF CUPS

WITH no other mode of transport than a rusted bicycle, I gave myself more than an hour to get to the railway station on time, but convoys of army vehicles had blocked the roads, and I was rerouted a mile around the town of Sligo. I rode through narrow streets packed with people and traffic. The atmosphere was weighted with dread and expectation. Rain glittered on the Union flags which flew tirelessly, decking every flagpole in sight, practically blindfolding the shops and gaunt-faced townhouses. It was market day, and pushing against me was a mixed bag of farmers with thick beards and smoking pipes, cattle dealers with shrewd dark faces, and a regiment of sales girls swaying to work in long black skirts. Even the statue of Queen Victoria, sitting on her plinth in Market Place, seemed a challenge to my presence. In the main square, a band of RIC men posted notices warning the Daughters of Erin that if they launched any further operations, serious military reprisals would be made. The notices ended with the slogan *God Save the King*.

I swerved on and off the shoulder of the cobbled streets dodging old women selling creels of wizened potatoes and churns of golden butter. The throng of horses and carts came to a halt for cattle and sheep, but trundled over flocks of banty hens. A milk-wagon horse expired outside the station, causing more delay, and then a bicycle transporting a tower of freshly baked bread collapsed in front of me.

Anxious at being late, I bounded into the station, aware of the attention I was receiving from a group of men in belted raincoats and soft hats huddled at the station doors. I assumed they were undercover police checking for wanted men and women travelling in and out of the town.

Fortunately, the train from Galway had just arrived. Among the disembarking passengers, I spied a man with a greatcoat which spread like wings as he stepped from his carriage. A soft black sombrero shaded his angular features and a voluminous silk tie flowed from his collar. His trousers dragged over his long feet as he strutted up and down the platform. In his wake stepped a woman with a clear, intelligent face.

Even before greeting him and smelling his familiar odour of carbolic soap, medicine and old books, I was seized by a deep tug of loyalty and tenderness to my mentor, William Butler Yeats, which was quickly replaced by anger and self-pity that he had left me to my own devices in such dangerous territory. A few days previously, I had received a telegram that he and Georgie had travelled to Ireland and were spending a night or two with Lady Gregory at Castle Coole in Galway before making their onward journey to Sligo. Their arrival could not have come soon enough for me. I embraced him warmly on the busy platform.

'I was afraid I might die,' announced Yeats, 'if I left it another day or even an hour to return to this wild coast.' His nose ran in the wind but he appeared oblivious to it. A group of tired-looking soldiers shuffled by in grey uniforms, making his habit and gait appear even more eccentric.

Georgie stood at his side like a silent guard. 'Willie has had the cold but is much better today,' she advised me. 'He was worried you might have made contact with his ghost and secured its release.'

Some of the crowd stopped to stare at Yeats and his young wife, as though they were royalty visiting their raffish kingdom of rain. On the adjoining platform, another train snorted with steam, anxious to leave. The carriages rocked as passengers boarded. The press of bodies, enthusiasm and noise threatened to swallow us up.

'I trust you've had a comfortable stay at Lissadell,' shouted Yeats.

'To tell you the truth,' I confessed, 'this supernatural quest is like a fever. Everyone treats me as though I'm contagious. I've found Sligo to be one of the most hostile places I've ever visited.'

The wheeze of the locomotive engine and its cloud of hissing steam drowned my words. In any case, Yeats did not appear to be listening. The tide of embarkation had captivated his attention.

'What a wonderful sight,' he declared. 'No longer do I feel like a shadow. Or an exile. In London, everyone pretends to be living. But we're all frauds, hiding behind our stacks of books in the British Library.' He turned round and surveyed the throng with the look of a schoolboy who'd been detained too long from play by his teacher. 'I've lost contact with Irish crowds, with ordinary people. I've lost touch with the forces working for Ireland's freedom.'

Georgie and I dragged Yeats along the platform. Behind us, a porter struggled with their substantial baggage, a collection of portmanteaus , boxes and trunks.

'How did you spend your time in Galway?' I asked and immediately saw some of the light depart their eyes.

'By your disappointed expressions, I suspect your experiences were less than fascinating.'

Georgie spoke for him. 'We sat at countless séances in servants' quarters, listening to blind old women say in Irish that the dead do not yet know they are dead.'

Yeats' words were tinged with a note of petulant complaint. 'Unfortunately, gathering evidence that the soul lives on demands many lines of investigation. And many encounters with terrible frauds.'

'Some mediums try to fool the world,' I said. 'Others just fool themselves.'

'But I intend to put some distance between myself and this

country's charlatans.' He stared at me, eyes glinting. 'I have come straight to the source. What have you been up to, Charles?'

'Peering into coffins and the minds of deranged Irish men and women. Do all your compatriots suffer from a monomania?'

'Only the interesting ones.' His shining eyes lighted on me and then darted away. 'What about the scenery?'

'I used to think I was a dedicated Romantic, but I've seen enough windswept beaches, brooding cliffs and enchanted forests to last me a lifetime.'

'Any sign of our ghost?'

I hesitated for a moment. The departing train, packed now, shuddered and began to slide along the platform.

'A few clues and scattered traces,' I mumbled.

'Do you believe her soul has returned?'

'I'm an occult investigator. What I believe or not is irrelevant.'

Yeats nodded as if in agreement, but his attention was distracted by the sight of a new-looking cast-iron lamp post beside the station house. He became very heated on the subject of municipal lighting and the lack of ornament to the lamp posts that were springing up all over Ireland.

'A curse on the municipal planning office,' he declared. 'What is the point of all this lighting, if everything it shines upon is ugly?' He stared about him ruefully. 'There was once a fine avenue of lime trees planted here. A curse to anyone who cuts down a tree or raises a building planned in a government office.' Then he grabbed my wrist and looked at my watch. 'It's time we thought about dinner. There will be eggs and fresh butter at the hotel, but I wonder will we have meat. I shall insist that our ghost-catcher should dine on the finest roast beef.'

We progressed through the crowd in fits and starts. Everyone seemed to be in our way. I spied a familiar figure leaning into a doorway that provided little cover, a tall, sinister sketch of a man with a black cap and a belted raincoat that flapped in the stiff Atlantic breeze like a warning flag. I felt a sudden stab of anxiety at the thought that I had become Wolfe Marley's latest assignment. I fought the sudden impulse to flee to the nearest library and bury my head in some tome on ancient civilisations, anything to hide away from this world of intrigue and constant surveillance. I glanced back when we were a little further down the street, and caught his gaze in the reflection of a shop window. He watched me intensely, as though I were a thief mingling with innocents.

When we arrived at the hotel Yeats and Georgie went up to their room and did not come down for lunch. I ate at the table alone, and after a further hour of waiting went upstairs in search of them. I knocked on the door of their room but there was no answer. I pushed it open. The dishes of the lunch they had ordered lay on the table, most of the food untouched. A cloud of incense wafted from the adjoining bedroom. Through the half-opened door, I made out the shape of Yeats kneeling in front of his wife. On the floor lay many loose pages of writing. His hands fluttered over the leaves, searching for a word or phrase. Now and again, he stared up at Georgie with pursed lips, his parchment cheeks glowing with two red spots of excitement.

I stepped closer, not making a sound. There was something different about Georgie. An attentive wife, usually she and Yeats were in constant conversation. Even while engrossed in books, they would regularly stop to read each other favourite phrases and passages, like-minded companions on a quest towards spiritual and intellectual enlightenment.

Sitting supine in an armchair that afternoon, she seemed to belong to no one, not even herself. Her hair had been untied, and fell about her shoulders. The skin on her temples shone translucently, and her eyelids were closed, the long lashes fluttering as though she had surrendered herself to some sort of trance. A page full of writing fell from her hand. Yeats quickly placed a blank one in front of her and she began to fill it with a strange jerking scrawl. While one hand wrote, the other sat on her lap, opening and closing. She was whispering to herself in a voice soft and without any form of emphasis, in the tone of someone reciting a text by rote. At times her writing switched directions, looping backwards in lines that ran off the page.

Something was being written through her; I stared in fascination. It was the first time I had witnessed the remarkable practice of automatic writing, a phenomenon that investigators believed was either a feat of free association or a mysterious communion with the spirit world.

Yeats did not notice me as I entered the room, so engrossed was he in studying her handwriting. I lifted up a handful of stray pages and read a tangle of riddles, promises and entreaties interspersed with references to a collection of ancient mythologies. I found it impossible to decipher any meaning in this Byzantine puzzle of words, but I noticed how Yeats raked through the scattered pages, practically grovelling at the feet of his beloved, as though she held the crown of his poetic genius.

Midway through some sort of astrological prophecy, Georgie stopped speaking and writing. Silence filled the room. Yeats stared at her with the look of a man abandoned in a labyrinth without a map.

A light breeze wafted through the curtains of the window, unsettling the pages on the floor. The air smelt of the sea. A sheet fluttered against my foot. I picked it up and read what seemed to be a stream of gibberish. Then I noticed something else. At first, I thought I was mistaken. When I was convinced I was not, I folded the sheet and slipped it into my breast pocket without Yeats noticing. Its style closely resembled another sample of handwriting that was fresh in my memory.

'No use having a theory if it tires you,' intoned Georgie, her eyelids still closed. 'The fatigue is the safeguard against excess.' Then she began snoring softly.

'Are you alright?' I asked Yeats.

He rose to his feet, waving the incense smoke away from his face. 'Mr Adams, you must tell no one about what you see before you. Since you and I last met, Georgie has been blessed with a stream of supernatural messages, which come in the form of automatic writing. This afternoon, I have been priming the pump with the most difficult spiritual questions.'

He sat down suddenly.

'You don't look well.'

'Indigestion.'

'From what?' I glanced at their uneaten food.

'The supernatural world. Georgie has filled thirty-two pages this afternoon alone.' He picked himself up, unable to hide a smile of satisfaction on his weary face. 'I never imagined that my young wife would become a conduit for hidden truths from the unseen world.' He lowered his voice in a confidential tone. 'Not to mention a fount of metaphors for my poetry.'

I was stunned. Here was evidence beyond doubt that Yeats had successfully switched muses from the untouchable Maud Gonne to his sophisticated city-born wife. Yeats had made Gonne into a living legend with his poetry, the 'perfect beauty' with 'cloud-pale eyelids, dream-dimmed eyes'. He had dared to dream that she might marry him; on several occasions he had proposed to her, and she had made the excuse that there were secret reasons she could never marry, before trampling on his ardour by marrying Major John MacBride, a nationalist hero in Ireland. However, Maud's rejections had not prevented Yeats from arranging an astral marriage with her spirit, and in lectures to fellow Golden Dawn members, he claimed to have met astrally with Gonne during sleep, once appearing to her as a great serpent.

'Come into my study,' he said, leading me back into the main room. Any space in which Yeats emptied his trunk of books and manuscripts he called his study.

'Let me offer you a glass of wine from the Pope's own vineyard at Avignon.' He beckoned me to an armchair and filled two glasses from a bottle he had ordered from the hotel cellars. He passed me a glass and sat in the armchair opposite. Raindrops twitching upon the windowpane filtered a sombre light across his face. I recounted my adventures since we had last met, including the sea journey to Ireland and my midnight meeting with Maud Gonne.

Yeats' pale face bore the touch of an old ghost. He ignored his glass of wine, and observed me with his hands clasped across his chest as though in solemn prayer. From time to time, his eyes shifted to the ceiling as though he were composing a poem from my jumbled narrative, picking out words here and there to weave into a flowing verse. Each time I stopped, he chewed his lips in concentration and then beckoned with his long-fingered hand for me to resume.

'A few things in your account have caught my attention,' he said at the end. Producing his pack of tarot cards, he laid a few suits before me. 'I discern the hand of the Two of Swords, the blindfolded maiden. The blindfold represents your story's complication and confusion, while the rippling waters suggest the need for intuition and perception.'

I interrupted him. 'A young woman has been murdered. This is not an exercise in reading the tarot cards. We should be looking for a motive and a murderer, not a suit of symbols.' My voice was sharp and accusative, and he looked hurt.

I went on to tell him about my strange encounter with Captain Oates, who'd seemed to be sitting down to dinner with a hallucination. Yeats nodded as I described the captain's bizarre behaviour.

'The captain is eating and drinking in the spirit world. This is promising evidence.'

'What do you mean?'

'He is being driven to satisfy their hunger. Did the spirits leave any physical trace? Did you notice any manifestations of light, or strange smells?'

'I noticed nothing like that. I believe the strange ritual was just a function of his delirium.'

'Delirium? How can you say that?' Yeats' back straightened and his face grew paler. 'If Captain Oates communes in such an elaborate fashion with a ghost might that not be evidence of its existence?'

'It is not evidence if only Captain Oates hears and sees it.'

'Who are you to determine what is evidence and what is not?' His voice grew shrill. 'You assume that Oates is suffering from madness and therefore you discount his evidence. Just because you are unable to witness such phenomena does not mean they do not exist.'

'I accept that. But how can we verify Oates' vision in an objective and scientific manner? Words can argue anything, but they do not make an unreal thing real, or an untruth truth.'

'The universe extends far beyond the realm of human perception and scientific explanation. All we can do is grapple with symbols to dramatise the reality outside space and time.'

'What kind of symbols?'

He paused momentarily. 'Let us say that for the sake of an analogy, Captain Oates observes a rainbow and comments on its splendour to his companions. Where does that rainbow come from?'

I blinked with uncertainty. 'We know that rainbows are formed when sunlight hits water spray in the atmosphere.'

'Yes. But where does it come from? It doesn't just appear out of nothing.'

'From the rain and sunlight.'

'No.'

'Are we talking about a higher deity?'

'Not at all.'

'I'm at a loss, then.'

'What we can say is that Captain Oates' rainbow, like his ghost, is the coming together of certain conditions at a certain place and time. Water vapour, light, his eyes and his consciousness. The same is true for his ghost.'

'I'm not sure I understand.'

'You understand perfectly. Rainbows and ghosts do not really exist in the physical world, in the sense that they can be touched or contained in any way. They have no existence independent of the set of conditions that make them visible to the beholder. Do you understand that? If there are five people observing a rainbow, then there are five rainbows. And if they all turn their backs, all five rainbows will cease to exist. The same is true, I hold, of ghostly manifestations.' The heat left his cheeks. 'Now, are there any further points of mystery in your narrative that you would like me to penetrate?'

I handed him Rosemary's notebook, but kept the photograph of Gonne in my pocket, not wishing to distract him. I explained how I had found it hidden in her room. He took time to flatten out the crumpled, slightly damp pages.

'What do you make of it?' I said after a while.

'Obviously she is trying to hide some secret information.'

'What sort of information?'

'Unfortunately at this point we do not possess the cipher to translate the code.'

'How shall we obtain it?'

Yeats shrugged. 'I have come across many ciphers designed to protect the secrets of the ancients and their Apocrypha. What I have learnt is that codes are usually assimilated from the environment of the code-maker. Until I learn more of Rosemary's environment I am powerless.'

'The list of names sounds like code words for people or places.'

'I'm not a horticulturist but the first two are names of roses. Perhaps they were the secret names of her lovers.' His brow clouded as he stared at the page. 'Indefinite possibilities emerge.' He tapped his fingers on the open page and stared into his glass of wine for a long time.

Finally, he said, 'There may be little else to this list but Rosemary's guilty conscience and some inconsequential but hidden facet of her life. She was afraid she might bring trouble upon herself if someone discovered the contents of the journal.'

I furrowed my brow. It was frustrating to think that the secret life of the murdered girl lay on that piece of paper, and that it was beyond the power of our intelligence to penetrate it.

Yeats leaned back and took on a meditative air.

'Do you have any further trials for our powers of reasoning?'

'What about initiation ceremonies.'

'What about them?'

'Do you know of any carried out by the Daughters of Erin under the instructions of Maud Gonne?'

'No.' He sniffed his glass and sipped it slowly. He seemed reluctant to talk about the subject.

'Does that mean you don't know of any, or that the society never conducted any?'

'Maud Gonne forbids such practices. She has given up on magic completely. As a convert to Catholicism she considers them satanic practices.' His forehead creased. 'Why are you so interested in Maud?'

'Her behaviour has aroused my suspicions. First, I meet her on the boat journey to Sligo, in the disguise of a Red Cross nurse. Showing off her theatrical talents, she engages me and an agent of the War Office in a conversation about the dead girl, without arousing any of our suspicions. To round off the melodrama she pretends to be caring for a dying soldier, who is returning to Ireland on his dying breath, but who is, in reality, her teenaged son. While in Sligo, she organises contact with me in a covert fashion and reveals that she knows a lot more about Rosemary than she hitherto demonstrated. In short she is a woman capable of significant subterfuge and deception.'

'If Maud lied to you, it was only a necessary omission to ensure her survival.'

'But this is about more than a simple lie. She reminds me of a *femme fatale* from a gothic opera. One in which all the stage sets are designed by you.'

'Congratulations, Mr Adams.' An ironical smile played on his lips and a flush of colour rose to his cheeks. The mention of her name seemed to tighten his entire body, leaving him quick to anger. 'You have unmasked Maud Gonne's true essence. How very shrewd of you. Your uncanny insight will help you progress through the Orders of the Golden Dawn. A number six at least, or even a seven.'

'Can you tell me where she's staying?'

'Of course I can't.' He gave a short, bitter laugh. It was obvious the mention of her name had pressed on an old point of pain – the trauma of unrequited love. 'My task in Sligo is to avoid Maud. The police consider me the most likely lead to her hiding place.'

'Who else might know where she is?'

Yeats bared his teeth. 'Try the War Office. They spend all their time spying on her.' He made a noise, expressing his contempt for their machinations.

'What is the significance of the coffin? I'm convinced it's the vital clue that will lead us to the killer.'

Yeats looked thoughtful. 'In Celtic mythology death is regarded as a solo voyage to a new world. And a coffin is really a boat built for one, solid and snug, ready for the long and stormy voyage to the hereafter.'

'Are you suggesting her burial at sea was some sort of ancient Irish ritual?'

'As a symbol, that is what it suggests. But then this is a murder we're studying...' His voice trailed off. I wondered if he was trying to divert my attention away from Gonne and her exploits. I guessed what was going through his mind. The fear that he might be tainted by Maud's treachery to the British Crown.

I sipped the rest of my wine. Yeats picked up a volume of poetry and stuck his nose between its pages, as if he were sniffing an expensive vintage, as if all books possessed their own aroma. I found myself concentrating on his lapel. Pinned to it was a brooch in the shape of a cross with a rose in the centre. I tried to clear my head, but a dizziness overcame me. I gripped the armrests of the chair. I struggled to make sense of the evidence before me. A procession of thoughts and questions flitted through my mind as images of the distinctive design flashed before me. Clarissa Carty and the medium in Edgware Street both wore similar looking necklaces. What linked them to Yeats? I could not find any point of reference between them. All that I could discern was a series of personalities cloaked in deception. What was illusion and what was reality?

'How am I going to successfully conclude my mission in Sligo if no one tells me the truth?' I complained.

'What do you mean?'

'What are you and Gonne hiding from me?' I demanded. 'What is the significance of the rose and the cross? Tell me something that is not another chimera. Tell me something I can make sense of.'

Yeats was silent for a few moments. He looked at me and shook his head.

'I don't know if I can answer your question.'

'Then tell me what binds you to silence?'

Yeats regarded me sympathetically. He was the model of avuncular authority. 'My dear Charles, if anything, you have created these illusions and layers of deception for yourself.'

'What do you mean?'

'You've had a difficult time in Sligo and you're weary.' He leaned forward and smiled understandingly. 'But there is one thing you must understand. The rose and the cross do not belong to your line of enquiry. They are part of the inner knowledge of not only the Golden Dawn but a host of cults that believe in the rebirth of the soul. I might trust you with the knowledge, but the Order would never forgive me if I divulged its secrets. They are for you to discover as you progress through the different stages of the Golden Dawn.' He eyed me closely. 'I can disclose that the elders of the society are following your progress with great interest.'

'Are you telling me this assignment is some sort of spiritual test? To determine my progress in the Golden Dawn?'

Yeats ignored my questions. He eased back his chair and stood up.

'Come, Georgie is still asleep. It is not too late to tour the beaches at Lissadell and clear our minds of these cobwebs.'

He pulled on a snug-fitting woollen jacket in midnight blue, and hovered over a vase of flowers before deciding on a red carnation to decorate his buttonhole.

'Besides, I was hoping to meet one of these notorious Daughters of Erin. I hear they are that brazen they wear men's clothes while on manoeuvres.'

In spite of my annoyance, I smiled inwardly at the thought of Yeats encountering a straightforward horsewoman like Clarissa Carty on Lissadell beach, and the flamboyant note his outfit would strike next to her boyish form and the wild waves of the Atlantic.

15

THE HANGED MAN

A MOUNTAIN wind swept down from Ben Bulben and moaned in the valley between the thorn trees. The wind had a chill edge, and carried the intermittent whining of some animal from the forest, a fox or a badger, a forlorn call for its mate that was strangely like singing.

Captain Oates leaned on the branch he was using as a walking stick and peered through a pair of field glasses, his grizzled face filling with the astonishment of a savage. He wore a uniform so caked in mud it was impossible to tell what colour it was. His body, which had lost much of its soldierly bearing, trembled slightly as his chest heaved up and down. He peeped through the binoculars at a ridge of pine trees, which looked no friendlier now that the sullen light of day had broken upon them.

It was a strange feeling, using his field glasses to observe a spirit that belonged to the invisible world. He fought the impulse to run away, to flee back into the ruined estate, but the desire to find out what had happened to Rosemary O'Grady was stronger than the urge to save his own skin. He shifted slightly. His movement upset a blackbird, sending it clattering into the undergrowth, and his close-up view of the trees wobbled. When he refocused, the trees were unchanged, or rather the darkness between the trees was unchanged. He scrutinised the bottom of the ridge, which was cut by a sunken lane, and thought he saw a flare of black hair float momentarily above a whitethorn hedge. A young woman's lank black hair.

Somehow, the binoculars helped him hold his nerve whenever he felt his grip on reality weaken. He returned his gaze to the ridge of pine trees. After several moments, a figure emerged from the gloom, a hooded female figure that beckoned him towards her. He put down the field glasses and rubbed the back of his neck. He raised them again and saw that the figure was still there, waving her thin hand at him.

The ghost's appearance made no sense. No matter who had murdered Rosemary, he was sure the killer's motive had nothing to do with him. Why then had she chosen him to haunt? What could he do to help? Perhaps he should tell her that she was on the wrong track. Reluctantly, he made his way up to the pine trees that were starved of sunlight.

Held in thrall by her swaying figure, he pushed through scratching branches. He followed her over moss-covered forest floors, through ice-cold rivers and crippled plantations of Scotch pine, entire ranks of which had been snapped in two by the assault of the Atlantic winds. Sometimes her figure appeared in front of him, and then behind, or to his left and right, circling him as though she were trying to make him lose his bearings.

The distance between them shortened. Eventually, he caught up with her on a cliff overlooking the sea. She stopped just ahead but did not turn around. Slowly she began walking towards the precipice, and he did the same. The churning sea was more than forty feet below, and a fall from the edge would be fatal. He heard a voice behind him. 'I'd like to go back now,' it said. He spun round but there was no one there. 'I'd like very much to rest. I've been following you all afternoon.' He realised the voice was his own, and his breath sobbed. Day and night, reality and dream, had merged to form a continuous whole from which he was no longer able to discern the particular parts. He could not remember how many nights had passed since he had discovered Rosemary's body at Blind Sound. All he knew was that she had come back to life and would not let his mind rest. He was exhausted now, so weary he could not trust his own faculties. The thought of losing control frightened him.

'I have to go back,' he shouted.

'Don't leave my path,' warned the ghost.

He wanted to sit down and rest, make some nest in the thick cliff-top grass and not move for a long time, but the spirit kept urging him on.

'This is not yet the place.'

'What place?'

'The place where I discovered their crime. A crime so great I was not allowed to go on living.'

'Why burden me with this? What do you expect to gain? I was not involved in any part of that terrible business. That's all there is to it.'

The spirit turned back from the edge and led him along the coast towards Blind Sound. The sun's edge disappeared behind clouds and they came across a sunken graveyard marked with boulders and a few headstones. She pointed to a cave in the ground as though it were a doorway out of a labyrinth. He clambered into the mouth of the cave, and slid down its wet passageway. The darkness gave way to light and soon he found himself crawling out at the base of the cliff. She was there waiting for him, standing at the top of a large slab of rock, motionless, apart from the fluttering of the wind through the hem of her long dress. He scampered after her but when he reached the rock, she had disappeared. He yelled. She reappeared further along the coast, waiting silently for him.

He puffed and panted as they crossed an undulating terrain of sand dunes. The sea boiled and the wind picked up, whining through the marram grass. Rain whipped his face. The pale beach seemed to stretch for miles under the sombre light of a storm. His strength began to wane as the day darkened to twilight. Beyond each horizon of sand dunes loomed another, so that the beach they were traversing never seemed to end. He began to feel like they were two sleepwalkers drifting towards the edge of the earth.

'Are you travelling across the sand for eternity?' he asked.

'Yes.' It seemed that time meant nothing to her.

The shoreline grew wild and bleak. The sea retreated so far from them they could no longer hear the sound of the waves. He noticed how fine the sand was on this vast beach.

'You promised to show me something.'

'That is true.'

'Then why keep us walking forever?'

She did not answer. Her hand rose in the air, pointing towards a set of rocks where the sea was suddenly booming. He was unsure of what she meant him to see. The gale blew hard and scudding clouds obscured the light of the setting sun. Perhaps she meant him to witness an echo of her last living moments. He watched carefully as twilight fell and cast its violet hue over the storm-tossed scene. The waves arched their backs higher and higher. He was about to give up and turn back when he caught a glimpse of a small dark object floating far out, just before it disappeared from view. He waited and the object reappeared, drawing closer to the beach. It was the head of a swimmer rising and falling with the waves.

The appearance of the swimmer was matched by a series of furtive movements on the beach. Two thickset men appeared from a nearby cave, prompting Oates to take cover behind a large rock. They walked to the water's edge and waited. They seemed oblivious to the plight of the swimmer struggling for his life. For a while, he seemed to stall, bobbing with the waves, gulping brine, and then a tall wave picked him up and carried him closer to the beach.

The swimmer slid down the long white chute of the incoming wave and rolled with the breaking surf, his chest bound by several coils of thick rope which stretched back into the sea. His body had barely come to rest when the two men surrounded him. They worked on him like a pair of brisk undertakers, efficient and professional, wrapping his form in white cloth. Then they undid the rope, and tugged on it, heaving together with all their strength. The rope sliced through the waves like a powerful glistening tail. The men sucked in their breath and pulled harder. A barrel popped out from the waves, and then several more, all bound together by the rope. When they had hauled all the barrels ashore, the men dragged the swimmer's body back to the cave. They returned for the barrels, rolling them across the sand and heaving them over the rocks. Soon they were all gone. The tide rose, covering the sand, washing smooth their traces. Oates reappeared from his hiding place. He had observed what the ghost meant him to see, two men recovering the body of a half-drowned swimmer as though his soul was their bounty, and a flotilla of barrels unspooling through the strength-sapping waves. A thought began to evolve in his head. He realised he was in great danger standing on the sands of Blind Sound.

It was almost dark and a storm had picked up when Yeats and I reached Blind Sound. We met a pair of horses pulling a cart loaded with barrels, and a man with his hat pulled low on the riding seat driving the animals ferociously onward with a whip.

Yeats clambered over the rocks to the little sandy beach but the force of the wind almost blew him back into my arms. His figure looked slight and vulnerable against the breaking waves. I scrambled after him. The shore had the pummelled appearance of a battleground. Crabs and shellfish packed the rock pools like soldiers in trenches, while the debris of a landslide lay strewn across the beach.

'We should be careful,' Yeats shouted above the wind. 'It's not only wrack from the human world that is washed ashore on this wild beach. Blind Sound is haunted by supernatural flotsam. On nights like these, shipwrecks and the ghosts of drowned fishermen ride the waves.'

I surveyed the narrow strip of beach, the grim rocks, the recessed façade of the cliffs that resembled a natural amphitheatre. Yeats raised his arms as though he were a high priest and the beach an altar built for the adoration of restless spirits. He began an invocation. I retreated, not wishing to break his concentration.

I picked my way over an uneven rampart of upended bushes, tree-roots and the boulders of a collapsed stone wall. A short distance further along the coast I could see an isolated hillock, half of which had caved into the sea. The waves had wormed their way in a series of tunnels that looked like slits along the base of the hillock. I clambered along the shore, sliding over slippery rocks, and got as close as I could to the caves.

The wind whistled through them, making a mournful piping kind of music, and I thought instantly of Orpheus visiting the underworld. I felt a mysterious pull towards the caves, and would have investigated further but my attention was caught by a figure emerging from the rocks between Yeats and the cliffs, staggering like a cripple towards the sea. His head was matted with mud and his uniform was torn. His face gleamed with sea spray. It was Captain Oates, looking wilder and more unkempt than the last time I had seen him.

I watched his crab-like movements across the sand to where Yeats was engrossed in his invocation. To my horror, the captain removed a revolver from his jacket and pointed it in the direction of Yeats. My heart seized up with fear. Only an hour ago, we were sharing a bottle of wine; now my mentor seemed a few degrees away from death. I roared at the top of my voice but the wind hurled my words back. A wave struck a rock beside the two men, rising high above them with explosive force. Yeats stood erect against the churning sea, oblivious to everything, his arms raised above his head, like a man about to disappear into a whirlpool.

I grabbed some small rocks and began throwing them in the direction of Oates. Fortunately, their movement was enough to distract him. He looked round with a haunted face and crept back to the gloomy rocks from which he had emerged. Pushing away the thought that the captain might be capable of killing, I gave chase, but there was no sign of him amid the rocks. The only possible hiding place was a small cave in the cliff face, its dark mouth frothing with waves. I stared at the entrance and waited.

Where else could Oates have run to? On this lonely bay, there were no forests to hide in or abandoned mansions to raid for food. There was only the sea and the treacherous-looking cliffs. What else could he do? I hung back waiting for him to reappear from the cave, as the crest of a huge breaker filled its mouth with churning water.

'Captain Oates,' I yelled, but all I heard was my own echo.

When the sea ebbed, I waded through the water and clambered into the darkness of the cave. It opened out into a chill galley-like chamber, its floor carpeted with seaweed. A rough ladder had been fashioned from rope and driftwood, and dangled from an opening in the roof, far above the reach of the tide. I climbed up into a smaller chamber. It was a dwelling fit for a hermit. The stone floor was covered with empty seashells and the bones of small animals. I crawled through the wicks of spent candles positioned regularly along the floor. The sheen of the wet rocks gave the appearance of countless eyes following my movements. After a few yards, the daylight gave out completely.

'Come out,' I called. 'I only want to talk.'

I waited for a while, shivering with the cold, my ears boiling with the magnified roar of the sea. Eventually I gave up and returned to the beach where Yeats was still standing motionlessly before the darkening Atlantic. I called out his name. He turned away from the sea in exasperation, his hair drenched with sea-spray.

'The storm is drowning out all communication with the spirit world,' he shouted. 'We should come back another time. When the sea is calm, or by moonlight. When the powers of Neptune are greatly diminished.'

Yeats was still convinced we should be trying to contact the dead girl's spirit. However, I was beginning to realise that Oates was the key. He was the man we should be talking to, but he was more difficult to communicate with than a wraith on the waves. A black mood of frustration hung over us as we departed from Blind Sound.

Yeats' dissatisfaction deepened when we got back to his hotel. The hour had passed during which he and Georgie usually conducted their final automatic writing sessions of the day. She had left him a note and retired to bed. If Yeats wished to seek advice from his spiritual guides, he was going to have to make contact with them without his clairvoyant muse by his side.

16

PAGE OF SWORDS

IT seemed a whimsical landscape designer had once passed through the grounds of Lissadell, leaving behind a sprawling collection of outbuildings and glass houses interlinked by paths of broken seashells and overflowing gardens, odd corners of which he had filled with sundials, pillars, and follies now grappled by ivy and honeysuckle.

Yeats had summoned me the next evening, along with a group of servant girls and former acquaintances of Miss O'Grady, to one of the estate's oldest buildings, a disused Roman Catholic church. The building was so overrun by creepers that only its entrance door was visible, a blackened arch of seventeenth century masonry; its sinister effect heightened by the sudden appearance of bats swirling out of nooks in the old stone.

Sauntering in as if he owned the place, Yeats led us through a low vaulted passage littered with the refuse of old nests and last winter's leaves. His footsteps were unnaturally loud, their hollow sound reflecting the emptiness of the church's inner sanctum. A table and chairs had been arranged in the middle of the floor for the evening's performance, a private séance, with his wife performing the role of medium. The poet had chosen to wear a tight-fitting, corn-coloured suit with a green silk tie and dark trousers that looked more like breeches. Stiffly squeezed into his jacket, with his hair flapping in two grey-black wings, he resembled a butterfly struggling to escape its exotically coloured cocoon. The thought flashed through my mind that his attire might do more harm than good in attracting the spirit of a dead woman.

Just before proceedings were due to begin, a figure appeared in the shadows of the doorway. Yeats froze at the sight of Wolfe Marley advancing towards us, his footsteps as heavy as Yeats' but without the echo, just a dull, scraping sound like that of a badger padding across the forest floor.

Yeats quickly recovered his poise, fixed his silk tie and with a little bow, welcomed the British agent to the séance. For a moment, I thought I detected an almost imperceptible change in Marley, his self-styled cynicism giving way to a flicker of reverence. He ducked his head and sidled to the back of the room where he found a seat behind the row of servant girls. He winked at me and produced from his damp coat a little leather-bound bible, which he patted as if for reassurance.

A set of drapes had been hung over the arched windows. The only light came from an oil lamp positioned on the central table at which Yeats' wife was already seated in an elegant high-backed chair. With the exception of Marley and myself the observers were all women, invited by Yeats to verify the identity of Miss O'Grady's spirit, should she deign to make her presence felt. The spooky atmosphere of the disused church had already enchanted them. The air vibrated with their deep concentration, their rapt faces barely registering Marley's late arrival.

Yeats began to pace the room, a sheaf of papers in his hand, walking his haunted tightrope. The séance was already running late, and a spasm of irritation flared upon his drawn features. A lover of rituals and decorum, Yeats could rarely ignore his sense of how things should be done. The upheaval caused by Marley's unexpected arrival had unsettled him. He returned to his meditations in a distracted manner. He murmured loudly, fidgeting with his pince-nez. He lifted them from the bridge of his nose, passed them back and forth between his hands, waved them in the air, and then slipped them into his breast pocket before finally gathering them up and folding them in their case, which he absent-mindedly left at the edge of the table, along with half his papers.

After a great deal of huffing and puffing, he completed his invocations and preparations. Then he turned to address his audience in a low voice.

'My dear guests, I must warn you that in a few minutes you will be surrounded by an invisible host of dead people.' He stared closely at the row of servant girls, his eyes charged with a magnetism that seemed to draw all the shadows of the empty church towards his strained features. 'In this very room several of your relatives may already be waiting, along with the ghost of Rosemary O'Grady.'

He invited the audience to ask questions of the spirits, if they felt strongly motivated. 'Don't hold back,' he urged them. 'Remember that if a question forms on your lips, it is because somewhere in the hidden universe there lies an answer.' He reassured them by adding that if anyone felt overpowered by the influence of a malign spirit, he would immediately conduct a ritual which would sever their connections with the harmful spirit.

His audience may not have understood him, but they did not seem to mind. It was enough to be in the presence of someone, who, in their eyes, had successfully invoked the spirits of the invisible world. They followed his every word and movement, as children do, safe in the knowledge that someone wiser than they would protect them from the pitiless forces of the wandering dead.

Their attention shifted to Georgie, who had shed her air of sober respectability in a way that would have shocked the North London branch of the Women's Fellowship, of which her mother was still an ardent member. She stood up, revealing a long black gown with three strands of golden rope tied around her waist. She raised a dagger dipped in wine and intoned the oath, 'I solemnly promise to persevere with courage and determination in the labours of the Divine Science.' Then she lowered herself back into the seat. Georgie was thoroughly steeped in the rituals and lore of the Golden Dawn. An adventurous, educated woman, she had joined the order four years previously, with Yeats as her sponsor, and had diligently climbed the order's ladder of knowledge, mastering astrological science and lunar studies, as well as the order's difficult colour and geometrical symbolism.

Her knowledge of the moon's movements, and the entire planetary and zodiacal symbols was so profound that she and Yeats could converse fluently in this private language. Lately, she had risen to the highest levels, and attained knowledge of the order's most dangerous practices, meditations on the secret Hindu symbols, such as the black egg of the spirit, which was believed to convey powers of clairvoyance and spirit channelling.

Marley leaned towards me and whispered, 'I hope they're not planning on sacrificing anything. Or anyone.'

Yeats walked over to one of the draped windows and opened it slightly. A breeze went straight through the room. Georgie's dark hair stirred. Her eyes were open but aimed past Yeats and the assembled spectators. They had the clouded look of someone in a trance.

'Do I speak clearly enough?' said Yeats in the deep, Homeric tones which told those assembled that they were in the presence of a great poet and orator, even if it made some of them squirm.

'Yes,' replied Georgie.

'What messages do you have for us?'

After a pause, she drew a strangely formed beast on a sheet of paper. Yeats beckoned me to his side to help him examine the figure.

'Is it a stag?' he whispered.

'No, a unicorn.'

'A portent clearly.'

'But of what?'

'I don't know.'

'But this is your field of expertise.'

'Sometimes the medium's symbols are indecipherable.

Sometimes they are a concrete expression of a thought so abstract it cannot be divined by mortal minds.'

Georgie began to write in her strange, jerking script. Yeats retrieved the page before it fell onto the floor. It read: 'Lie down every afternoon for thirty minutes between two and three and meditate on the heir.'

Yeats sighed. He kept his voice low. 'It's Martha.'

'Who?'

'One of Georgie's more maternal spirit guides. She's all "baby-baby". The conception of a Yeats heir is top of her agenda.'

'How many spirits does Georgie have?'

'So many I have not yet recorded them all.' He sighed. 'Some are what I have termed "frustrators", spirits of evil intent who try to disrupt the flow of communication with false information and lies.'

I stared at his wife, imagining the countless spirits floating above her, colourless and shapeless shades in search of form, lost souls hovering between life and death. I wondered whether Rosemary's ghost was among them.

With a flourish of her pen, Georgie began writing words upside down. Four times she inscribed the equation 'sword=birth' followed by another 'fish=conception'. She announced she would bear a son in a year's time if Yeats performed the necessary rituals.

Yeats coloured at the outburst. 'Enough of this baby talk. Can't you speak of anything else?' he hissed.

Her voice coarsened. 'We instruct Saturn to melt into Venus.'

'What?' replied Yeats. 'Again, tonight? But I'm exhausted.'

'Not too exhausted to pose question after question.'

'I'm not an animal. I can't live up to these demands.'

The servant girls, who had been watching the exchange with fascination, turned to each other and giggled. So far, Georgie had maintained an enviable serenity. Yeats glared at his young wife as though she had brought this humiliation upon him deliberately. He dropped his gaze, feeling mocked. His hands, a middle-aged man's slightly gnarled, sun-spotted hands, sat clasped tightly between his knees.

'You haven't answered my question,' he persisted.

'You're trying to get away.'

'Away from what?'

'Your marital obligations.'

Yeats closed his eyes and groaned.

'There is a blackness within you that keeps bubbling up. Can't you stop being so gloomy and pay more attention to the needs of the medium?'

While Georgie spoke, she doodled. A rash of triangles drawn like daggers spattered across the page. Yeats grew pale. He stood up and moved to the other side of the table where the bottle of wine sat with some glasses. Turning to me, he whispered, 'I'm under attack by my chief tormentor. A malign spirit called Leo who introduces himself with the symbol of a dagger.'

'I'm not going to let you off so lightly,' said the voice.

He knocked back a glass of wine in a single gulp. 'Oh yes you will.'

'Drinking will only heighten the fatigue.'

His hand shaking slightly, he filled another glass.

'You must keep up your obligations.'

'I must? Why? Who says I must?'

I rose and was about to say something but he threw me a look that made me hold my silence. Georgie stopped speaking and seemed to sink into a deeper trance. Yeats relaxed slowly, like a man who had appeased an intimidating child. The air in the room changed slightly. The smell of roses wafted from the window. Yeats held Georgie's hand and she returned a timid pressure, gazing at him with mute eyes.

I leaned toward Marley and whispered, 'What do you think?'

'Mesmerising,' he replied. 'A haunted church, a beautiful medium in a trance, a deluded poet seeking the hidden secrets of the universe, and a room apparently full of mischievous ghosts. I'm captivated.' A light had been switched on in his eyes, as if a pinch of humanity and imagination still burned there.

Yeats addressed the spirit. 'You must understand we have not come here to discuss domestic matters. The last time you monopolised the séance. I command you, let the other spirits speak.'

Several minutes passed and Georgie did not utter a sound. Then her voice softened. 'I see a young lady. She has a message.'

'Yes?'

'I cannot hear. She is too far away. Now she is drawing closer.'

'What is she wearing?'

'A dress embroidered with flowers.'

The smell of rose blossoms was so strong I stiffened. I tried to push away the fantastical idea that somewhere in the room the spirit of a murdered young woman had just stepped out of the pitch black of eternity.

'She is very afraid.'

'Why is she afraid?'

'She says there is a hostile influence in the room. She is pointing to someone in the corner. A malign influence with bristling grey hair. If you won't drive him away she'll scream.'

'Is she referring to a demon or the actual presence of a man?' Yeats glanced at Marley.

'All men are demons in her eyes.'

Yeats paused. 'Then am I a demon, too?' He raised his chin in wounded defiance.

Georgie's voice thickened. 'Why not? Aren't you a man?'

'Then your chosen medium is the soulmate of a demon.'

'A demon and his soulmate.' The voice gave a low chuckle. 'What a stirring combination.'

'I want to hear more about the murdered girl.'

'She has a story to tell but doesn't want to speak to you. She says the room is not safe. She'd rather talk to you on the beach at night. Under the influence of Neptune.'

'I have taken all precautions possible to make the church safe.'

Georgie's voice changed tone again. 'You still wish for a son to consummate your marriage?'

'What has wishing for a son got to do with this séance?'

'Because it involves the medium. Some men torment their wives wishing for a son. They have no idea of the havoc they create. You should be content that her blood is healthy and the children will be well.' The voice continued, insinuating, probing sensitive ground. 'The medium doesn't think you are capable.'

'How am I not capable?' Yeats struggled to speak with authority, but his voice broke into a bleat.

'She fears you lack the passion. She knows about your secrets.'

'What secrets?'

'That you're still in contact with Iseult Gonne. That you wrote to her during your honeymoon to let her know how unhappy you were. Is that correct?'

I could sense Yeats' tension. He had become captivated by Iseult after agreeing to take charge of her introduction to London's literary society in the summer of 1916, and had proposed to her immediately after her mother Maud Gonne spurned his latest proposal. However, the affection she showed towards him was more in keeping with that of a young woman to an adoptive father and guardian, rather than a suitor in love.

'To a degree.'

'How often do you write to her?'

'I don't know. Barely once a week. I've only met her twice, since the wedding.'

At this revelation, a buzz of conversation erupted from the audience of servant girls. Distracted, Georgie's eyes fluttered and she awoke. Yeats sat down, sighing. The spell was broken, the moment lost. Even though he was a renowned poet and orator immersed in public affairs, he was still capable of being surprised by his young wife, of being caught short by the interrogative gifts of her spirit companions.

In spite of my best attempts to mollify Yeats, his embarrassment made him resentful and reluctant to talk to anyone after the séance. Without uttering another word, he swept out through the heavy doors of the disused church with Georgie hurrying after him. I made to follow them but found my path blocked by Marley. He was determined to share his opinions about the séance.

'Mr Yeats surprised me this evening,' he said, staring at me intently. 'He has come all the way down from his ivory tower and shown himself to be a man of flesh and vulnerability. A harassed husband and soon, I fear, a harassed father.'

I avoided his gaze.

A note of contempt sounded in Marley's voice. 'Tell him he should stick to his poetry.'

'Are you suggesting the séance was a failure?'

'A successful fraud, rather than a failure,' he declared. 'No more than that. One of the most beautifully acted deceptions I have ever seen. The medium's performance was a *pièce de résistance* that would grace the Abbey stage any day of the week.'

'What makes you so sure?'

'What other conclusion can one draw? It's obvious the ghosts don't exist. Besides, I suspect the medium is attempting to have a row with her husband.' He grinned. 'Perhaps even seduce him.'

'But that's idiotic. If she was, surely she'd be more discreet about her intentions.'

'Sometimes an argument in public is a safer way to defuse accumulated marital tensions.' Marley walked over to the table and inspected the pages of Georgie's handwriting. 'No one else in the room saw or heard the spirits. Only one person did, and she purports to have no conscious memory of their communication. The only evidence is her scrawled handwriting and a series of doodles.'

One of the servant girls drew back the drapes that covered the windows with a dramatic swish. In the distance, the mountain of Ben Bulben lay dark as a crypt under a gathering rainstorm.

'How can you be so sure she's a fraud? Yeats is a world expert on séances and mediums.'

'And so is Georgie. I understand she has been a member of the Golden Dawn since the age of seventeen.'

'If she is a fake, what has she to gain? She didn't earn a penny for her performance tonight. Besides, the séance practically descended into chaos. Why humiliate her husband by creating these so-called "frustrators"?'

'Mrs Yeats gained something more important than money tonight.'

'What was that?'

'Her husband's undivided attention. The more she holds it, the less time he can give to his former loves. Don't you see? The "frustrators" are crucial to the fraud. They add confusion and stall for time. Otherwise, Yeats would want to publish the messages from the otherworld immediately, and reveal them to the world as proof that spirits exist, that there is a reality outside ours. No. Every hoax needs an element of failure. Georgie is happy writing endless reams of nonsense and speaking in her strange voices. As long as she has Yeats' interest, the charade is worth continuing. And anytime he presses for results, she introduces the evil spirits to create confusion and delay. Look at what happened this evening. The "frustrators" did not allow Rosemary's ghost to speak because she was never there in the first place.'

Marley chuckled as I stared doubtfully at the pages of automatic writing. Remarkably, his face had relaxed. The more sinister world of spies and subterfuge had loosened its grip on him, if only for a moment. 'To tell you the truth, I enjoyed this evening's performance. It was more fun than a trip to the theatre to watch the captivating Maud Gonne.'

'You should get out more often, if that's the case.'

'You're one to talk.' He stared at me knowingly.

I felt his disbelieving mind search out a new target. 'Do you have me under surveillance?' I asked warily.

'Do you think I'd tell you if you were?'

I hesitated to reply.

'Unless you and Mr Yeats have devised a method of vanishing magically from the scene, I suggest you avoid Sligo's beaches, especially at night.' His face darkened again. I could sense the firmness of his suspicions. They were a stronghold, an unassailable vantage point from which he could launch pinpoint attacks on my integrity. Under his cynical gaze, I grew acutely aware of an unfounded sense of guilt.

Marley added, 'I need hardly remind you what the punishment for treason is.'

'Trying to make contact with a ghost is hardly treason.'

'Let me save you and Mr Yeats the bother of any further botched séances or embarrassing paranormal investigations. Rosemary O'Grady was a fanatic. Of the same mould as Maud Gonne. Generally speaking, fanatical women are unpredictable and dangerous creatures. They resist being controlled. They are cold-blooded and have no fear of death, and they don't always obey orders or stick to plans.'

'What orders had she been given?'

'My sources tell me she was at the centre of a plot to bring German weapons by submarine to Sligo.'

I tried to absorb the implications of what he had said.

'This was an international conspiracy that threatened the British Isles as a whole. A plot hatched to plunge Ireland into chaos. I want to stress to you that withholding information about the Daughters of Erin and their intentions is tantamount to treason.'

'I have nothing to withhold.' I thought of the Ireland I had encountered so far, and wondered whether it was not already slipping into chaos.

'We are merely asking your cooperation if you come across any information about gun smuggling.'

'Am I being recruited as a spy?'

'We are seeking your cooperation, as a loyal British citizen.'

'So if I should uncover a plot to smuggle weapons I should contact you.'

'That is correct.'

Marley backed off with a smirk. I left the church in a hurry. I had the strong feeling that any further spiritual investigations conducted by Yeats in public would not involve his wife as a medium. He was under considerable strain and I feared he might try to free himself from the smothering and unfamiliar constraints of marriage by doing something desperate like contacting his former lover, Maud Gonne.

17

EIGHT OF CUPS

CAPTAIN Oates picked his way over heaped landfall, broken fencing, treeroots ripped from the earth, and strange-looking stone slabs sticking up at odd angles like headstones amid the sea pebbles. If he had not been tracking the mysterious movements of a large sailing boat, he would have stopped to examine the slabs. As it was, he would not be diverted from his surveillance. He had been following the boat's course all evening. He watched it through his field glasses, sailing westward, riding the tide, then labouring hard against the currents, its hull low in the breaking water. He knew that the spring tides poured quickly between the rocky promontories of the bay, and that more nimble boats had been squeezed to smithereens between its rocky jaws.

He watched the boat inch its way through an obstacle course of raised sand beds and sharp rocks until it was about to slip past the headland, when it mysteriously swung back to port and returned into view, threading its way back across the bay. Finally, he had found something worth studying in the wind-tossed oblivion of the Atlantic. After months of interrogation, the turbulent waves of Blind Sound were delivering their secrets.

Darkness fell, and a light began to wink every ten minutes or so from the boat. It occurred to him that its crew were signalling someone on the shore. He was about to look for cover when he heard a noise from the rocks behind. Automatically, he felt for his revolver, realising as he did so the futility of the movement. He turned, prepared to explain that he was out for a stroll and had been observing the movements of what might have been porpoises or basking sharks swimming out in the bay.

However, he offered no such explanation when he saw who was advancing towards him. It was someone who no longer had an interest in porpoises or sharks, or boats that might be smuggling weapons or contraband. A figure little more than a deeper shade of black unfurled against the black cliffs, gradually forming into the thin shape of a woman with a hood obscuring her face.

Oates stood rooted to the spot, at once alarmed by the return of Rosemary's ghost and reassured, the way one feels when confronted by a familiar face in a nightmare. A fresh surge of sea-water washed against his feet.

'Why are you following me?'

'Why do you ask?'

'Because I need to know.'

The ghost did not reply. Her hooded face was like a vortex threatening to pull him in.

'The least you can tell me is whether you're here to do good or evil.'

'I'm here to give you a message.'

'What sort of message?'

'That you are at risk of serious harm.'

'From whom?'

'Forces over which you have no control.'

'Supernatural forces?'

'Human forces. Of the most dangerous kind.'

He was aware of the sea at his back, the forward rush of each breaking wave, and the sound of what might have been a boat's hull smacking against the churning water.

'What were you searching for every time you waded out into the bay?'

The ghost backed away, her head hung low with the submissiveness of someone trapped in an eternity of waiting. The sound of rough voices rose from the sea.

'I heard a report that it was just seashells."

'Not seashells. Men.'

What type of seductress are you, he wondered.

'Germans, to be precise,' said the ghost.

'What did you want from them?'

Her voice turned cold. 'Guns. Bombs. Weapons for the Daughters of Erin. I was tasked with finding a suitable bay along the Sligo coast for a German U-boat to land safely. I waded out and measured the depths of the water and the movement of the tides in every cove and inlet for miles.'

'Is that what you were doing the night you were murdered?'

'Yes.'

'What else happened that night?'

'I discovered that the Daughters of Erin were being betrayed. I collected all the tell-tale clues but couldn't work out who to trust with the information.'

He thought to himself that that was the problem with belonging to a secret revolutionary society. Who did you trust to report your suspicions?

'I found out there was never going to be any weapons arriving at Blind Sound. Only contraband. Alcohol mostly.'

Oates thought of the girl with the fire of revolution burning in her head, wading out in her long dress every night into the Atlantic. A fluttering sound filled the air behind him, like that of wind moulding the canvas of a sail. A curtain of luminous sea mist passed between them. The wind dropped, and the waves grew softer, the sea denser.

The figure of the ghost seemed distracted. Something was different about her tonight.

'You must go now,' she urged him. 'If you stay here any longer, you'll face the same death I endured.'

'And what was that?'

'The smugglers will hide you in a coffin and let the sea swallow you up.'

'Then I will make the sea spit me out.'

'Come with me now to the top of the cliffs. Up there you

will see everything with absolute clarity.'

Oates stared up at the moonlit cliffs, the crumbling rocks that gave onto the direst drops. He knew of higher cliffs but few were as imposing as the overhanging cliffs at Blind Sound. Again, the ghost urged him to leave, as though he were stubbornly clinging to a sinking ship. He sensed a note of growing exasperation in her voice. The wind rippled through her long black gown. She shivered.

'Sometimes I can't help wondering if you're not dead at all,' he said. 'That you might be more alive than I am.'

Her form was immediately charged with energy. She sidestepped him and jumped onto a rock. 'Tell that to the priest who buried me.'

He climbed the rock and clutched at her long gown. It struck him that he could be as wanton as he liked with a ghost.

'Your heart is healthy,' said the figure. 'Pulsating in its own blood. I see it. I feel it. But mine is rotten and shrivelled.'

'I want to see your face.'

'You can't look at me,' she whispered urgently.

His hand pulled at her gown, tore it apart. He felt cold flesh and fell back in surprise. She seemed to be sighing but it might have been the sound of the wind flowing through her torn robe.

'I still can't see your face.'

'Don't come near me,' she warned. 'It's the face of a living woman you want to see.'

She was agitated. Her body trembled.

'Then why do you tempt me?' There was hurt in his voice.

'I have taken my life to the grave.'

'I'm not afraid to join you.'

'If you want me there is no need to go to the trouble of dying. There is a better way.'

'How?'

She removed her hood and revealed the silhouette of her face. The wind whipped her hair against her cheeks. He reached out to brush it aside but at that instant, an oil lamp flashed from a nearby rock. Its intermittent beam distracted his eyes. Someone was advancing towards them. The ghostly figure of the girl flickered against the light and then disappeared swiftly from view.

'Don't go,' he shouted into the darkness. But she was already gone.

He looked up. Two men, bare-chested and muscle-bound, were trotting towards him with oil lamps swinging in their hands. He had seen them before, the night the swimmer had been dragged ashore tied to an anchor rope. Their malevolent faces surrounded him, the grey hairs on their chests matted from the sea.

'Who were you talking to?' they demanded. He could smell the salt tang of the Atlantic.

'A ghost.'

'Are you fooling with us?' said one of them, removing a knife from his belt.

'Wait,' said the other. 'It's the captain. The chief wants to speak to him.'

He bounded into the darkness but they ran after him, diving onto his legs, the three of them scuffling together. Oates tried to roll down the beach into the sea, his body lacquered with sand and seaweed, but he was no match for the two men with their wide shoulders and powerful gripping arms. They were well-rehearsed gymnasts of violence; in the light of the oil lamps, their shadows threw fierce somersaults against the sand and rocks. Soon they had overpowered him, pinning his body to the soft sand, raining down a barrage of blows. A whimper emerged from his dry throat, a plea for mercy. He gulped down cold air that reeked of blood and salt.

'That's enough,' said a voice from the rocks. It spoke loudly but without conviction. A figure stepped into view. At first, Oates believed he was safe when he recognised who it was, a fellow member of the Crown forces, but when he stared into his eyes, any hope that he might be saved rapidly dissolved.

'That wasn't a ghost you saw, Captain Oates,' growled the voice. 'Ghosts don't hide their modesty behind cloaks and hoods. After all, who ever heard tell of a lost soul worried about a rip in its gown?'

18

KING OF PENTACLES

ON his home turf, Yeats was a master in the theatre of disorientation. His figure ghosted through the alleyways and side streets of Sligo town with an apparently aimless sense of direction, as though he were running blindfolded through a labyrinth. In reality, he was following a series of secretly rehearsed markers: a broken water pump, a tiny windowpane filled with the vivid greenery of shamrocks, a flaking statue of the Virgin Mary holding vigil in a damp gable wall.

A thin drizzle had been falling since we left the séance, thickening the visibility and soaking the spirit of the town's inhabitants, forcing them to retreat within their shuttered houses. I hurried after Yeats, my brisk steps faltering at every watery crossroads, more alleyways spiralling off into the sodden gloom, my feet crunching and slithering as the cobbled pavement gave way to slops of manure and household waste.

At points along the journey, I glanced behind, looking for a telltale shadow, the sheen of a policeman's uniform, or a face hidden beneath a low-brimmed hat. I kept imagining the lanky figure of Marley standing in darkened doorways, patient as a heron waiting for the right moment to strike at its prey, but the only form of life I saw was a solitary cat, which fled at my approach, a half-eaten fish head trailing from its mouth.

Yeats pushed on until he spotted the final mark, a small thorn

bush growing from a rotten chimney. We turned the corner of
a building that looked frozen in the act of collapse, and found
ourselves in a narrow street of shops, dumpily built, their walls
bulging like the sides of a boat, the eaves of their roofs barely at
head-height. I stared into windows so dark they looked as though
they had absorbed a century of shadows. A visitor unused to Irish
ways would have glanced over the several dusty jars discreetly
displayed behind the glass and not realised the buildings were
shops at all.

A shout answered Yeats' knock on the third door, and we
stepped into what appeared on first impression to be a long,
tightly packed wardrobe of unstitched greatcoats and brightly
coloured dresses, but turned out on closer inspection to be a small
but gruesomely packed abattoir. We pushed through the hung
carcasses of sheep and pigs, sodden rags of flesh brushing against
our heads. The sawdust-covered floor carried the imprints of
bloody boots; offal smeared the distempered walls. The pungent
metallic smell of something that was not quite organic hung
in the air, which, mixed with the bloody smell of meat, made a
sickly cocktail that had my stomach retching.

'Why have you brought me here?' I enquired between gasps.

'To prove that Georgie is not the only one who can eavesdrop
on ghosts.'

I miscalculated the height of a step and fell against a row of
carcasses. They parted like a grisly curtain and revealed what
appeared to be a keg of gunpowder, the source of the unusual
metallic smell. Hurriedly, I followed Yeats to the back of the
room, trying not to show my surprise. Yeats appeared ignorant of
what lay concealed behind the carcasses.

The head of a little old man appeared from behind a butcher's
table with a ruffled look of surprise, like that of a priest disturbed
from the inner sanctum of his confessional. His hair was stiff
and wild, and his eyes had a slightly haunted look, as though the
invisible world was enacting its strange myths just at the corner
of his gaze.

'My dear Mr Yeats,' he exclaimed, rubbing his hands. He

hurried to the door, hung up a 'CLOSED' sign and turned the key. 'I have exactly what you're looking for.' He led us into a back room that was even smaller than the one we had left.

'Who's this?' I asked.

'Owen Ahearne.' Yeats practically cooed when he said the name. 'A butcher by trade, but he's also Ireland's greatest expert on phantasmal acoustics. In his youth, he studied under Madame Blavatsky's guidance at the Theosophical Society. Last year I invited him over to London to instruct the Golden Dawn on his latest research on metallic mediums; man-made devices which can tune into celestial conversations.'

The back room was so small that standing in its middle, Ahearne could reach all the shelves that lined the walls. They were filled with Victorian apparatus and curiosities, new-fangled radio devices, and trumpet-like instruments, which collectively gave the room the impression of a secret listening station. The upper rows displayed books on magic, packs of illustrated cards and glass cases containing daggers and other heraldic weapons. From a lower shelf, Ahearne removed a long wooden box.

'Does it work?' asked Yeats.

'I haven't even opened the box,' he said quickly. 'Haven't had a moment to see what's inside.' His repetition made me suspect that he was being less than truthful. 'It arrived yesterday from the manufacturer in Germany and I immediately stashed it away. I was afraid the British War Office might orchestrate a raid on my shop.' Ahearne's face changed again. His eyes darkened. 'Did you make sure no one followed you here? Did you take the roundabout route, the one with the secret markers?'

'Yes, yes,' reassured Yeats.

Ahearne eyed me closely. 'Who's your companion?'

'This is Mr Charles Adams. He's come to Sligo to clarify the circumstances of Rosemary O'Grady's death.'

He turned to me with brightening eyes. 'And what have you clarified so far?'

I divulged my findings. 'That the police have yet to find a

crime scene, locate any witnesses, or establish a credible murder suspect. Which is very discouraging.'

'It suggests to me the police have no interest in solving the crime.'

'Worse. The police say Miss O'Grady was an arsonist, a smuggler, a rebel, a woman of loose morals who was the victim of a botched initiation rite. They have suggested she might have been killed by a secret coven of her comrades who employed the sea as their efficient undertaker.'

Ahearne's breathing grew shallow, his voice agitated. 'I hope you're not going to peddle this conspiracy and hide the plain truth.'

'Which is what?'

'That British agents were behind her murder,' he wheezed with anger. 'In the same way that they are behind everything sinister that happens in this country, from the smuggling along the cliffs to the spreading of propaganda that a German invasion is imminent. The only thing they don't control is the movement of apparitions and faeries. At least not yet. Mr Yeats is trying to ensure that the land of spirits remains loyal to Irish nationalism.'

'A revolution always needs its recruits,' replied Yeats with a weak smile.

'I have a well-placed informant that is involved in this case. He tells me that the Constabulary are planning a massive round-up of Republicans. Are you quite sure no one followed you here?'

'Not even a cat,' replied Yeats.

Ahearne's reference to an informant puzzled me. It suggested that a British agent based in Sligo was in collusion with Republican networks. His use of the phrase 'well-placed' pointed a finger of suspicion at Grimes, or perhaps even Marley. In a way, it made sense that Maud Gonne and the daughters of Erin were operating under the protection of some influential individual with the British forces.

Ahearne eyed us suspiciously. 'My confidant tells me that every second person in this town is in the pay of the British King,' he muttered, 'including you and Gonne. Or have you forgotten?'

'If you mean the pension in recognition of my literary achievements, it's hardly a fortune.'

'But enough to ruin your reputation as an Irish nationalist.'

'I'm not bothered about reputation. I'm more interested in character.'

'If by that you mean contradictions and flaws then you have an abundance of character.' The dry skin of the old man's face wrinkled as he smiled.

'Now you're being cruel.'

'I'm only insinuating that you might be human after all.'

'And what about Maud? I don't believe you understand her predicament.'

'I understand she's a rich Englishwoman still receiving her father's war pension. Since the English shot her husband, she's been dressing up in black and playing the martyr's widow. The plight of the Irish is her hobby-horse, an adventure that keeps her from settling down to domestic life. Besides, I have it on good authority that she can't be trusted.'

'Who told you that?' Yeats was indignant.

'Her husband, Major John MacBride.'

'But he was killed for his role in the Easter Rising.'

Ahearne grinned.

'You haven't tried to make contact with him, have you?'

'I didn't contact him.' Ahearne tapped the wooden box. 'He contacted me.'

It took a moment or two for the implication to sink in. The revelation brought colour to Yeats' cheeks.

'You've been using the listening device,' he said. 'You told me you hadn't opened it.'

Ahearne blinked slowly like a preening cat and looked at Yeats with an insolent expression. 'How could I resist?'

Yeats turned and gripped the door handle. 'We must be on the move,' he declared.

'Where are you off to now?'

'To Blind Sound with our German gift.' He patted the wooden box. 'By the way,' he addressed Ahearne, 'you shouldn't believe everything the spirits tell you. Especially a vainglorious lout like Major MacBride.'

Early the next day we rode out of Sligo on two horses provided by Lissadell Estate, the wooden box strapped to the back of Yeats' saddle like a cowboy's rifle. We still kept watch behind us, and turned every time the horses twitched their ears. The only sounds we heard were the steady clop of the horses' hooves and the trickling sound of water, which filled the high spring hedges like an immense whispering whose throat was every dripping bud and thorn. After half an hour of riding, we began to feel reassured that no one was following us.

'Marley thinks Georgie is only pretending to contact the otherworld,' I said. 'He fears you have spent so long pursuing the spiritual that you have lost your common sense.'

'Marley is infected with the Anglo-Saxon mind,' replied Yeats dismissively.

'What do you mean?'

Yeats stared at me and composed his reins. 'We Celts and you Anglo-Saxons might look much the same, but we see things utterly differently, and we each live in our own worlds. The English have a tendency to analyse and simplify the world, which is why so many great men of science come from your stock, but you run the risk of turning the world into a children's story-book with everything reduced to the simplest terms, everything separated and spelled out as clearly as possible. I suspect it is the result of your great need to explore and colonise primitive civilisations.'

Yeats had taken his mind off riding, and his horse seized advantage, pulling at the thick grasses that grew along the roadside. He yanked his reins, flicked his whip along the animal's shoulder, and we ambled on.

'The true Celt is magical by nature,' he continued. 'He does not try to reduce the mysterious to predictable laws. Nor does he lose sight of the pure, the elevated, and the spiritual. His world is a realm of changeless beauty and sensual ecstasy, a garden flooded with brilliant sunshine.'

I stared at surroundings that hardly belonged to the realm of the gods. We were in the gullet of a wet valley, the air thick with drizzle, the fields and hills turning several shades of green darker than anything I had witnessed before. Our sodden horses moved in a slow mechanical way, reminiscent of a dream, as though we had strayed into a rain-lover's hallucination. The flowering blackthorn hedges floated by as high as our thighs, the white flowers lighting up the dismal scene. For a while, the only sound was the swishing of the horses' flanks through the overgrown verges.

Yeats stopped ahead of me, and I was grateful for the rest.

'What's wrong?' I asked, seeing the look of alarm on his face.

'The horses are spooked.' Beads of perspiration, not rain, formed on his brow as he struggled to keep the reins low on his agitated mount. The beast backed nervously into mine like a stubborn pony.

I saw what had made his horse stall. Over the hedge, a cordon of policemen were moving stealthily towards a dilapidated cabin in the middle of a stone-walled field.

'Stay at ease,' he said to me, as though I was the one getting fidgety and not the horses.

I turned my mount round and stared at the police raid unfolding before us. I recognised the burly figure of Inspector Grimes disappear into the darkness of the cabin and emerge moments later, rolling in front of him a train of wooden barrels. One of his men lit a straw torch and threw it onto the cabin's rotten thatched roof. A flickering glow took hold. The crackling sounds of fire caused a fresh wave of agitation to pass through the horses. Yeats' mount stamped its feet, swung its hindquarters round, whinnied and lifted its forelegs high into the air, its eyes widening with terror.

'Give me some space,' growled Yeats, fighting to control the animal, but he was losing the struggle. The animal bucked with its hindquarters and swung its powerful long neck to the left. Yeats slipped to the side, clung on for a moment, and then, in a moment of desperation, pushed himself off the rearing animal.

He fell backwards into the ditch, his head swinging back sharply as he hit the ground.

'Is everything alright?' I asked.

'Do I look alright?'

'You don't sound too worse for wear.' I enjoyed the comical sight of the celebrated poet and dandy upside down in a ditch full of mud and dandelions.

'Just smelling the delightful hedgerow flowers,' he said, picking himself up.

He looked a little shaky so we changed mounts, my horse being the more restful of the two. A short while later, we met Grimes and his men emptying the contents of the barrels into a road-side stream. The policemen had been working hard. Their beards were matted with sweat, their uniforms covered in dust and straw, evidence that they had been rummaging deep in hidden corners and crevices. Behind them, a tall lean figure stood urinating into the hedge. The yellow stream sprayed over foaming branches of whitethorn blossom. The figure turned and did up his buttons. It was Wolfe Marley, his collar raised higher than usual against the fresh mountain winds.

'What are you searching for?' inquired Yeats.

'Barrels of buttermilk,' said Grimes.

'Why the show of strength?'

'Because they belong to the devil.'

Marley grinned. 'Inspector Grimes is an Ulster evangelical. To the true Bible Protestant, the devil's buttermilk is whiskey and porter.'

'We're rounding up illegal contraband and smugglers,' explained Grimes, his eyes burning with the fire of the zealot. 'The coves and creeks of this coast are ideal for smuggling. On moonless nights, a train of ponies climb the local cliffs laden with gallons of brandy and chests of tea. The contraband is concealed throughout the country in run-down houses or hidden in haystacks. Sometimes buried in graves, painted black and disguised as rocks, or dug into holes in gardens and meadows.'

The Inspector examined the horses carefully. I could see his eyes searching for illicit goods, hidden weapons, a secret stash of brandy. His eyes lighted on the wooden instrument case strapped to Yeats' saddle. Exhibit 'A' were the words about to form on his lips.

'We carry no smuggled goods,' said Yeats. 'And have declared our dutiable merchandise. Good day to you.'

He squeezed his horse through the policemen. Marley and Grimes stepped back quickly. They watched us intensely as though convinced we were wrong-doers, as though we might be loaded with a supernatural cargo that could not be confiscated.

We drove the horses over haggard bog land scarred with turf-diggers' trenches. A few dead trees raised their heads like the antlers of tussling stags. We trotted to the crest of a hill from which we could see the silver strand and black cliffs of Blind Sound hovering in a sea mist. Nothing moved in the soaked landscape. Yeats' face looked exhausted, shot through with the fatigue of the previous evening's spiritual trials. He hunched forward as if about to nod off to sleep.

'Tell me, is Georgie aware of what happens during a séance?' I asked.

'No.' His answer was curt. After a few paces, he elaborated. 'While the spirits' critical powers are awake, hers sleep. She is quite literally a medium, the conduit through which the spirit guides deliver their instructions.'

'Instructions?'

Yeats flinched. 'Yes.'

'I thought their messages were a font of metaphors for your poetry, the foundation of your philosophy on the afterlife.'

'Yes. But, unfortunately, the spirits have proved highly inefficient,' he said ruefully. 'Three-quarters of what they deliver is devoted to matters so personal it is completely unusable in any book of philosophy or poetry. At least one that will pass the censor's eye. When I press them on intellectual matters, they tell me I am not yet ready to know the truth. They say it will take time.'

'How long?'

'A thousand years,' he said with a despairing sigh. 'In the meantime they are strangely preoccupied with the marital bed. In fact, if they were alive I'd suspect them of being avid proponents of the theories of Marie Stopes.' Yeats' gaunt throat twitched a bitter laugh that never reached his lips.

The horses stopped and scuffed their hooves on a narrow bridge over a stream running wild between black rocks. The play of shadow and reflection agitated the animals. They sidled nervously. Yeats opted for a few calming words of poetry, reciting several times 'Smooth flow the waves, the zephyrs gently play', until we were able to steer the animals across. Unfortunately, he was unable to cure himself of a similar affliction. The note of protest in his voice expanded.

'After the first few dazzling days, when great truths seemed to emerge from their messages, the negative spirits began to take over the séances. And then our marriage bed.' The horses stopped unexpectedly, ears twitching. Then they moved on.

'For instance, at a particular time of the month, they order us to make love twice in a certain position, so that a child might be conceived. They have promised me a boy, a reincarnation of a Butler ancestor, as long as I keep satisfying Georgie. As long as I love her and don't leave her. As long as I stay with her and ignore the distractions of Maud and her daughter Iseult.'

I had seen Georgie furtively reading reports on Marie Stopes' research in the hotel sitting room. Her theories stressed the husband's duty to give his wife sexual satisfaction. Yeats was too much of a scholar, I feared, to ever become a happily married man or a devoted father. He needed clues, signs and instructions, even in his relationship with women, but in home life there were none.

Georgie's bouts of magical writing were a ghostly form of therapy, I began to suspect, a cunning wifely strategy to ensure that her sexual appetites were being met by her middle-aged and reluctant husband. It was no secret among occult circles that Yeats suffered from sexual inhibition and shyness. I had often heard him after several glasses of wine refer to the female's nether regions as 'those dark declivities'.

'Shouldn't a marriage be based upon freedom rather than coercion?' I asked.

'Precisely. But I am being suffocated by these spirits. I shall not submit to their authority any longer. I don't care what tactics they deploy, what warnings or threats they issue. And I refuse to submit to a woman, to be a slave to her demands.'

His cheeks were flushed with colour. At first, I thought that his vigour was returning but then I worried for the state of his mind. His emotions were threatening to well up and overpower his reasoning.

'I want the life I had before marriage. I want to be able to make mistakes, to have faults, to be selfish, to be human.'

We were passing Lissadell's stables and the high whinnying noises of horses recognising each other filled the air. Our mounts snorted and stretched their necks, their tails afloat behind. We leaned forward and with considerable effort managed to settle them.

'I think her spirit hates me,' said Yeats. 'She is full of anger. Female anger.'

'Whose spirit?'

'Rosemary O'Grady's.'

'She entrusted a vital mission to you.'

'Why me? What do I know about her life? What do I know about murder?' He laughed bitterly. 'My country is descending into chaos, my wife is desperate to conceive while I am not, and here we are forced to play the roles of Sherlock Holmes and Watson. We'll be lucky not to end up with knives in our backs.' A sick look came over his face as if he were suddenly suspended over a precipitous cliff. It struck me that since he had fallen from the horse he had been unusually garrulous and forthcoming on personal matters.

'How do you feel from your fall?'

'What fall?'

'You came off the horse about twenty minutes ago. Abruptly. You must have struck your head.'

He glared at me indignantly. 'But we've been riding splendidly all afternoon.'

'We changed horses after the fall. You're on the quieter beast.'

Yeats examined his horse's head. He closed his eyes and went deathly pale. I pestered him with several medical questions and diagnosed a mild concussion. I advised him we should head back to the hotel immediately.

'Nonsense,' he replied. 'I'll walk it off.'

He dismounted and pressed his head against my saddle. 'Are you alright?' I asked, my anxiety for his health rising.

'Of course,' he replied. His long arm reached round to check that the wooden box was still in place. He unslung it and tied it round his shoulder. We secured the horses to a tree and walked the final stretch to the beach at Blind Sound.

19

SEVEN OF CUPS

I HAD discovered, as part of my induction into the Golden Dawn, that Yeats was fascinated by mechanical contraptions and outlandish inventions, which might be used like Marconi's radio to tune into the invisible world of spirits. In the past year, he had carried out experiments on all manner of devices from adding machines to gramophones and radios powered by glowing crystals. However, his poetic genius was amply matched by a complete lack of scientific understanding, and even his most rigorous investigations and autopsies on the machines failed to reveal any genuine secrets.

On the beach at Blind Sound, I watched him remove from the box a long golden trumpet with copper wands and buttons running along its sides. Inscribed along the horn of the instrument were the words 'The Soul of the World'.

'Another talking trumpet,' I remarked.

'Yes,' replied Yeats. 'But this one has been tuned to pick up a sound that never stops. One that constantly rings out from mountain tops and cities, from the upper realms of the sky to the depths of the sea. The spirit of the world as it changes from moment to moment.'

I took a step back. Yeats' occult claims no longer dazzled me but this one was blinding. 'The spirit of the world will speak through this piece of metal?'

'You can smile with incredulity but I've seen it used for that very purpose.'

'Where?'

'In an attic overlooking one of the busiest thoroughfares in London.'

'How does it work?'

'The details are shrouded in absolute secrecy.'

'There's a surprise.'

'A secret to which the trumpet maker has made me privy.'

Yeats began adjusting the controls of the instrument, and explained to me what he had been told. Assuming that I understood metallurgy, he spoke some gibberish about the alloys of rare metals used in the moulding of the trumpet, and a ground-breaking Teutonic theory on pistons and communicating chambers, which the instrument used to amplify vibrations beyond the range of human hearing. He held the trumpet aloft as though he were the champion of a new technology that would revolutionise the world of spiritualism. Then he lowered the instrument, and dropped his voice. 'Of course, there is a risk of embarrassment and failure. The creator might be a fraud after all. Which is why I have elected to trial it on this far western shore.'

He readjusted the copper wands and tapped at a glass dial positioned next to the instrument's mouth. The grey light of the waves illuminated his face as he laid the trumpet on a makeshift altar of stones. Mumbling in Latin, he traced a pentagram around the structure.

My patience snapped. 'What is the point of all this?' I shouted above the wind. 'Why is there a need for such gadgetry and dramatics? Why so much spectacle and ritual? Why all of this just to hear a ghost speak. Isn't it enough that we just listen? Shouldn't the mode of contact with miraculous beings be simpler and less artificial?'

Yeats did not reply.

'I no longer wish to be part of this pointless spectacle,' I announced. 'I shall climb the cliffs and observe your folly from a distance.'

'Quiet,' ordered Yeats. 'I want spectators not critics. Your ticket of admission is your silence. When the show is over, you will have your opportunity to applaud or boo.'

If there had been a door to slam on that empty beach, I would have done so. Instead, I walked briskly to where the sand gave out to rocks and the debris of landslides. The cliff looked unassailable but I felt strangely braced after my outburst. I took a final glance back at Yeats, who stood motionless, arms raised before the churning sea. A flock of seagulls materialised out of the spray and then disappeared. If Blind Sound was his temple then the cries of the gulls were the ringing of its discordant bells.

I found a precipitous path, worn smooth by the passage of nailed boots, and clambered my way upwards. The path was virtually invisible from the beach, but it cut an unmistakable route along the south-facing cliff. Small boulders had been assembled to help one negotiate gullies, and treads cut into the rock where the path fell away, just wide enough to hold a man-sized boot and allow one to sidle across, face pressed to the wet stone. On a small promontory, I rested for a moment. Gulls and cormorants swooped feet away, against a churning backdrop of waves and grey oblivion. The sound of hungry chicks in their nests echoed from higher up the cliff. I felt a piece of wire dig into my back, and turning to the cliff face, found a crude handle, suspended above a small crevice. I pulled the handle and uncovered a string of tin cans filled with turf ash and reeking of something that smelt like paraffin. It was a makeshift string of lights, I realised. I sat down and contemplated my discovery.

I could follow the line of the path below me by the shine on the rocks upon which countless boots had sought footholds. Who had used the crooked path? I wondered. Who had left behind the fine web of their repeated journeys? A short-cut for fishermen to a favourite perch, perhaps. But why the string of lights? Something to do with the night. Smugglers signalling from a vantage point to boats out in the bay? Perhaps, but I lacked the evidence to prove my supposition.

The sound of Yeats' incantations disturbed my thoughts.

His shouts, carried in snatches by the wind, sounded childlike in their glee and enthusiasm. I made out the names of several mythological deities and familiar invocations in Hebrew and Latin. The wind rose and his chant merged with the tumult of the waves into a single pulsing voice, as though the black cliffs themselves were speaking in a restless tongue.

I checked for any sign of Captain Oates on the beach, but the only figure was Yeats. I pushed off again, following the rest of the oblique track until it petered out in a lichen-covered cleft. I was about to turn back when out of the corner of my eye I saw a shadow swinging erratically against the cliff. I crouched as a horrible clacking sound filled the air. I glanced up in time to see a cormorant swoop, its beak opened in attack. I ducked as it flapped its wings, beating the air about my head. Waving my arms in self-defence, I shuffled along the narrow ledge, but the bird's violent movements knocked me off my balance. I grabbed at empty air and fell into a roaring wind, which drowned my bellow of alarm. The air was sucked from my lungs, and I fell more than twenty feet. My last vision was of an upended beach with a dark figure running sideways towards me, dimming to a hazy sea-green and then deep blackness.

I must have slipped into some sort of dreamland, for the next thing I knew the ghost of my friend Issac was lifting me to my feet on a beach by an alien sea, a floating bazaar of mysteriously crested waves and changing shapes rising and falling in the wind-whipped foam.

'Look how the waves are in constant motion, ebbing and flowing with the tides,' said the ghost. 'You still don't understand the force that drives them. It is the key to understanding the mysteries that beset you.'

He pointed with a bony finger, and I saw the black-haired head of a young woman bob above the waves, and then another. Soon the sea was full of girls, faces pale and skeletal, rising out of the water, their breasts covered in seaweed, their pale legs riding the swell of the waves. A cry sprang into the air, a rallying call, and then the charging women began to chant and whoop. The sound of their howling overwhelmed the roar of the sea. It came from everywhere, filling the air, demanding vengeance for some unmentionable crime. I cowered on the sand, unable to move, as the white wall of their bodies tumbled around me. I braced myself for the impact but their agitated forms passed right through me and dissolved into the sand.

When I came to, I could sense the presence of someone close by, gazing at me intently, speaking a strange language. I tried to understand the figure through its eyes but it was like trying to search for a way out of a maze.

'Are you still in one piece?' asked the voice.

My eyes fluttered fully awake. To my relief I found myself lying a safe distance from the breaking waves. Yeats stood over me with an anxious face. 'I turned and saw you fall,' he said.

I struggled to my feet, but a wave of lightness kept me on my knees. My fingers clawed at the wet sand.

Yeats stared up at the ledge from which I had fallen. 'What happened, Charles? What made you forget that your body is subject to the draconian law of gravity?'

'A cormorant knocked me off my feet.'

'These cliffs are heavily populated with their colonies. Many's the fine feather pillow has been plucked from their nests.'

I told him of the strange vision I had experienced while unconscious.

'What else did you see?'

'That was it.'

'Let me hypnotise you.' His gaze was greedy, penetrating.

'Hypnotise me?' I replied in alarm.

'I want you to return to your unconscious and reveal the symbols hidden there.'

'You think the dream contained a message from the otherworld?'

'Without doubt.'

I thought of Clarissa, and it struck me that the vision might have more to do with my repressed fears and desires concerning the Daughters of Erin.

'My role is that of an investigator. I have no wish to become a channel or a medium.'

Yeats looked hurt. His thoughtful expression became grave and vaguely threatening.

'Forgive me,' I said, 'but I have been infected with curiosity over what happened to Rosemary O'Grady. Not curiosity over whether her spirit has returned but a desire to discover how she was killed and who her killer was. And that is not possible if you insist on turning me into a vessel like Georgie.'

'Then I'm tempted to knock you unconscious again. For the good of this investigation.'

'For the good of the investigation or your own good?'

'What do you mean?'

'I'm not the one seeking answers from spirits about my personal life. Nor am I gnawed by self-doubt and fears of madness. That is why you ferret out every half-sighting of a ghost, every shilling séance, every new contraption to communicate with the dead, because you are unable to make up your own mind, because you are haunted by ghosts of your own making.'

Yeats stared away deep in thought.

'I fear you will interpret what I have said as the harshest of criticism,' I said, 'but I speak from the heart. Out of friendship.'

'It's true,' he said. 'I may be wracked by indecision from time to time. But is that not the case with the male of the species in general? We'd rather have our gods make our decisions for us.'

Or our wives, I thought to myself.

The wind dropped and a jagged whining sound rose above the crash of the waves. I tried to pinpoint its source, as it echoed against the cliffs in a broken rhythm, coming and going like a strange wail. Yeats stared at the trumpet with a triumphant gleam in his eyes as though the sound was emanating from its golden mouth.

'What is that?' I yelled.

Yeats held his breath, afraid to make a sound. The wail grew louder, fulsome as a chorus, and then faded altogether.

'What on earth?' I said.

'Wonderful,' breathed Yeats. 'Here is evidence at last that the trumpet works.'

'But what does it mean?'

'I have no idea.'

Whatever it was, it sounded the very opposite of an angelic choir. It started up again, with greater rage and intensity, the harsh, grating sound of something trapped in the cogs of a machine. I wandered off, leaving Yeats holding the trumpet, muttering incantations under his breath.

The sound grew louder as I approached the caves. The dark cliff chambers magnified the noise, drawing out its twisted melody. I clambered along a wet terrace of rock to find a wooden barrel thrashing in the waves, its metal bands grinding rhythmically against the rocks. On its sides, the words 'The End is Nigh' had been daubed in white paint.

A voice from behind spoke with a panting breath. 'That piece of contraband is now the property of His Majesty's Crown forces.' I turned and saw Inspector Grimes' cold blue eyes as he climbed over the rocks, a battalion of his policemen in tow, while, beyond them, Yeats hurried in our direction, the wind flapping the dark wings of his coat.

'We thought we'd follow you to see what little games you're up to,' said Grimes. As usual, there was something gloating about his sweating face. He spoke as though his arrival on the beach had been a triumph of police detection. 'This is a dangerous coast, Mr Adams, the haunt of smugglers and rebels. That barrel might be full of brandy or gunpowder.'

His men surrounded the barrel and rolled it onto the beach. They sat it upright, and began working on prising open the lid with knives. They were eager to discover what bounty the sea had delivered. However, the wooden lid had expanded in the water and sat clamped tightly in place. Grimes pushed his way through, grabbed one of the knives and applied the pressure of his substantial frame to the makeshift lever. With a final ferocious heave, the lid gave way. Immediately he staggered backwards.

I peered into the barrel and saw the roughly curled head of Captain Oates floating in a dark pool of water. His shoulders were slumped, his hands tied behind his back, his knees tucked up, like a crippled puppet spinning slowly from its few remaining strings.

Yeats appeared and looked with confusion at our grim faces. A foaming wave washed against our feet and the sides of the barrel, sloshing the water within. The corpse moved gently, not living human movement, more like that of a huge dying fish, floundering within the creaking barrel. The head sank beneath the water. Under Grimes' instructions, the policemen pulled the collars of the corpse's uniform, so that the face was clear again, chin tilted upwards, standing drunkenly to attention, froth bubbling from the gaping mouth, the defeated, wide-open eyes looking too small for the bloated face.

Grimes inspected the floating body, squinting as if he might see some lingering essence, some spirit escaping from the captain's remains. He straightened up again, and his face went dark with suspicion.

'Captain Oates has been murdered,' he announced.

Not just killed or drowned, like Rosemary O'Grady, I thought.

'He was a good man, a loyal servant to the Crown,' fumed the Inspector. He stared at the sea, his eyes blazing with anger.

Yeats said nothing. His eyes widened at the sight of the barrel being emptied, and Oates' body, loose-limbed, heaving onto the sand, the uniform bloated like an air bladder. Yeats' body sagged, his knees crumpled and he fell sideways.

'Someone get a doctor,' I said urgently as I rushed to the poet's aid. 'He was suffering from concussion earlier.'

An hour later, a doctor arrived with a hearse pulled by a pair of horses for the body of Captain Oates. Yeats was just stirring back to consciousness, and promptly fainted again at the sight of his transport. The doctor checked his vital signs and organised a stretcher to lift him into the hearse along with the corpse. It was just as well that Yeats remained unconscious as they set off on the journey back to Sligo.

'The coward has gone, and now I am left with the fool,' said Grimes approaching me with an air of menace. 'I want you to accompany me to Sligo Barracks, Mr Adams, while Ireland's poet laureate recovers from his fainting fit.' He smiled thinly at my reluctant reaction. 'Don't be alarmed, it's just an informal visit. You're not under arrest.'

'If I'm not under arrest then why should I go there?'

He shrugged. 'I thought you might be interested in meeting the ghost of Miss O'Grady.'

20

O

TEN OF PENTACLES

SLIGO Barracks and gaol were less a building and more a sprawling block of darkness contained within high walls protected by a barrier of rotating spikes. Opaque leaded windows, no larger than household bibles, ensured that little light penetrated the depths within. A group of women were holding a protest with placards at the gates when the Inspector and I pulled up. They had travelled from evening Mass to shout out the names of loved ones beneath the greasy railings. As we passed, they made the sign of the cross.

'Be gone, ye unbaptised heathens,' roared Grimes.

He led me through a series of iron doors which slammed behind us with a heavy clang. We passed a row of cell doors that must have opened into spaces no larger than coffins. The place reminded me of a dingy public bathhouse. A poster on the walls illustrated the difference between a dozen different types of human parasite. A fire hose lay coiled in the corner, and water gleamed in the cracks of the stone floor. I tried to affect the attitude of a welfare committee member inspecting the prison conditions.

'It must be difficult running a prison during a time of great unrest,' I said, in a foolish attempt to fill the cold void of the corridor.

'Influenza helps,' he replied gruffly. 'Last winter's epidemic cleared out more than half the cells. Of course, we filled them again within a month.'

A guard checked me for concealed weapons and removed my notebook and pen. He stopped just short of inspecting my head for lice. Grimes fiddled with some keys hanging from a chain, barely suppressing a cruel smile.

'Are you prepared to make contact with the dead, Mr Adams?' he asked. He appeared to enjoy the look of uncertainty that flashed across my features. 'You'll soon see that our newest prisoner is a little different from the usual thugs and hooligans we apprehend.'

A tray containing an untouched bowl of congealed porridge and a mug of thin tea sat by the door. 'She is refusing to eat. I believe the tactic is called a hunger strike. But then starving oneself shouldn't be too difficult for someone who is supposed to be dead.' He swung back the grille with a heavy clunk. 'Let me introduce you to the ghost of Rosemary O'Grady.'

For a moment, I was mesmerised by the sight of the young woman sitting serenely in a corner of the cell. She was dressed in a long black cape with a hood. Her appearance had changed since the last time I had seen her. There was a white pallor to her cheeks and dark petals of sleeplessness lay beneath her eyes, an effect produced, I realised, by heavy make-up. It was Clarissa Carty dressed up as a stage ghost.

'Who is she?' I enquired, afraid to take my eyes off her in case my alarm betrayed me. It occurred to me that the Inspector might already know we were acquainted.

'A Daughter of Erin.'

'Why have you arrested her?'

'Because we believe she is behind the murders of Rosemary O'Grady and Captain Oates.' He watched me closely. 'Don't you recognise her?'

'Not at all.'

'She was the fiancée of Richard Denver. She says the two of you are friends.'

We both stared at her without speaking.

'Look,' said Grimes. 'Look at the way she is smiling.'

She was motionless, staring at the dank wall before her, smiling as though she approved of everything that was happening to her.

'Does she know we're watching her?'

'Yes,' he replied. 'She wants us to see her smiling. She wants us to believe that she is afraid of nothing.'

'What evidence do you have against her?'

'We found her with a magic lantern, a device used by charlatans to conjure up the images of ghosts. She confessed to haunting Oates to drive him out of his wits and divert suspicion.'

'That's plausible, but why would she kill him, or Miss O'Grady, in the first place?'

'Jealousy. The two of them were competing for the attention of Captain Oates.'

'But Captain Oates was the enemy.'

'And Miss O'Grady was the prettier. These women think solely in terms of violence and murder. Her thwarted desire to be loved by Oates was transformed into a desire for revenge.'

Grimes beckoned me away from the cell door and led me down the dank corridor into a small room that had a haggard, functional look, ready for any purpose its inhabitants saw fit to pursue. I felt unsure of myself. If this were an interview room, I expected something a little more formal, a desk, a flag, a portrait of the King. I wondered what previous unfortunates had been brought through the same door, and what fate had befallen them within those four blank walls. Someone banged on a door in the next room; the noise was raucous, like that of many fists. A shiver crept up my spine.

The Inspector removed his cap. 'This is one of our guest rooms,' he said with a smile that was not at all welcoming. 'Our visitors seldom complain about the lack of furnishing.'

In spite of the room's dank cold, he was perspiring along his forehead. Trickles of sweat curled along his thick sideburns. A pair of fists kept doggedly pummelling the other side of the wall. So far, all I had seen from the Irish Constabulary was normal police work, or at least nothing that necessitated direct medical intervention. However, that was about to change dramatically.

Grimes stared at me closely, as though he badly wanted something I had, but didn't know how to ask for it.

'As an Englishman, do you swear to stand against the Irish insurrection and the leprosy of Roman Catholicism?'

'Your oath is phrased a little too strongly for my liking.'

Grime's face darkened like a dying lamp. He drew out a baton with a flourish and swung it into my left side, just below my ribs. I slumped against the wall, in gasping acknowledgement of his brute strength.

'This is not the time to play the pedant, Mr Adams.'

The knocking on the wall stopped and the room went quiet. Grimes stood above me, staring at me attentively. The lack of noise made everything seem far away, like it was a game, or a play I was watching, as though he were only pretending to torture me.

He hauled me to my feet.

'It's time to drop the fairy-tale act, Mr Adams. Miss Carty has admitted to everything. There were never any ghosts.' Another blow landed on my ribs.

'What have I done to deserve this?' I wheezed.

Grimes snorted in derision. 'We know of your secret alliance with Maud Gonne and her bloodthirsty rebels. Who knows how deep your betrayal of your country goes?'

'What do you mean by betrayal?' I now felt well and truly trapped within the maw of Sligo prison.

'I believe your purpose here is to sow confusion and disrupt the work of the police and His Majesty's Crown forces. With all these daft rumours flying around about spirits and diabolical possessions, your ploy was to distract us from something much more sinister.' He strode back and forth. 'I want you to tell me about the German plot.'

'What German plot?' I stared at him blankly, wondering who was the one indulging in fairy stories.

'Where is Madame Gonne, the provocateur and spy?'

'I don't know.'

'What part does Mr Yeats play in this treacherous fabrication?'

'None.'

He lost his temper and yelled in my ear, 'You're a spy, Mr Adams.' His hands flexed around his baton. 'Who are you? What is your role here?' He poked the baton into my ribs.

'I'm a secretary to the Order of the Golden Dawn.' I grimaced against the pain.

He pushed me forcibly to the floor, as though he were about to club a dog.

'I'm an Englishman, not a spy,' I complained. 'I don't belong to any violent organisations and I'm not plotting with the rebels.' I breathed in tightly. 'I have a right to be questioned in a fair and appropriate manner.'

'Fair and appropriate's alright in England. But we're far from England now. Don't you know it's not only ghosts that have a habit of disappearing in this part of the world?'

I braced myself but the unexpected rustle of a newspaper behind us interrupted the Inspector's line of direct questioning. I turned and saw Marley rise from a bench in the shadows by the door, and walk casually towards us. He had been watching the entire interrogation.

'That's enough, Inspector,' he said and ordered him to leave the room. Grimes pulled his cap low over his sweating forehead and slammed the door behind.

Marley smiled at me, it seemed, without malice or cruelty.

'I want you to confide in me, Mr Adams. Tell me about this trouble you've got yourself into.'

I sensed that he and Grimes were playing a game, and that his gentler approach was part of a carefully orchestrated plan to break my mental defences.

'If you and Mr Yeats had any common sense you would see how your so-called supernatural investigations seem to everyone else. The self-indulgent antics of two morbid schoolboys. If these weren't such dangerous times, they'd be the stuff of comedy.'

'Our investigation is guided by the instructions in Rosemary's letter. Our object is to move beyond the surface of things.'

'You're still intent on searching for this ghost even though Clarissa Carty was obviously behind the hauntings.'

'If anything, I'm more curious than ever.'

'I'm beginning to suspect you and Mr Yeats are the fanatics, not the Daughters of Erin.'

'Two people have been murdered,' I declared. 'Surely, we can't allow evil to triumph. Even if it is on one small remote beach. It will go on to contaminate the rest of the country.'

'These things are best left in the hands of the police, who are convinced they have arrested the perpetrator.' His tone remained mellow. 'Why do you ignore my warnings and keep returning to Blind Sound?'

'When someone dies there is a theory that for a short while their spirit lingers in that place.'

'Rosemary's murder allows you to prove a theory?'

'And in so doing find out how she died.'

'Assuming you make contact with the right ghost.'

He stared at me for a while. Neither of us spoke.

'I'm still wondering what to do with you,' he said eventually. 'I've listened to your self-justifications, and I've heard what Grimes thinks of your involvement with the Daughters of Erin. Who do you think I should put my faith in?' He began pacing the room. 'I didn't get to be where I am today by believing in the excuses of suspects,' he warned me.

For a moment, I felt overwhelmed by the sensation that the room was retreating deeper and deeper into the corridors of the prison. Taking me further and further from freedom and the normal rules of a civilised society.

Marley watched me with his sceptical eyes, without blinking. I could see that he was indeed a loyal servant to the machine of the Crown forces, unwavering in his cold devotion, standing by while fellow Irishmen were flung into the grinding teeth of the same machine.

'Rosemary's ghost brought you to this gaol,' he said. 'Now that you know there was no ghost, what you do from now on is entirely your own responsibility. Will you allow yourself to be deluded and tricked like Captain Oates, or will you turn back from this dangerous precipice?'

'What do you think?'

'I'll be honest,' he sighed. 'I don't care. But I can tell you there is no mystery to be uncovered at Blind Sound. I want you to consider your actions very carefully. I want you to think of what's best for a man with Mr Yeats' reputation, to keep going forward, or turn back.'

'Surely, that's up to Mr Yeats?'

'Of course, but the point is Mr Yeats does not always know when to turn back. Like every Irishman he's haunted by his own ghosts.'

'Really? What ghosts are haunting you?'

He never answered my question. To demonstrate that he was in control, he led me briskly out of the room and back down the corridor. However, something told me that not even he was fully in command of what was happening.

I told him that I had heard rumours of a Republican spy within the British forces in Sligo. He showed little sign of surprise at my claims.

'Do you have any names?, he asked.

'None whatsoever. I only know that the source is highly placed.'

'That is indeed very interesting, Mr Adams.'

However, he seemed unconcerned, which suggested to me that he wasn't the informant.

'It would be a good idea for you to mention this to Inspector Grimes,' added Marley, and then he left me at the prison gates.

'That was your final warning, Mr Adams,' he shouted after me.

A cold sea breeze swept through the town, scattering the abandoned placards of the women protesters. A silvery moon caught glinting reflections in the wet cobbles as I crisscrossed the empty streets hoping to find some breathing space for my confused thoughts.

The jealousy of a love rival seemed too simple an explanation for Rosemary's death. Nor did it explain why her body was washed ashore in a coffin. I wondered had Clarissa been acting alone in her plot to haunt Oates, or had she the support of the Daughters of Erin and Maud Gonne? Ghostly tricks usually required the efforts of more than one person. Were they part of a political campaign to frighten Oates out of his wits and render him so powerless he could be manipulated like a puppet? A feeling of unease welled within me. There was something about the picture I could not see clearly. My head burning with questions, I left the grim coldness of Sligo gaol behind and headed straight for Yeats' hotel.

When I went up to their rooms, I was alarmed to discover that Yeats' condition had worsened. He lay in his wife's arms, his breathing fast and rasping. I examined him quickly, feeling a feverish temperature, but every time he awoke, he complained of the cold. The doctor arrived before midnight, and after taking his temperature and pulse, assured us that the patient would survive. However, he made us promise that Yeats would receive no visitors or experience any form of disagreeable emotion or excitement for at least three days.

21

O

THREE OF SWORDS

THE next Sunday morning, Sligo was all church bells and
shuttered windows, men doffing their hats and retreating out of
the rain into the darkness of doorways. Even the winding streets
that dissolved into the pouring griminess seemed redolent of a
particularly Irish form of self-effacement, designed to misdirect
the visitor, suggesting there was nothing here worth investigating
or bothering about.

The cobbles were wet and my squelching footsteps echoed
in the quiet streets. I turned round several times imagining the
echo of my feet might be the footsteps of a pursuer, a shadowy
agent or a policeman in black gumboots. I ran across an empty
square. Seagulls flapped their wings and flew high over the roofs.
I waited breathlessly in a doorway, surveying the soaked square
and only emerged again when I was sure no one was following
me. I stayed close to the walls and leaking drainpipes until I
arrived outside Yeats' hotel.

I ordered a pot of tea in an eating-house across the street,
through whose rain-swept windows I could watch the entrance
to the hotel. I sat in a dark alcove while a waitress moved a greasy
cloth back and forth across black tables, and watched me with
melancholy eyes. When she had finished wiping the tables, she
took down the pictures of boats hanging on the walls and began
cleaning them. The paintings were by a local artist, and depicted

sailing vessels that frequented Sligo's famous harbour. I was distracted by one of the names of the boats, *Cheerful Charlie*, inscribed upon its sleek stern. It was one of the codenames in Rosemary's journal.

Shortly after two o'clock, a young woman dashed out of the hotel. She was dressed in a dark raincoat beneath which the flannel of her dressing gown flapped as she ran. She paused before crossing the street, and seemed to stare straight at me. At first, I did not recognise her. I had not seen Georgie for a few days. She looked different. There was no longer anything calm or soft about the expression on her face. Her cheekbones were sharp and her eyes hollowed like that of a prisoner unused to daylight. Her face carried an expression of panic, a desperation that had probably been rising all morning. She ducked under a few shop awnings and, without a backward glance, disappeared into a public house.

I rose and made my way into the hotel and upstairs to Yeats' rooms. I told myself there was no cause for alarm or secrecy. The building was sunk in the afternoon calm of a provincial hotel, and the Yeatses were its only guests. The previous day, I had gleaned from the porter that Georgie would leave the hotel every afternoon while Yeats slept. Her excursions usually took her to the nearest pub, he told me, where she would order three gins with orange juice, one straight after the other.

The door to their rooms was unlocked. Slowly, I pushed it open. Beyond the columns of books, I made out the gaunt shape of Yeats, fast asleep on a reclining chair in what seemed like a strange cross between a fur suit and a bathrobe. His velvet blue sleeping cap matched perfectly the padded slipper on his left foot, but on the other he wore a black gum boot. I wondered had he injured his foot, or had Georgie misplaced the other slipper. A strong odour of sweet perfume, antiseptic and oddly, of cats, wafted from the room.

A specialist had travelled up from Dublin the previous day and dismissed my diagnosis of concussion in favour of Malta fever, an exotic illness transmitted through contaminated milk. He had recommended that Yeats should have bed-rest for seven days after his temperature returned to normal. During that time, he was only allowed custard, jellied consommé and three spoonfuls of brandy a day. Even by the standards of romantic poets, Yeats was a determined hypochondriac and wholeheartedly embraced the role of convalescent. However, the idea of anyone other than his young wife tending to his fevered body reduced him to tears. Hence the absence of a nurse and the desperation on Georgie's face as she escaped to the pub during his afternoon nap.

Careful not to disturb the slumbering poet, I made my way down a narrow corridor towards the bedroom door. A pale, fox-like face flashed in a mirror within the room and stared at me. I stepped back, heart racing. Dishes clattered in the kitchen below. On the street, a lamp man was busy illuminating the gas globes, casting a waxy glow through the windows. A coach drove past, its iron wheels ringing on the cobbles. When I looked again the face had disappeared. Perhaps it had been paranoia, an hallucination of some kind, or the reflection had been mine all along, startling me with its look of haunted unease.

I entered the bedroom and walked to a bedside cabinet upon which lay some drawings of Yeats' ancestors, a set of tarot cards and a collection of detective novels. Beneath the table, I found a heavy trunk with a lock but no key, which a search of the rest of the bedroom failed to uncover. I crept back to the study. I surveyed the contents of the room and my eyes alighted on a cuckoo clock on the wall that had stopped working. The hands were frozen at nine o'clock, the time Yeats and Georgie usually finished their evening interrogation of the spirit world. I crept over to the clock and opened the door to its cogs and wheels. Jammed against the winding mechanism was a silver key. I crept back to the bedroom with the key and opened the trunk.

From my perusal, I concluded that the reams of notes within were either the most extensive supernatural researches ever recorded by a creative mind, or the misguided product of a grand *folie à deux*. Georgie's script was thickly packed into a collection of folders which would have created an ocean of paper had I spread it on the floor. Fortunately, it had been catalogued with the poet's customary scientific zeal into the different voices or avatars, as Yeats called them. In some ways, it was a futile attempt to bring order to a thousand lines of madness. Out of this shifting ground of childish complaints, recycled dreams and philosophical gibberish, he had identified at least a dozen different spiritual 'instructors', as well as an untold number of 'frustrators', whose sole intention seemed to be to prevent Yeats from mastering the complex symbols and concepts relayed by the 'instructors'.

I opened the folder belonging to Leo, the spirit whose writing I had earlier noted very closely resembled that of Rosemary O'Grady's letter. The most conspicuous feature of his messages were the repeated reminders of secrecy, and the conspicuous manner in which they followed Georgie's personal agenda, frequently taking her side, praising her, while criticising Yeats. The spirit often drew attention to Georgie's physical needs, when she felt lonely, tired or hungry, or when she needed more attention or physical fulfilment in the marital bed.

I next came across a series of calculations and geometric designs. I stared at the shapes and numbers. What was it about them that struck me as oddly familiar? As though I had seen them perform another role, under a different guise. The way they formed a list, like a calendar of dates. What did I almost understand? I realised that I had found a clue not to the mystery of Yeats relationship with his young wife, but to something more secretive, something cruel and premeditated, the murders of Rosemary O'Grady and Captain Thomas Oates.

The sound of a soft pair of feet running up the stairs interrupted my reading. I bundled the folders back into the trunk and slid under the bed just as someone arrived at the door of Yeats' study. I heard Georgie call his name softly, but there was no answer. She hurried breathlessly into the bedroom, and without glancing in the direction of the bed, stepped into the adjoining bathroom and began running water into the tub.

My back burned where I had grazed it against the metal

springs of the mattress. I lay miserably, face pressed to the musty carpet. Remembering that the 'instructors' had forbidden any third party to peruse the script, I refrained from making my presence known, even if it meant that under the circumstances I was at risk of committing a significant indiscretion with Yeats' wife.

A minute later, Georgie emerged into the bedroom, undressed and collected her bathing robe. She was on her way back into the bathroom when something made her stop. My heart froze with anxiety. Her bare legs went rigid with something other than the cold. I glanced across the floor and noticed the trunk sticking out from under the cabinet.

'Willie,' she called again, this time with a note of impatience in her voice. She padded over to the trunk and flipped back the lid. After sorting through the papers for a few minutes, she gave an angry exclamation and hurried out of the room.

A muffled exchange between her and Yeats reached me through the wall. In a slightly slurred voice, she remonstrated with him about the unlocked trunk. His entreaties came back sounding confused and weakened by sleep and ill health.

'You promised me not to touch the scripts in my absence,' she hissed. 'Honestly, if a herd of buffalo had tramped through them, they could not be in a greater mess.'

Yeats made some reply and Georgie's voice shot back louder.

'I'm beginning to suspect you're trying to kill off my ghosts.'

'Kill off who?'

'Thomas and Anne. What have you done with their messages?'

'Hush.'

'Tell me the truth. You don't want to hear from them any more, or at least you wish to edit and amend their comments beyond recognition.' Her voice rose hysterically. 'You'd rather they were cast into the oblivion of eternity.'

Yeats sounded fully awake now. 'Am I permitted to tell you there is too much gin on your breath?'

Georgie's voice thickened with guilt. 'I know you disapprove of their instructions.'

'This is not the time for such a conversation. Wait till I am well and you are more sober, and then I will tell you what I think of their messages.'

'I want you to tell me now.'

'What do you want me to say?'

'Confess that you are planning to do away with my ghosts.'

Yeats' voice lost its meekness. 'The spirits will hear us. I beg you to be quiet.' I heard his body fall back against his chair. The sound of his racked coughing brought an abrupt end to the argument.

The carpet was soggy from the forgotten bath as I crept out the bedroom. When I stepped past the study door, Georgie was attending to Yeats with the weary concern of a wife who had married a man more than two decades her senior. Her mouth was grimly set as though she were storing up words for the spirits' next marital lecture.

22

NINE OF SWORDS

AFTER his coughing fit, Georgie made Yeats bathe in the cast-iron tub and then retire to bed. She fed him warm consommé and rubbed goose fat over his wheezing chest. She removed the proofs of his latest book of poetry that he had been trying to edit, and placed one of her detective thrillers firmly in his hands.

'The doctor warned you not to tax your mind.' She glared at him, her mouth set in a frown. Then she receded into the darkness of the room. The last thing he saw was her scowling mouth hanging by the closing door like that of a bad-tempered Cheshire cat.

Yeats dropped the book. He felt wrung out, exhausted to the core of his being. Fortunately, the soup and Georgie's massage had a lulling effect on him, so that when he rested his head against the pillow, he found himself drifting off immediately to sleep.

His mind slipped into a vaguely familiar fairyland of rain and wind making wavy patterns over glimmering bog land. Images flashed before him, propelled by his burning fever and the lingering agitation of their row. A man with a dark coat and a hat like a detective in one of Georgie's thrillers stood on his own, examining a body in a ditch. When the detective rolled the body over with his foot, the water-logged face of a monstrously overgrown baby stared back at him. He blew a whistle in alarm, and suddenly policemen were rushing out of bog holes and trenches, forming numerous coiling paths across the bog land, which swarmed thickly towards the detective. Before they could reach the baby, however, it roared with a mighty force that blew them all backwards. The baby roared again, and the policemen joined in, all of them roaring in unison with such devastating intensity that they were like frogs in danger of bursting their heads.

When he woke up it was the middle of the night. He tried to draw back the heavy blankets, but was reminded that the fever had reduced him to an enfeebled state. He tried to interpret the images of his nightmare. Dear God, he wondered, am I in danger of losing my head over this baby Georgie so desperately wants?

From the sound of his wife's hushed breathing, he guessed she was awake also. Their row had made everything seem so alien, its lingering hostility altering the shape of their bed, its orientation in the darkened room, even the outline of her body, as she lay turned away from him. It seemed to him that he was sharing his bed with not only his sensible, well-educated wife but a dark subcontinent of scolding female voices.

For the past fortnight, they had been trying to conceive a baby, a son, who would not only be a reincarnation of one of his ancestors, but become the future leader of an Irish republic. The child had grown in their excited imaginations to the status of a new messiah, a redeemer, but Yeats found the entire process taxing, more complex than that of writing a volume of poetry or one hundred plays. The spirit 'instructors' had ordered them to conduct complicated rituals and meditations involving swords and green ribbons and pentagrams. Night after night, they lay in the different positions of the compass, surrounded by symbols of the four elements, mindlessly following the erotic directions given to them.

At the same time as all of this overwhelming physical intimacy, he felt himself being pushed ever further to the margins of her life. They had been making slow but efficient progress together on their spiritual quest, but now he found himself tipped back into unknown sexual territory. Rather alarmingly, the body of the woman whom he had fallen in love with was soon going to change and grow in unfamiliar ways. The idea of his unborn son in her expanding belly disturbed him, its embryonic body advancing towards him like an unstoppable beast. The burst of water and blood that would herald his son's new life would also ring in unpleasant domestic changes. He would be deprived of the total attention of his wife, upon whom he had come to depend, and disturbed day and night from his poetic reveries by the squalling noise of an infant.

Georgie, however, had taken on a radiance, a ghostly shimmer as though the new life she was inviting into her womb had put her in touch with a heightened level of reality. He was unable to get over the indignant suspicion that she was withholding something from him, something more than the biological secret of creation.

He shifted his body, making the bed-frame creak. He guessed that it was sometime around three o'clock, the hardest hour to get back to sleep. It would not be daylight for another four hours at least. Georgie turned on her back and even though she did not speak, he could tell that she was lying next to him with her eyes wide open staring at the ceiling. For a while he did not move, wishing her to think he was fast asleep. The next thing he remembered, a church bell was tolling, and a band of moonlight had crept across their bed. It was much later but not yet dawn.

His thoughts kept returning to the trunk containing the script, lying there on the bedroom floor, a repository for all the answers to his provocative questions about life and death. He yearned to shake the bundles of pages that had been flung from her feverish hand. The wish to shake anything close at hand left him trembling. In the darkness, he felt overwhelmed by anger, and furiously rotated his body beneath the covers.

This time she could not ignore his agitation. Without uttering a word, she rose and lit a candle. With her usual composed motions, she chose a detective novel from the pile on her bedside table, sat back in bed and began reading.

After a few minutes, he muttered darkly, 'It is quite clear that for you there is no abyss.'

She put down the book and lay back in bed. Neither of them moved.

'Aren't you going to snuff out that candle?' he said.

She got up and put out the flame. The slightest vibration of their breath seemed magnified one hundred times in the darkness. He tried to control the rise and fall of his chest. The possibility rose in his mind that either Georgie or her ghosts were bent on torturing him for past misdemeanours, and that his desire to create a new philosophical system from the script was doomed from the outset. Philosophy had a structure, but so too did madness to a lunatic. Perhaps her automatic writing contained no spiritual guidance, no messages from the gods, no history or mythology, just an endless stream of free associations and behind it all a dead silence. A silence as deep as that from within the rocks and cliffs of Sligo's rugged coast.

He sighed heavily. The life of a poet was a difficult one, with many setbacks. One could easily lose touch with the currents of history, with what really mattered. Then there were the months of silence to deal with, the loss of purpose, the sickness of body and mind. What was he doing back in Ireland? He had wandered onto the stage of important events, wanting to be a part of their pattern, their ebb and flow, but somehow the tide of history had cast him aside.

He had not suspected how serious the younger generation of revolutionaries were in their planning, but then the Easter Rising had taken the entire country by surprise. Nor had he envisaged the public's reaction to the court martial and execution of its fifteen leaders. The rebellion had been extreme, insane even, but something about it, in hindsight, seemed beautiful and fitting and terrible. Intuitively, he could see that their intentions had been correct, but he baulked at the violence their actions had triggered, the cult of blood and sacrifice to which they had devoted themselves. He wanted to invent a way out of this predicament for his fellow countrymen with whom he had a permanent and unshakeable bond. It was his responsibility. How could it be otherwise for Ireland's leading poet?

His mind returned to the trunk on the floor, which now resembled an indefensible outpost of his imagination, one that lay open to all sorts of assault and battery. He wondered was the script a means of diverting his attention from the problems of his marriage and his country, a way of escaping the world of politics and marital responsibilities, an opening not into the self, but into lunacy?

In the darkness, he listened closely to the sound of her chest. He realised she was controlling her breathing, pretending to be asleep. He reached out and touched her on her chest, above her heart, but she did not flinch. How very different she was from her rivals in love, those reckless and passionate women who had vexed his heart for decades. So much more calm and remote and disciplined. She lay beside him feigning sleep as if nothing could waken her. Perhaps it was the same skill she used to convince him she was slumbering during their séances.

A coldness came over him, the coldness of death itself. He thought of her automatic writing and wondered what had been play-acting and what had been genuine contact with the spirits. His suspicions increased, tearing up whole masses of rooted belief. The morbid thought struck him that he was wedded to a fraud, a charlatan, the most subtle con-artist he had yet to meet in his thirty years of investigating the paranormal.

'Why are you playing at being asleep?' he asked, his voice husky with dread.

She did not reply, as though answering that question might prompt her to talk about other subjects she was too afraid to discuss. He closed his eyes and the question 'What else are you playing at?' came easily to mind but with great difficulty to his lips.

He felt the bed shake slightly as she moved away. Perhaps she had guessed the question that was preying upon his mind.

'I'm not the one playing at inventing a religion,' she replied, her voice sounding calm.

'How am I playing at inventing a religion?'

'All your unanswerable questions about mystical patterns and symbols.'

'We are entering a time of great upheaval. A new age should have a new religion.'

'Is that why you stayed with me rather than chase after Gonne and her daughter? The script taught you that I was worth loving.'

Yeats closed his eyes. A numbness hit his heart. 'I never thought you weren't worth loving.'

'But I always felt it.' She pronounced the words carefully, making sure he heard them. 'Those frantic women you surrounded yourself with. How could I compete with all that melodrama, all that nervous energy? You only stayed with me because I can do what your Mr Adams seems incapable of. I can catch your ghosts, channel their messages, reveal their secrets. You love me only because you are an artist and I supply your outlines. I draw the shapes while you paint in the colours and take all the credit. If I had known the true state of affairs, I would never have consented to marrying you.'

He felt his chest tighten and another coughing fit come on.

'Your accusations are smothering me. Why are we putting such effort into having this child if you believe I do not love you?' The coughing choked the rest of his questions.

Eventually the fit subsided and a silence grew between them. It continued for a long time, so long he drifted back to sleep. He was brought back to consciousness by the sound of her voice, so small and quiet that the words were hardly there, like those of a ghost already fading from view.

'Goodnight, my dear Willie,' she whispered.

23

NINE OF CUPS

I BARELY recognised my reflection in the darkened window. My coat no longer held me at my shoulders, while my face looked hollow, my eyes restless and sunken. A fiercely guarded bundle bulged under my thin coat. I realised I was turning into my own idea of a mad Irishman obsessively carrying his secrets next to his heart. Without hesitating to knock, I pushed open the door to the cavernous shop and stepped inside.

Ahearne stood at his bloody counter. His eyes conveyed an expression of restrained contempt and curiosity.

'Ah, the snooping Englishman, I'd thought I'd seen the last of you.'

'I'm sorry to disappoint you.'

'How do you find Sligo?'

The ruinous estates, the turbulent Atlantic, the rebellious women on horseback, at that moment all were unexpectedly uplifting to me. I felt as though I had stumbled upon the secret heart of Yeats' poetry. Perhaps I truly had gone native, and become a fully signed up resident of Sligo's fairyland of mists and misfits, where all the signposts of reasoning lay trampled face down in the mud.

I placed the bundle of papers on the counter and asked Ahearne for his assistance in deciphering the strange messages contained within. I explained how I had taken the pages from

Yeats' script and that they showed striking similarities with Rosemary O'Grady's letter and her journal.

'This is not a reference library,' he snapped. 'Besides, I'm afraid of angering Yeats' ghosts.' His fingers tapped lightly on the packet and then withdrew.

'How?'

'They don't want anyone, even Yeats, to understand the message of the script. They send him symbol after symbol to crowd his mind and confuse him.'

'Then why bother communicating with them in the first place? Why would they not want Yeats to know the truth?'

'Because we are all mortal and flawed, especially a literary genius like Yeats. Only a god should know the truth. We mortals tend to be deaf to the things we need to know the most. For instance, Yeats should pay more attention to his young wife, while you should buy a ticket for the next boat back to England.'

I explained the connections I had made. 'In these pages from the script, the writing is the same as Rosemary's letter to the Golden Dawn. Even the geometric designs and dates match those I found in her journal.'

His eyes sparked with interest.

'I came to you because Yeats told me you were the greatest expert on the occult on this island.'

Pleased at this compliment, Ahearne held out his hand and I passed over the packet, thinking guiltily of the unseemliness of letting this strange little man eavesdrop on Yeats' ghosts.

He scanned eagerly through the pages, rasping their corners with his dry fingers. 'His little scribbler has been busy. Are there any more of these?'

'Hundreds upon hundreds. These were the only ones I had time to take.'

Ahearne licked his lips. Sweat formed on his pale forehead. He stared at the inky writing that spread in all directions, and the clusters of drawings that grew along the margins.

'I have an idea what these patterns might represent,' he said. He turned to one of the volumes on his shelves. After several minutes, he raised his head and said, 'Progress, definitely progress.'

However, it was at least a further half hour before he closed the reference book.

'What light do you think these symbols will shine on Rosemary's death?' he asked.

'I'm not sure. I have a vague idea they might explain what drew her to Blind Sound. But perhaps there's nothing remarkable about the lists at all.'

'The messages from the script are remarkable. Truly ground-breaking. They possess a licentiousness and daring I have rarely encountered in the spiritual world. I had never thought our ethereal companions could be so charged with sexual energy.'

'But what about the dates and geometric signs,' I interrupted. 'Do they refer to cult rituals? Some kind of initiation ceremony?'

'No. I believe they have nothing to do with ceremonies or rituals.'

'What then? Politics? Revolutionary tactics?'

'Not these either.'

'Do you have any idea at all?'

'The connection between Rosemary's journal and the spirit messages is the universal magic of the number twenty-eight. They are both moon charts. Rosemary's, as far as I can interpret, was recording the sea's sly tides, while the spirits are tracking the secret female tides, and in particular, the menstrual cycles of Yeats' wife.' He flattened out the pages of the script. 'We see here the great circle of twenty-eight lunar phases with precise instructions as to how often and in what positions to have intercourse. I shan't explain the code any further for fear of making you blush. Suffice it to say, these are details which should be confined to the Yeats' bed chamber.'

They had been, I thought to myself. Now I understood why Yeats, an international expert on the occult, had been less than keen to publicise his wife's expertise at automatic writing.

Ahearne turned to Rosemary's chart. 'Here we see the same circle of twenty-eight phases along with what are possibly water depth recordings, times and locations.'

Ahearne's theory made sense. I saw how both sets of numbers and drawings were based upon the lunar calendar. One of them was written by a woman desperate to conceive a baby, while the other by a woman secretly recording the lunar phases of the tides to help a submarine or boat make a clandestine landing on the Sligo coast.

Ahearne's eyes shone with admiration. 'Rosemary was attempting to plot a navigational course for smugglers along a very treacherous part of the coast. Her task was far more difficult than that of a helmsman with a compass and sea maps under his nose. She had to work out the meaning of the waves and the tides, as well as measure the depth of the water at different points in the bay. The sea is a secret world, more secret than the invisible world of spirits, and just as full of portents and clues.'

Ahearne watched me with eyes that looked neither old nor weak. He was aware of the windfall of leads his breakthrough offered to a ghost-catcher. However, I removed the bundle of papers reluctantly, as though they comprised a trap of my own making.

'Do you want my advice?' he asked.

'Of course.'

'This is a much more delicate investigation than even Yeats first realised.'

'How?'

'There is a political dimension. Irish Republicans will not want their movement mired in scandals involving murdered smugglers. Be careful of what rash steps people like Gonne might make to preserve their good name, and remember she has a powerful protector working within the Irish constabulary.'

'Who are you talking about? Inspector Grimes?'

'I never betray my informants.'

I left Ahearne's shop and wandered aimlessly through Sligo's side streets, wondering how I was going to proceed with the evidence that Rosemary had been involved in smuggling. Almost immediately, I was aware that I was being followed. They had no faces, these shadows; they were more like phantoms. I paused at a street corner, waiting for them to approach, but for some reason they held back.

In the silence, I could hear the wash of the sea. It seemed to be slowly wandering towards me, over the roofs of the houses. I came across a river and followed it down to the harbour. I could just make out Rosses Point and the cliffs of Blind Sound through the evening sea mist that had settled over the coast. I walked to the pier's edge and stood contemplating the waves as they lapped against the grey walls.

I went over in my mind the complicated chain of events that had begun when a young woman's body drifted ashore in a coffin, and ended with Captain Oates' murder on the same beach. I tried to digest the fact that Rosemary had been a smuggler, and Clarissa's claims that a man in some sort of uniform was involved in the background, pulling the strings. Had it been Captain Oates or a member of the local Constabulary? Nothing was as it seemed. The collection of evidence and the establishment of a chain of proof was so much more difficult set against the murky backdrop of a country on the brink of rebellion. Two people had been killed and an innocent girl awaited trial. How was a secretary from London, intent on finding physical evidence for the existence of spirits, going to discover what really happened? And what if I did manage to look into the dark heart of Sligo and discern the face of a murderer? What then? Who could I trust to tell my suspicions? A feeling of impotence rose within me, along with a sickly sense of dread.

The throbbing sound of wind and water on the move distracted me from my thoughts. I looked up in time to see a sailing boat round the pier as slowly as a piece of driftwood. Its sleek lines contrasted sharply with the waddling tubs of moored fishing boats and the dark hulls of steamers. There was no one on deck, but somehow I sensed the presence of an invisible hand controlling its movements. The wind rippling through the sails carried the boat on a lazy pirouette towards the open sea. I stared at the name painted on the side, just visible above the lapping waves. *Cheerful Charlie*, it read.

When the boat reached the end of the harbour wall, a figure appeared from below and began adjusting the rigging. The wind moulded the sail, filled it taut, and soon the boat was slipping beyond the lamp-lit frontage of the harbour and skidding across Sligo Bay, a ragged line of surf rising from its prow.

Darkness advanced, a moonless night, I thought, perfect for smuggling. I was about to return to the town when I noticed a light shining from the harbour master's cabin. Through its window, I spied a moon-faced man studying a large sea chart that kept rolling up like the spring of a watch.

I knocked on the door and greeted him good evening.

'An Englishman, sir?' he asked.

'Yes.' My throat constricted as though I was trying to swallow a piece of gristle. How strange it sounded to be an Englishman. And how curiously dangerous a word it seemed in the gathering darkness.

However, the master's face was open and friendly. 'Lost on your evening stroll, sir?'

'Not quite. I'm trying to find out who owns the sailing boat that just left the harbour. The *Cheerful Charlie*.'

'I can't disclose such details.'

'Does it belong to a member of the Crown forces?'

His eyes said yes. Then a wary look overtook him. 'Are you a British agent, sir?'

'Yes,' I lied in a clipped tone.

'You and your comrades will be very busy tonight then, sir.'

'We're always busy.'

I bid him goodnight and walked back to the end of the harbour pier. The boat had long since disappeared into the unknown gloom. I stared out at the tortuous cliffs of Blind Sound and watched as a small winking light sent out a secret signal from the black rocks. For the first time since arriving in Sligo, I felt a firmness and clarity to my thoughts. A sense that I could penetrate the mysteries surrounding that remote western shore.

24

NINE OF RODS

THERE was no moon above, just a canopy of silver stars creating a pattern of glittering fish scales on the sea at Blind Sound. I paid a tinker to get me there on his pony and trap, and he rode like a soul escaping the gates of hell. It was past midnight when he dropped me off.

The force of the sea-breeze I encountered on the beach made me feel as though I was still being pulled by a galloping horse. I leaned forward and traversed the beach, guided by the booming of the waves and the stinging wings of spray. In the darkness, I felt that the silver strand was a narrow bridge between two voids, the sea on one side and the black cliffs on the other. I found shelter behind a large rock, and making myself as unobtrusive as possible, sat and watched the faint light playing on the waves.

I didn't have long to wait. Two swimmers, bare-chested and muscle-bound, emerged from the waves with thick ropes tied around their waists. They dragged themselves onto the sand. As soon as they had their breath back, they began hauling on the ropes until a string of barrels floated ashore. They lifted the barrels one at a time, and walked them through the slippery rocks and boiling surf until they reached the mouth of the cave. There was something practised and disciplined about their movements. After they had delivered the final pair of barrels into the cave, they clambered in and disappeared from view.

I crept after them, aware that I was stepping into a dangerous void. I had spent so many days in Sligo staring into the deep unanswering gloom of Blind Sound that it had taken on a terrible beauty, one which I desperately wanted to fathom. The cave loomed before me, its arched entrance like a man-made tunnel running east into the heart of the cliff. The tide had filled it with rushing water, which the smugglers had used to float their contraband out of sight. I could hear the echoes of the barrels knocking against rocks as the incoming water sent them cannoning deep into the tunnel. I waded into the water and felt myself sink into a heavy load of seaweed that rose and fell with every wave washing into the cave's recesses.

I waded deeper, feeling the current of the tide rippling around me, moving at increasing speed. Every now and again I caught the echo of someone barking orders from deep within, and a ghostly ripple of light play upon the slick tunnel wall.

I kept moving until the water grew shallow and I felt soft sand beneath my feet. The tunnel rose slightly and led back to another opening to the sea. The Atlantic swelled and broke against a steeply sloping beach. I stopped. The men and the barrels had disappeared. There was nowhere for them to have gone, except back into the ocean. I returned down the tunnel. The tide had ebbed making my return journey slightly easier.

As I explored the cave, the voices returned, as though the men had been waiting in the shadows for me. I heard the moan of wood rubbing against rock and the scolding voice, shouting orders. A ribbon of light appeared in the water beneath a jutting rock draped in barnacles and seaweed. Beside it was a small iron wheel, which I had missed the first time. I turned it first clockwise and then anti-clockwise. It groaned, and slowly the barnacle-crusted rock began to shift. It wasn't a rock at all, but a solid iron gate, cleverly disguised, which concealed an entry to a secret tunnel. I kept turning the wheel and the gate opened fully, the seawater rushing in, dragging me along with it. Pieces of a loose-fitting jigsaw began to lock together in my mind. The opening and closing of the gate acted as a sluice, which might account for the mysterious behaviour of the tides and currents in Blind Sound. I swam with that slick and furtive current and pulled myself onto a narrow ledge running alongside the gulley.

Traces of the men's echoing voices lingered and then faded. I sat without moving, listening intently, feeling the tension in my shivering body, the taste of apprehension in my mouth. Crouching, I made my way deeper into the tunnel, feeling my way along sharp outcroppings. There was nothing but silence and darkness. Even the wash of the sea was muted. The smugglers must have made their escape along this secret tunnel, I thought.

Eventually, the rock wall gave way to earth and crumbling shale; the salt smell of the sea was replaced by the odour of soil and organic matter. My hands felt around strange smooth shapes embedded in the soil like fossilised roots and eroded rocks. I pressed on, my instinct still warning me that I was in grave danger. The smugglers might be waiting somewhere ahead in countless invisible nooks. Or they might be inches away from my groping fingers, ready to launch an ambush.

Soon I saw a flickering light and heard the men whisper less than fifty yards further up the tunnel. Their hoarse voices brought a level of intimacy to the gloom. They were murmuring about coffins and dead bodies. I moved forward as quietly as I could but my feet crunched on something skeletal and friable. The whispering stopped and the flickering light vanished. Minutes later the light reappeared on the cave wall, only this time it was closer, brightening and fading with the steady rhythm of a pendulum. Flickering shadows jumped towards me. They were advancing towards me with their lamps.

Slipping and falling, I clambered back the way I had come. The ground was interspersed with rocks and I kept catching my feet. My clothes were torn and my fingers covered in blood from the repeated falls. I kept going, hoping to smell or hear the sea, or glimpse starlight on breaking waves. I plunged back into the pitch-black water of the gulley, but the sea's hazards proved more unpredictable and less easily avoided. A rogue barrel riding the current came rocketing up the cave and struck me across the head. Knocked sideways, I coughed and spluttered, my throat scalded with brine. I moved back up the cave, watching out for the dangerous silhouettes of escaped barrels. The lack of light made the network of caves and tunnels appear more labyrinthine than they actually were. Unfortunately, the sea was rising through the interlocking caves, cutting off my path to Blind Sound. I was forced to crawl back up the tunnel to try and make my escape via dry land.

I tried to read the air by listening and sniffing. The updraught of salt air fought with the mineral smell of earth. The muffled sound of men moving in cramped confines was broken into echoes and garbled by the advancing wash of breaking waves. I found myself a niche, and tucking up my knees, sat and waited.

I was convinced the smugglers were still searching for me, but when the sound of their voices faded and then vanished altogether, I began to suspect they had made good their escape. A while later, I jerked awake, horrified to have fallen asleep in that dark chamber that was as cold as a crypt.

I spent the next few hours trailing miserably through a lattice of pitch-black tunnels until I was absolutely spent of energy. In the seething darkness, I might as well have been trapped in a spider's giant web. In places, the roof had collapsed, and great slabs of earth shifted out of place like a fallen deck of cards. I came across lumps of broken wood that must have acted as supports for the tunnel roof. Another set of cards shifted out of place in my mind, one bearing the faces of Maud Gonne, Clarissa and Captain Oates. How much did they know about this tunnel? I wondered.

At one point, I felt a breath of cold air on my face. Higher up on the wall, my fingers found the lower rungs of a metal ladder, leading to a hidden cleft. I clambered up the ladder and saw that it led to an exit hole. A view of the starlit sky hung above as from a distant window pane. I climbed further and waited a few feet beneath the exit, listening tensely. At first, the only sound was a sea breeze ruffling through marram grass. Then I heard voices approach, low cautious voices. They were searching for something. Small stones and twigs crunched underfoot as the men above extended their investigations. The tension made my stomach knot. I heard the scrape of stone against stone and then a disturbingly hollow clonk as a slab of rock was shifted across the exit hole, sealing me in pitch blackness. The cool draught of night air was replaced by the iodine tang of seaweed welling up from below. I wedged my back and shoulders against the rock but it would not budge.

For the first time of my life, I felt the terror of being buried alive. I crouched against a hollow in the cave wall, thinking that it might end up being my grave. I felt a tail slither across my leg. There would be rats, mice and other vermin living in colonies close by. I ran my tongue over dried lips and tasted blood. My mouth felt full of salt, and as time passed, I grew thirstier. I could hear groundwater trickling from the roof of the tunnel. I knelt and tried to catch the drops in my mouth but with little success. By a stroke of fortune, my groping hands found a rock that had cracked into the rough shape of a bowl in which water had formed a little pool. I raised the rock to my parched lips and drank slowly. The water was slightly warm, with the faint metal tang of groundwater, but delicious.

I slipped back into an uncomfortable sleep, and awoke cold and stiff, staring at a pale light creeping from the upper end of the tunnel. Daylight at last. I pushed my back against the wall and looked around me. While I had slept, someone had removed the slab of rock covering the opening. I sensed my surroundings in fits, moments of clarity alternating with confusion. The oddly shaped rocks, I now saw, were human bones, and the pieces of wood the splintered remains of coffins. The tunnel had wormed its way through some sort of cemetery. I shuddered when I realised the rock bowl I had drunk so greedily from was in fact the upper half of a human skull. When I realised that I had sought refuge amid the remains of human skeletons, my stomach convulsed with nausea. Falling on all fours, I ejected its contents in a stream of vomit. My mind was still churning through the horror when I heard the low tones of men's voices from above.

One by one, a group of black silhouettes assembled around the light of the exit hole like dark birds gathering on a branch. Suddenly, I was alert to every detail happening around me. I thought of the collapsed graves, the landslides on the beach, Rosemary's body enfolded in a twenty-year-old coffin, and the pauper's coffin found by Gonne, and the entire malign operation became clear in my head.

I rolled to the side and tried to clamber back down the tunnel but the figures cut off my only escape route. In the pale light, I saw Inspector Grimes' face bending over me, his inquisitive eyes examining me closely. He wore his uniform but he seemed larger, swollen with menace, like one of the floating barrels. More figures slipped out of the darkness and crowded around him. They weren't wearing their police uniforms, but I recognised most of them. The only person I didn't see was Wolfe Marley.

'Welcome to my crypt, Mr Adams,' said Grimes, his bulk crowding out the light, his gun so close to me I could smell its oiled metal casing.

'An insatiable curiosity mixed with a death wish, that's the fatal flaw with you ghost-catchers,' he said. 'You must have known that by coming here tonight you would risk everything, including your life, but foolishly you had to see for yourself.'

I scrabbled against the wall, searching for a stone or a piece of bone, but it was pointless trying to resist. I was a panicked amateur surrounded by a gang of professional criminals.

'All you had to do was take my advice and stay away from Blind Sound. You could have left Sligo at any time, but you didn't and now you're going to pay the price.'

'The same advice you gave to Captain Oates.'

Grimes did not blink. It was like talking to a statue. 'So have you figured it out yet?'

'What?'

'The puzzle.'

'What puzzle?'

'Why the body of a nineteen-year-old rebel was found washed ashore in a coffin from the last century?'

'Puzzles are always easy when you know the answer.'

Two of the men pitched towards me and snapped back my arms, forcing me to arch my neck. Under Grimes' instructions, they began binding me with tight ropes.

'Your problem is that you approached the mystery with too many assumptions and preconceptions. You believed that Rosemary died because of some complicated ritual or bizarre accident, but the answer was much simpler than that. We killed her because she discovered our secret smuggling tunnels. We placed her body in a coffin for the same reason every corpse is placed in a coffin, to bury it and put it beyond sight forever. Obvious isn't it? End of puzzle.'

'So why did the coffin wash ashore?'

'The solution to that question lies in the nature of the sea.' He surveyed the human remains embedded in the tunnel walls. 'I see you've been making yourself at home in the stranger's bank.'

'What is this place? Some sort of burial ground?' My hands, tied behind my back, groped at fistfuls of dirt but were unable to throw them. Grimes circled and paced around me, like a predator waiting its moment to spring forward.

'The ground around us was used during the last century to bury unidentified bodies washed up on the beach. Disasters at sea, sailors and fishermen washed overboard, suicides swept away by rivers. Because their Christian names weren't known, the unfortunate souls couldn't be buried in consecrated ground. Over the decades, the sea has eroded these tunnels into the bank, and carried away parts of the graveyard. The night we killed Rosemary we came across a coffin that was intact and decided it was the best hiding place for her corpse. We buried the coffin back into the tunnel wall, as deeply as we could. We assumed that if the coffin was ever found it would be simply buried again, no questions asked. After all, the unknown dead command no one's attention. We hadn't counted on a sea storm eroding the wall and washing the coffin from its resting place right before the prying eyes of Captain Oates.'

'What about the swimmers with ropes?'

'Have you ever stopped to consider how difficult the business of smuggling is? The sea is the worst criminal of all. I wrecked several yachts along this coast not to mention the loss of countless barrels of merchandise. I discovered the only safe way to bring in the contraband was to have swimmers tow the barrels in on a rope. Even then, I lose a third of my bounty. The tide that rises through these tunnels has sucked away a fortune in brandy.' He crouched in front of me like a dog about to bare its fangs. His men drew closer, bristling with violence.

'You're no longer a policeman,' I accused him. 'You're a smuggler and a murderer.'

My words were cut off by an oil rag stuffed into my mouth, which forced my tongue down my throat. I gagged as someone pulled a sack over my head. The smell of oil stung my eyes and made my breathing laboured.

'Unfortunately for you, we can't stop now,' said his voice, the only firm thing in the darkness. 'This is our prime time, our window of opportunity. What do you think will happen when the insurrectionists rise up and overthrow British Rule? What will happen to the Irish Constabulary then? Where will we go? The War Office will abandon us to our fates in a country run by priests and peasants. The contents of these barrels are our pension, our security against a hostile future.'

I writhed against my captors. I kicked back with my legs and struck my head against a sharp rock. Then everything went black.

When I returned to consciousness, I found myself trapped in a tiny cavity with only enough space for my curled up body. I held my breath and wriggled my shoulders, and the tiny cavity swung into motion, rocking back and forth. I was floating in some sort of barrel or tub. I called out but no one answered. I listened to the slow-paced sound of waves washing against the sides, solitary as the tolling of a bell, and lay still waiting for God only knew what.

25

QUEEN OF CUPS

YEATS was unable to remember for how long, how many hours or days he had spent in the hotel bedroom, recovering from his illness. His mind floated away from his body and wandered through the dirty side streets of Sligo town and out to vantage points along the wild coast. He spied the wreckage of great estates, laurel and clematis running with abandon across the once flourishing gardens. He saw unbridled horses galloping across dawn-bleached beaches, young women full of anger and longing sinking into the deathless foam. He watched as phantoms that could neither touch nor hear nor see led him through secret tunnels of churning water to the dreaded gateway between this world and the next.

His mind drifted in and out of sleep. A weary tenacity swept him on like a swimmer too weak to fight the current. His mind flitted through the events of the past month, sorting through the countless gestures and expressions he had observed. He kept imagining himself returning exhausted through the deserted streets of Sligo, to find Georgie waiting for him like a guard at the threshold of a darkened room, her arms crossed, a frown on her lips. A powerful wind rushed through his mind and the room filled with fluttering pages. 'Whose wings are these?' she asked. But it was only the inescapable pages, falling and rising between them, pages crowded with words, smudged and urgent and full of wretched spelling mistakes, pages like the state of his mind, bursting with rage and frustration.

When he switched on the bedside lamp and sat up in bed, he could still see her face and page upon page of her writing flash before his half-closed eyes like flickering images from a magic lantern. He was so agitated he could not sleep, and his eyes, desperate to go on searching for the meaning behind the words, left his weakened body and floated down into an abyss of lurking terrors, half-human beasts, unborn children and screaming birds, all whirling in a gyre beneath a stormy sky that resembled a monstrous black rose.

Later in the night, he was aware of Georgie slipping quietly into the bedroom. The dark illuminations of his mind had vanished, leaving him with the sobering realisation that it was not the spirit world that had dragged him back to Sligo, but the influence of a more mortal hand. Someone a lot closer to home. With this insight, he felt the silver cords binding him to the ghost of Rosemary O'Grady fall away one by one. The letter addressed to him was a piece of pure fiction. A fragment of ridiculous fantasy.

He could see the motivation behind it, now. At one stroke, the letter-writer had swept him out of reach of the Zeppelin bombers, as well as the clutches of Gonne's daughter Iseult and the entire London literary and spiritualist scene. She had cleverly whetted his appetite for spiritual investigation as well as pulling on his emotional heartstrings. She had manipulated him completely.

All his feelings of insecurity about his marriage resurrected themselves. How little he had learned about life in his fifty-two years, to allow a twenty-five-year-old woman to deceive him on so many levels. But then, he thought, modern women mature much more quickly than their male counterparts. Georgie might not spend sleepless nights pondering metaphysical problems, but the light of wisdom shone clearly from her face. Perhaps life would be much easier if he simply allowed himself to be guided by that light.

He broke the silence. 'My ghost-catcher tells me there are no ghosts, Georgie. Just you and me.'

A load fell from his shoulders immediately, and he decided to show all his cards when she didn't reply. 'It was you that sent me Rosemary's letter, wasn't it?'

He felt her stiffen. Clearly this was the question she least wanted to hear. She had been counting on his natural discretion to prevent him ever mentioning the subject.

'Please don't talk,' she urged him. 'You'll tire yourself out. I can see the colour has completely left your cheeks.'

He savoured the small victory her response had delivered. Minutes before, he had been filled with the insecurity of a husband confronted by a woman who was more like a stranger than a wife. For her part, Georgie seemed to grow more vulnerable. She fidgeted distractedly with the edge of the blanket, the colour rising to her cheeks. For a moment, he feared he might have pushed her too far.

'Is this what you've been thinking about during your fever?' She talked as if she was trying to gain time.

'Yes.'

They both sat in bed, saying nothing for a while. They listened to the wind blowing fiercely against the window pane. Somehow the remorseless wind was reason enough for them to continue lying together.

'I'm not ashamed of what I've done,' she said in a calm voice. 'I was working to save my marriage.'

'Is that meant to make me feel ashamed? Are you suggesting I am the one to blame for this tower of deceit?' Any sense of satisfaction he had felt suddenly vanished. 'If your aim is to shame me to make yourself feel better, then you are wasting your time.'

'I wasn't the only one who deceived you.'

'Who else then? Who else had a hand in this mess of lies?' He thought of Maud Gonne, Iseult, Charles Adams, the other members of the Golden Dawn.

'You deceived yourself.' She waited for him to absorb what she had said. 'But don't you see how necessary it all was? You merited a great lie, one designed to bring you back to Sligo, where your country and its people need you.'

'And what about the automatic writing? Is that a complete fabrication, too?'

'After we were married, you wouldn't speak to me. You threw yourself into your books and letter-writing. I had to express myself somehow.'

'By all means, a woman should express herself.'

'But you made it impossible. Your ghosts and your past loves oppressed me. Marriage oppressed me. I was in dread of losing my identity. I needed some form of expression.'

'You should have articulated yourself in verse or prose. Kept your feelings on record, if only for ourselves.'

'I was afraid of your criticism.'

'I would have understood.'

'No. It is so different for you. You had the good fortune to be born a man. You have the automatic freedom to express yourself, without taboos. You can write whatever you want to write, say whatever you want to say. When you married me, I became the wife of a great poet. I was voiceless, a new bride trapped in a roomful of old ghosts. No wonder then, that I made them speak for me.'

Yeats sank his head back on the pillow, and stared at the ceiling with the look of a man watching his cherished dreams dissolve like mist into the darkness. How easy it is to be deluded by the wonders of the imagination, he thought to himself. He pulled the sheet up to his chin and closed his eyes. He was aware of Georgie settling down beside him, following the same sequence of movements as every other night, smoothing the bed sheet and plumping up her pillow, loosening her dark hair and placing the pins on the bedside table. He felt her seek out the familiar hollow of her pillow. Neither of them spoke for what seemed a long time.

'Willie?' She reached out to him suddenly.

'Yes?' He held her hand.

'Am I demented?'

'No more than any other human, I would say.'

They lay side by side, holding each other, until the drifting irrationality of their waking life dissolved into the cold sanity of sleep.

26

PAGE OF CUPS

GRIMES followed his men back up the tunnel, reluctant to leave, a man contentedly reflecting upon the end of another dangerous but profitable mission. It had been a good night's smuggling rounded off with a satisfactory conclusion to the problems caused by the prying Englishman. He recalled the pathetic sight of Adams' limp body as he was sealed inside the barrel, deriving a grim amusement from the watery fate that awaited him. He stopped suddenly, and crouched low in the tunnel. The sight of a strange light drifting against the cave wall had interrupted his self-congratulatory thoughts.

'What's that?' asked one of his men. 'Some sort of signal?'

Grimes snuffed out his lamp with his fingers and ordered his men to do the same. They waited as the light grew closer. A figure in plain clothes was illuminated. A man with a black cap and a long belted raincoat approached them. It was Marley, looking disappointed, as though he'd arrived too late at a much anticipated sporting contest. He was surrounded by other men in plainclothes, more British agents. They gathered around the smugglers quietly.

'Where is our ghost-catcher?'

'Floating out to sea.'

'Like Captain Oates?'

'Yes. He's found what he came looking for. His trip to Ireland is complete.'

'That is disappointing. I had hoped he would experience the full effects of the British justice system in this troubled land.'

The cave walls sighed with the echo of a wave rippling in from the sea.

'What do you want?' Grimes' eyes glittered.

'One less murder. I want to take Adams to Sligo gaol where he will face a summary trial for treason.'

If Grimes was surprised, he did not show it in his voice.

'What do I get in return?'

'The address of a house.'

'Whose house?'

'Maud Gonne and the Daughters of Erin.'

I lingered in a suspended state of shock, between amnesia and agony, shaking with the coldness of the water that leaked through the barrel's cracks, tossing and turning within its creaking walls like a man falling a long way. The more I moved, the more the barrel rolled with the waves so that it felt as though I was floating far out to sea, but I could still hear the reassuring hiss of surf pounding upon a nearby beach. The water was stingingly salty, rising all the time around my cramped body, and I fought hard to find a breathing space. As each moment passed, it took more and more effort and concentration to get a breath. I was struggling to keep my chin out of the water when, above the grating of the barrel against the rocks, I heard what sounded like a commotion, voices shouting from somewhere nearby.

A muffled sound and a shaft of piercing daylight from above told me that someone had opened the barrel lid. I twisted round and fell through the opening into the sea, my arms still tied behind my back. A trail of air bubbles exploded from my mouth as I went under. Then a hand came through the water and pulled me by the neck back to the surface. More hands joined in, dragging me onto the beach. The hood fell off me, but I was so busy struggling for each wretched breath that I could not identify who my saviours were.

When I had finished coughing up seawater, I found myself

lying on a flat beach under a calm sky. The sea was an expanse of unruffled blue, so silky it seemed composed of air rather than water. Waves rose and fell with the faintest of slaps upon the beach. Marley stood over my drenched body as though I was the reluctant subject of a complicated water ritual.

'I hate to dash your spirits Mr Adams, but I'm not the rescue party you'd hoped for.' His face looked genuinely sorrowful as he produced a pair of handcuffs. 'I've waited a month for this opportunity.'

'You could wait a while longer,' I replied, rising to a sitting position, my body still shaking from the cold water.

'It's too late for you. I've come across men like you before, never knowing how deeply in the mire they're stuck.'

Grimes and his men stood behind him like a group of harmless spectators, as though there had been no violence that morning, as though they were out for a gentle stroll on the beach.

'You knew about the smuggling, too?'

'Better than that. I helped orchestrate it. Why wait for a conspiracy to be hatched when you can create one yourself? I work for the British Admiralty. We spy on everyone, including the Irish Constabulary. We've known about the smuggling for some time, but we've tolerated it, even encouraged it, because it helps us achieve our aims.'

'Which are what? To break the law and murder innocent people.'

'To weed out misfits and troublemakers like yourself. Like Rosemary O'Grady and Captain Oates. In the greater terms of war and peace, smuggling alcohol and tea is acceptable, but smuggling weapons and plotting a rebellion is not. Which is why we tolerate Inspector Grimes' little hobby.'

'Does that mean tolerating murder, too?'

'Inspector Grimes is a patriot, in spite of his murderous tendencies. Besides, we could never let it be known that he was involved in criminal activities. Think of the negative propaganda, the loss of trust in his Majesty's forces that would ensue.'

'Then why rescue me from the barrel?'

'Just taking care of the loose ends. The murder of another Englishman might attract too much attention to this part of the coast.' He placed the handcuffs around my wrists. 'I'm sorry, Mr Adams. It's time to give up the ghost. In fact, it's time to give up everything.'

Men with guns half-dragged, half-pushed me into the back of a motor car, the leather seats of which were surprisingly warm and comfortable in the spring sunlight. Marley climbed in beside me, while Grimes and the other policemen crowded into the back of a lorry which we followed back to Sligo along the coast road. I tried to console myself with the thought that at least I had discovered how Rosemary's body came to be washed ashore in a coffin. It was a fate I had narrowly avoided myself. I could have ended up a corpse in a barrel of water, I thought ruefully, rather than one hanging from the end of a rope in the courtyard of Sligo's notorious gaol.

'First I want to take you on a little detour,' said Marley, as the car swung into a lane sunken between tall thorn hedges. The lorry rattled ahead of us until we came to a stately house overgrown with creepers. I watched as the policemen bundled out of the lorry and forced their way through the house's red door. Gunshots rang out.

'I warned the bastards not to use live rounds,' cursed Marley. More gunfire and the sound of glass breaking echoed from the house, which I now recognised as the address Clarissa had taken me to on the night I met Gonne and her Daughters of Erin. The handcuffs forced me to sit hunched over, but I was able to crane my neck and look out the side window.

I watched with a sickening dread as the policemen tore the place upside down. Garments and pamphlets fluttered from the windows. A fire broke out in an upstairs room. I leaned back as the reflection of yellow and orange flames intensified across the car window. The sounds of wood splintering erupted from within the building. I listened intently to the trapped sounds of the fire, fearful of detecting a female shout or cry, but heard none. The policemen found a stash of poteen and were soon roaring drunk, waving the bottles wildly in the air. One of them staggered through the red door wearing a veil he had torn from a religious statue. The urge to add feminine touches to their uniforms was one of the less violent side-effects of their drunkenness. They discovered a pile of haberdashery and were soon dancing around the house with corsets over their jackets. Oddly, there was no sign of Gonne or any of her female militia.

Marley was scrutinising me closely. 'Don't worry, Mr Adams, your friends are quite safe.'

'What do you mean?'

'I tipped them off before saving you from that barrel.'

'Why?'

'Because we belong to the same side.' He ordered the driver to take off. My last view of the house was of Grimes prowling the grounds with his gun and a look of frustration on his reddened face.

'Gonne works for the British Admiralty?'

'No. Quite the contrary. She's a true Republican, an evangelist in that regard. A woman of selfless character, even though she operates outside the normal rules of society.' He leaned back comfortably in the seat. 'When I first met Gonne at the Abbey theatre, I thought to myself, there's the woman for me. But I wasn't the only one to fall for her charms. You saw her take over that mail boat. Every man on board was enthralled by her presence. If she wanted to enlist you to her cause, she would have had you. If she has a weakness, it is that she cares nothing for men. That is her only flaw.'

The motor car headed back along the coast.

'You should have come to me with your suspicions and spared yourself a brush with death,' said Marley. 'Don't worry, we're going to put a stop to that Ulster bastard Grimes.'

Maud might have been a professional in the art of disguise, but I realised I was now in the hands of a true expert at subterfuge.

'There are many of us helping the Republican cause, working in the shadows,' continued Marley. 'I was on the mail boat to help Maud's safe passage to Ireland. We came to Sligo to hatch a conspiracy plot.'

'What do you mean?'

'Maud travelled to Sligo so that the Admiralty might believe a German submarine was due to make landfall soon along the coast. In fact, the actual submarine was supposed to land much further south, near Galway. I informed the British Admiralty office that the plan was underway, and waited for Grimes to detect the suspicious activities of the Daughters of Erin along the beaches because we wanted the army to focus its attention here, rather than in Galway. At first, I couldn't understand why he didn't collect the clues in triumph and proclaim to his superiors that he had uncovered plans for a German invasion.'

'So Gonne came here to wait for a submarine that did not exist?'

'Yes. A ghost submarine if you like. Men have died over less.'

'However, Grimes did the very opposite of what we expected. He advised the Admiralty that the plot was a diversion. He guessed that the red herrings which had been laid were precisely that – a false trail. What we didn't know was that the *raison d'être* of Grimes' life is smuggling. Every piece of contraband that lands on this shore does so with his permission. He knows every cove and smuggler's path and has them operating when the conditions are right. The last thing he wanted was the place saturated with soldiers looking for a submarine.'

I stared at Marley, trying to fathom why he was telling me all this. I concluded that he was too much in control of the situation to be lying.

The motor car swung round the coast road, and we suddenly found ourselves watching a startling mob of horsewomen tumble down the hillside. There were cart-horses, ploughing horses, donkeys, and ponies of all sizes and descriptions, mounted by women and girls in black rags and tatters, coats, shawls and fluttering cloaks. Some rode on saddles, others none, some had leather-like reins while others made do with straw ropes. They rode from hiding places in the high ground around the cliffs, and at first sight of the car came galloping down the hill-side in an avalanche, yelling, shrieking and cheering, knocking each other over, and jumping the ditch onto the narrow road with such galloping haste that many of them were sent across the road and into the bog land on the other side. However, enough remained on the road to form a thick cordon around the motor.

Marley's face remained impassive as he unlocked my handcuffs.

'What's going on?' I asked in confusion as the horses knocked against the car, heaving it from side to side.

Marley spoke almost to himself in wonderment, 'Who'd have thought a secret society of young women, their blood vessels bursting with the urge to procreate, would prove such an effective ambush party.'

He removed a folder from his coat and opened it before me.

'I am entrusting you with this important task, Mr Adams, because you have two advantages over me. The first is that you are an Englishman, which in the eyes of the authorities makes you a more credible witness. The second is your daft obsession with ghosts, which oddly makes you more politically reliable. I want you to present this evidence to the judge who is due to open Clarissa Carty's murder trial this afternoon. He and the solicitors representing the prosecution and defence are all from Dublin and trustworthy. This is our best opportunity to have Grimes convicted as a criminal.'

He handed me the folder and I glanced through its contents.

'What do they mean?'

'You thought you were sent here to investigate a ghost. Instead, you've helped uncover a ruthless smuggling ring. This is a documentary record of Grimes' activities over the past month, including copies of boat ownership certificates. If the authorities search the boats they'll find evidence of smuggling.'

My hands were numb from the handcuffs and I struggled to sift through the folder.

'Clarissa told me you found Rosemary's journal. In it, she catalogued the movement of his boats, the amount of contraband, and the nights that the smuggling took place.' He pointed to a thin piece of brown paper. 'Here are notes from Sligo's harbourmaster. They detail how Grimes' boats sailed in the direction of Blind

Sound on the nights Rosemary and Captain Oates were killed.'

The documents appeared genuine, and I began to believe that they weren't part of a devious interrogation tactic. I felt their reassuring heft in my hands.

Marley smiled thinly. 'Part of me wanted to keep the documents and use them in a more tactical way, as and when required, but you forced my hand.'

'You were planning on using them for blackmail?'

'You see through me so easily.'

Horses stamped on the road before us, their riders calling out to each other in Irish. One of the beasts reared close to the side of the car, its mouth lathered in foam.

'If you think anything of Ireland and England, and the value of justice, you will ensure that these fall into the right hands,' said Marley.

A thundering roar from behind warned us that Grimes' lorry had caught up with us. A swarm of thickset policemen jumped from the back of the vehicle and approached the horsewomen with guns and black truncheons drawn.

Marley opened the door and shoved me outside. 'I'm going to count to five and then I'm going to shoot my gun in your direction.'

The advance of the policemen panicked the horses with many of them rearing into the air. I reached up and a female hand grabbed mine and helped haul me onto a horse's back. I ducked down beside her, and squeezed my heels into the animal's hot sides. My last view of Marley was of him withdrawing a gun and aiming it into the air.

27

QUEEN OF PENTACLES

THE DAUGHTERS of Erin provided me with a labourer's cap and a jacket for disguise. As they hurried me through Sligo's side streets, I realised why I wasn't afraid: I possessed the lethal calm of a man who knows he's drowning, swept up by events far beyond his control. I had lost my grip on the runaway world of Irish politics and revolution. In every direction, I came up against my own gullibility and ignorance. Much easier to allow myself to be carried along by these wayward currents. I had come to the painful realisation that the complete collapse of the spiritual side of my investigation was of secondary importance. All that mattered now was to secure Clarissa's release and let the authorities know the truth about Grimes.

Several hundred yards from the courthouse, I came to an abrupt halt. The area around the building was crowded with protesters demanding Clarissa's release. My female guides slowed, bumped into people, were swallowed up by the crowd, and then reappeared again at my side. By the time we reached the cobbled square in front of the courthouse, we were one with a pressing throng, swept along by the determined thrust of Clarissa's supporters. At one point, I turned and through the sea of faces caught a glimpse of Grimes' cold blue eyes and haggard moustache, as he scanned the faces of the protesters.

A column of policemen snaked through the crowd and began

interrogating the female activists, pulling at their headscarves, arresting some of the young men who had joined in the demonstration. They were hunting me down, I realised. I pulled my cap tighter and sank my head between my collars.

The policemen shifted their scrutiny when a ripple of excitement broke out in the square. A makeshift platform had been erected right in front of the courthouse, and a tall woman, majestic in flowing black robes, took centre stage. Even though her face was obscured by a black shawl, I could tell it was Maud Gonne. Her appearance had a mesmerising effect on the crowd. I expected a public rant, but instead she spoke with the quiet dignity of a mourner attending a deathbed.

'Daughters of Erin, we are here this afternoon to protest for the honour of Ireland. We do so at risk of suffering, for it is not easy for us women, some of us old and feeble, to come out like this. Roughly handled and bruised, our clothes torn, we will fight to save Sligo from the disgrace of convicting an innocent woman, a true Republican, while the real murderers triumphantly flaunt their crimes before a cowed people.'

At this point, a swarm of police pushed their way through to the platform, and a roar of protest rose from the onlookers as Grimes' men began to dismantle the stage from under the speaker's feet. Gonne tried to rally the crowd once more before the police overwhelmed the remnants of the platform.

A shrill whistle pierced the roars of the protesters as a policeman pushed through the crowd and grabbed me by the jacket. In the distance, I saw Grimes pointing in my direction, his face furious. He ran at full tilt, cutting a path through the throng. As I struggled to get away, one of the Daughters of Erin jumped on my captor's back and knocked off his cap. His face was morose and beefy, grimacing stubbornly as he clung onto my coat. The girl grabbed hold of his big jowls and shook them violently. He wheeled round and round, trying to shake her loose, his face growing redder and redder. She flung her hands round his throat and gripped tightly, until, finally, he fell and released me from his grip. Another RIC man appeared out of the crowd and attacked the girl with the butt of his revolver. She fell from the policeman's back, her head bleeding, and staggered against a wall.

'This is no time for fainting,' urged Maud from her disintegrating platform, whereupon the woman shook herself back to life, and threw herself once more onto the capless policeman. Several more women joined in, raining blows upon his red face.

Grimes pushed open the valve of a fire hydrant and directed a skin-blistering jet of water onto his officer and the attackers, skittering them across the cobbled stones, blasting them away from their victim. Even when they tried to clamber onto their feet, the water kept gushing against them, sweeping them to the ground once again, pummelling their drenched bodies with the force of countless fists. The policemen gathered in a circle to watch, stirred to excited laughter by the sight of the soaked women writhing beneath the iridescent spray, their long wet dresses moulded against their bodies, their scarves and shawls floating down the gutters.

Grimes redirected the spray at the rest of the crowd, cutting a swathe through the square. He was intent on flushing me out. I kept my head low and moved to the thickest part of the crowd, which pressed around Maud Gonne as she evaded the clutches of the policemen. Holding herself erect, she jumped onto the back of a cart, which was hurriedly hauled through the crowd by a group of her supporters. Somehow she kept speaking, addressing her people as they followed her to the top of the square, and then down a side street.

'A great transformation is taking place in our beloved country,' she shouted at the top of her voice. 'Our suffering people will know justice and peace, and their children will understand the great meaning of the blood sacrifice, of struggle and hope. I ask you not to fear what lies ahead.'

As usual, there was more than an element of theatricality about her delivery and her disregard for the threats of violence and chaos breaking out around her. She kept proclaiming to the crowds as though the seething town were a battlement on which she toured triumphant.

In the minutes after she disappeared from sight, she still ruled the square, and her voice continued to echo against the buildings. Then the sound of gunfire broke out followed by the sound of someone feverishly blowing a whistle. In the panic, I ran up the steps to the courthouse and took shelter within, just as a pair of court guards pulled the doors across and barred them tightly.

The trial had already opened, although there was no sign of Clarissa in the dock. I took a seat at the back of the public gallery and prayed fervently that the judge would adjourn the case soon so that I might get a chance of grabbing his attention without committing contempt of court.

The judge began the slow process of empanelling the jury. Among the twelve selected were three landlords' agents, a solicitor, a vicar and three retired Army officers. The judge went on to warn that the court would not give way to the moral pressure of the defendant's hunger strike or the protests of her supporters in the square. Nor was it possible to consider the defendant an ordinary female. Consequently, her sex should not affect the merit of the question of detention or release. The defendant was being tried for the aggravated and premeditated murders of two innocent victims, he told the court. Although she was purported to be a lieutenant in a Republican female militia, there was little indication that either crime was a political act.

Flanked by prison guards, Clarissa entered the court wearing a dark cape. From the evidence of her sharpened features, she had lost weight. Her eyes were so shadowed they appeared bruised, yet when she cast them over the public gallery, they flashed with feeling. She drew her hood more closely about her face and made her way to the dock. One of the guards stopped her in her tracks and ordered her to remove the cape. Her face blazed and she glared at him. He tried to forcibly seize her by her shoulders, but she skilfully eluded him and threw off the cape herself. The packed gallery gasped. Her head had been completely shorn by the prison wardens. The scabs where the razor had nicked her scalp were still visible. Her bald head gave her face a glowering expression.

At this point, a commotion broke out in the hallway beyond the court. The doors flew open and Grimes pushed his way past the guards. He paused briefly to remove his cap in front of the judge. A livid red band stretched across his sweating brow.

'Your Worship, I call on you to allow me to arrest that man,' he said pointing an accusing finger at me.

Clarissa stared at me; Grimes stared at me; the entire public gallery turned to regard me with astonishment. The judge frowned and also stared in my direction. He raised his gavel but then lowered it when the room appeared to settle. 'The court does not approve of disruptions, or such lawlessness,' he said, staring heavily at Grimes. The Inspector's mouth slackened. He tried to think of something to say but then thought better of it.

The rest of the court kept watching Grimes, expecting another outburst from the clearly angry Inspector, whose eyes were very much on me, his mouth twisted in a sneer.

'Your police work, no matter how pressing, must wait until the end of this hearing,' the judge admonished Grimes.

Ignoring the tension within the courtroom, the judge spent the next half an hour berating the Daughters of Erin for bringing scandal and social turmoil to Sligo.

'You are even more of an abomination to Ireland than we had dared to suppose,' he said. 'Not only are you traitors to your country and your class but also to the fairer sex, and a disgrace in the eyes of polite society generally.'

A hiss of indignation rippled through Clarissa's supporters. The judge then lectured the jury on their role and warned them not to read certain newspapers, which were intent on covering the trial in the most sensationalist manner possible.

Time seemed to stretch as the judge spoke on about some obscure points of law. I began to sweat and cough, while Grimes' face appeared to cool and grow at ease; across the crammed room his features were utterly calm. I was trapped within the very heart of Sligo's judicial system, next door to his gaol, with his police officers likely filling the hall outside the courtroom. He stared at me like a man who knows his quarry has reached the end of its running.

The judge adjourned the trial until after lunch and the court rose as one. As soon as the judge disappeared through a side-door, I produced the folder of documents and made a beeline for the defence counsel, a young man whose side profile looked oddly familiar. From behind, I could hear the thud of heavy feet as Grimes pounded towards me. However, I was confident he was too far away to reach me in time. I was within touching distance of the solicitor when a pair of court guards blocked my path. I tried to push them aside, but they promptly grabbed me by the arms and threw me against a wall.

The solicitor turned and eyed me with surprise. Recognition dawned on both of us. He was one of the freed Republican prisoners I had talked to in the hold of the mail boat.

'Let him through, officers,' he said. 'I know this man. He is an Englishman charged with an investigation in connection with this trial.'

I hurriedly explained the importance of the folder to Clarissa's defence. His young face creased in puzzlement as he flicked through the papers. Grimes spotted the documents and for a moment staggered as if he'd been struck a physical blow. He almost fell to the floor but then he pulled himself together. His voice rose to an hysterical pitch.

'Whatever he has handed you, I swear it is a lie, on my honour as a gentleman and an officer.'

'If you are not aware of what is in the folder then how can you be sure it is a lie?' said the solicitor. He turned and examined me. 'I shall be making an application to have this man made a witness of the court. He will come under its protection and be exempt from any harassment. If you try to arrest him, I will have you charged for contempt of court.'

Grimes face showed the strain of a man making fresh calculations, working out the odds, trying to determine if there was another way of levelling the playing field.

'This is a British Court in the British Empire,' he declared. 'You don't have proof of anything.'

But the solicitor ignored him. My sense of time returned as I was led into an antechamber and asked to recount my tale in front of the judge. Even though there were discrepancies, mixed-up dates, shadows lingering around some of the events in my account, for the first time since landing on Irish soil, I felt a sure sense of knowledge and control in what I was saying. I no longer had the sensation that I was floating through a plot created by others, chasing invented ghosts, half-waking dreams and dead silences. Ireland itself grew less dark and secret.

As I spoke, I could hear the protesters outside the courthouse. The square rang to the sound of their voices; they were in victorious mode, singing low heroic chants, confident that their country's destiny now lay firmly in their hands. For too long Ireland had been a ghost-country, appearing and disappearing in the great cycles of time, hovering in between remaining a loyal colony and being born as a glorious Celtic nation. It had haunted the minds of its people with its tragic mythology for long enough. The Easter Rising had been the revolution to end all that. Everything was changing utterly, because the country had finally encountered blood and reality, and now the modern forces of democracy and the social conscience of political leaders would help a new nation be born. Ireland's exile from the land of faeries and enchanted dreams was just beginning.

28

THE MOON

THE SCENE around me changed completely. Gone were the protesting crowds, the narrow streets, the dark throngs of policemen, the severe political speeches, and the glowing-eyed presence of the captivating Maud Gonne. I was standing in a bathing costume, half-immersed in the icy waters at Blind Sound, enduring the slap of the waves against my belly, and gazing in cold amazement at Clarissa as she emerged from a vigorous swim.

'I thought you wouldn't come,' she said. Her eyes were bright with exhilaration.

'Neither did I.'

She beckoned me to wade in further but the cold had rooted me to the spot. In addition, I felt a natural reluctance to follow her signals. This black rose and her sister rebels had not only fooled me, they had almost led me to my death. I had mistaken them for angels, but in reality, they were soldiers.

'I still haven't got over how you deceived me,' I complained.

'Life is full of deceptions.'

'If you want to leave Sligo, I can take you with me. Just give me a day or two and I'll arrange your passage to Liverpool.'

'You know very well that I wouldn't survive long, so far from home.'

'Longer perhaps than in a country swathed in blood.'

'I'd rather die happy, fighting for what I believe in, than pine away in a foreign city.'

In one swift, agile movement, she plunged beneath a breaking wave and disappeared from view. I envied her sense of destiny and political vision. Now that she had been released from prison, she had no special interest in the supernatural, or in reaching new levels of consciousness. She knew who she was, and her role in the fate of her nation. She also belonged to an enchanting corner of Ireland, one that I was reluctant to leave, this south-roaming beach, the slow-paced sea, the great hanging slab of Ben Bulben.

I turned to look back at the shore, and made out the figure of a young man standing by the rocks. He was wearing clothes like those worn by my fellow students at London University College. For a moment, all I could think of was the journey I had made from the drab examination hall where my fellow student Issac had died to this remote, western shore. Once, my friend's appearance would have filled me with fear and despair, but that time was over. The figure waved once, twice, and then disappeared.

I turned back to the grinning young woman as she re-emerged from the waves.

'You still have one more ceremony to complete,' she said.

'What are you proposing? To initiate me into the Daughters of Erin?'

'Close your eyes,' she ordered.

I obeyed and felt her hand push my head under the next wave.

'It's time you left behind the spirit world for good, Mr Adams,' she said. The surf engulfed me immediately, and I encountered the deepest of underwater silences. I opened my eyes to a flash of contained luminescence, my arms and limbs flailing, creating spirals of bubbles, which twisted like smoke into ever changing shapes. I experienced a sense of weightlessness and peace, as though the sea were spinning an illuminated web around me, one that encompassed the haunted, sweet netherworld of the moon, the ebb and flow of its tides, and all the intersections between the visible and invisible worlds. Their forces combined to drag me downward like a funnel, a whirling gyre, but then, just as I thought my lungs might burst, the tumbling ceased, the swell abated and the sea loosened its grip on me.

When I resurfaced there seemed to be more sunlight dancing on the face of the waves. I gulped for air, my blurred vision taking in Clarissa's sloping shoulders, her pretty eyes and mouth, the skein of iridescent crystals covering her skin. For several moments, we floated in a silk-like sea of aquamarine that looked as though it might hold us together for an eternity. I felt a quickening in my heart, as if my soul had returned to my body, pulsing with enthusiasm to live. For months, it had been lost, a captive of dark labyrinths and tunnels, searching for other wandering souls, other wounds.

'The ceremonies are no more,' she shouted, just as another wave caught our bodies, lifting us in its long rolling roar of thunder, and carried us towards the dark shore.

AUTHOR'S NOTE

After leaving Sligo in the early Spring of 1918, William Butler Yeats and his wife travelled to Galway where they supervised the reconstruction of Thoor Ballylee with the intention of turning it into their family home. Over the summer, they filled it with hand-hewn unpolished furniture, designed by a Dublin architect, as Yeats was determined his castle should be free of 'ugly manufactured things'. They also settled back into serious spiritual work, devising the philosophical system that would underpin his most famous later poems and form the basis of the book *A Vision*.

In a burst of sexual exuberance, Yeats abandoned contraception and began showing his young wife the 'Mars' in him, as he euphemistically put it. With pregnancy hanging in the air, they undertook urgent horoscope casting, and soon Yeats was contacting the spirit world again in the hope of securing his male heir.

On February 26, 1919, Georgie gave birth to the first of their two children. Yeats wrote of the news immediately to his closest friends. He recounted proudly how Georgie had not cried at all through the pains. She had burst into tears only when told it was a girl.

Yeats exhorted his spirit guides for an explanation, but they were unavailable for comment.

ACKNOWLEDGEMENTS

I would like to thank my agent Paul Feldstein for his tireless work, Ion Mills, Claire Watts, Frances Teehan and all the people at No Exit Press for doing a wonderful job in bringing this story to life, Martin Fletcher for his helpful suggestions, and Adrian and Fiona McFarland for helping to provide the inspiration for the book's horse-riding adventures. I'd also like to acknowledge my debt to various biographers of WB Yeats and Maud Gonne, in particular, Susan Johnston Graf for *WB Yeats: Twentieth Century Magus*, and Brenda Maddox for *Yeats' Ghosts*. My knowledge of Yeats was also deepened by reading Richard Ellman's *Yeats: The Man and the Masks*, Roy Foster's *WB Yates: A Life: Volume 1: The Apprentice Mage*, and Margery Brady's *The Love Story of Yeats and Maud Gonne*. I should point out that any errors or outright lies woven into the story are purely my own. I'd also like to thank Damian Smyth and the Arts Council of Northern Ireland for their financial support and assistance. Finally, I extend my deepest gratitude to my wife, Clare, my children, Lucy, Aine, Olivia and Brendan, and to Paul and Kerri – the beaches are eternally for you.